BROKEN
COMPASS

BROKEN COMPASS

Supernatural Prison World #1

Jaymin Eve

Broken Compass:
Supernatural Prison World #1

Copyright © Jaymin Eve 2016
All rights reserved
First published in 2016
Eve, Jaymin
Broken Compass: Supernatural Prison World #1
1st edition

Also by Jaymin Eve

A Walker Saga - YA Paranormal Romance series (complete)

First World - #1
Spurn - #2
Crais - #3
Regali - #4
Nephilius - #5
Dronish - #6
Earth - #7

Supernatural Prison Trilogy - NA Urban Fantasy series

Dragon Marked - #1
Dragon Mystics - #2
Dragon Mated - #3

Sinclair Stories

Songbird - Standalone Contemporary Romance

Hive Trilogy

Ash - #1
Anarchy - #2
Annihilate #3

Stay in touch with Jaymin:

www.facebook.com/JaminEve.Author
<ins>Website:</ins> www.jaymineve.com
Mailing list: http://eepurl.com/bQw8Kf

This is for all of you who have been thought of as weak. May others finally see your strength.

May you finally see your own strength.

Catch up on the Supernatural Prison World

There are magically hidden towns around the world which are entirely occupied by supernatural races. There are five races: Shifter, Vampire, Magic User (witch/wizard, sorceress/sorcerer), Fey (Faerie), and Demi-Fey (Ogres, trolls, harpies, gargoyles, mermaids, etc). They all live together in relative peace.

Bordering many of these towns are prisons which house supernatural criminals. These crims are contained there to keep the world, and humans especially, safe from them. Humans do not know about these races, except for the Guilds – specially chosen families who help the supernatural communities acquire things in the human world, and integrate if needed.

Stratford, Connecticut is the supernatural prison town in the USA, controlled by a council of five powerful supes, one from each of the races. Maximus Compass has just become the vampire leader. His brothers (quads) Braxton, Jacob, and Tyson, are the shifter, fey, and magic leaders also.

These quads are newly elected to their leadership role, after having defeated the dragon king in an epic throw-down battle. The king was trying to take over all of the councils around the world. He failed. But there has been much carnage left in his wake.

The quads are pack mates with Jessa Lebron, wolf shifter, and her twin sister, Mischa Lebron.

This is Mischa and Max's story.

Other terms

True Mate – A fated mateship. Mates will have a physical and mental connection. Only between supernaturals of the same species (i.e shifter and shifter).

Chosen Mate – A mateship which is chosen between supernaturals. Length of time is up to the couple involved. Can be between any of the races, and sometimes even with humans.

Half-Breed – The offspring of supernatural and human mating. They generally have nothing more than some advanced senses. Live normal human lives.

Hybrid – Offspring between two different supernatural races. Vampire and shifter offspring will be a hybrid of both races. Weaker in some ways than full blooded race members.

Dragon Mated – Dragon shifters are not genetic, and cannot be inherited. They are only born when a dragon soul chooses to bond with a supernatural. The two become dragon mated. Very rare, and very powerful beings are dragon shifters.

CHAPTER ONE

Maximus Compass

Each night the emptiness claims me and each morning I force myself to awake. Aimlessly, I wander the streets of the human world, feeding to survive. At times I briefly contemplate ending it all, but I refuse to leave my brothers or Jessa.

Speaking of my number one girl, a buzzing illumination indicated I had another text. She was relentless, never letting me wallow in my misery.

Jessa babe: *Maximus Compass, where the fuck are you? Seriously, dude, I'm as fat as a house and my eyes are literally falling from my head I'm that tired. Mainly because two babies are kicking the shit out of me every night. I need you to come home. Braxton won't stop feeding me. I'm starting to waddle. WADDLE.*

An actual smile forced its way across my face. She was the one light in my darkness, the reason I was heading in the direction of Stratford. Though I wasn't sure I could step into the community again.

That was the place my mate had ... *died*. I was able to say the word now, but it still burned like the hottest fires of hell. I needed to start accepting what had happened. Truth was, the guilt was killing me. Guilt and pain. I hadn't protected Cardia. I was too busy trying to save everyone else. My duty should have been to her first, and yet it never was.

I didn't deserve a true mate, and so the fates, those evil bitches, had taken her from me. I wanted to kill them. But, unfortunately, that was impossible.

My phone buzzed again.

Jessa babe: *I'm serious, Max. You need to come home. There's stuff happening, the shifter bears are planning some sort of coup against Braxton. We need you. The council needs you.*

She was pulling out the big guns now, reminding me of my responsibility, of my brothers. I missed those assholes. We had barely been apart since birth, and it was our birthday soon. Twenty-three. And yet I felt like I was a thousand years old. Old and completely done.

I hit her back with a brief text.

On my way.

That was all she needed to know.

CHAPTER TWO

Mischa Lebron

Curses were ringing out as I stepped through the front door of the Compass home.

"Are you goddamn kidding me? For shit's sake! Purple ... who needs ten different shades of purple? And what the hell is magenta?"

Hearing a whole lot of swearing was not unusual when popping into the home my twin, Jessa, shared with her dragon shifter mate, Braxton. The first few times it happened I'd taken off at a run, convinced that for anyone to be shouting like that they were either being murdered or going into early labor. She was expecting twins and no one could be sure when they were going to arrive. But now I knew better. Lately, the usual culprit of her ire was when someone ate the last piece of cake.

Never touch a pregnant shifter's cake. This mantra was now drilled into me, and I was not likely to forget. Of course, this time it was clearly something else. The color purple had her all a tizzy.

I hurried as fast as I could down the hall, but with my own impending pregnancy I wasn't exactly in running shape. Yep, my twin and I had decided we should do everything together, including having our first babies.

"Jess," I yelled, to let her know I was on my way, before remembering that was pretty much redundant. Bad habit from my human days. She was a wolf shifter, and would have heard me before I even made it across the front porch.

"I'm in the dining room, Misch," she bellowed back. And then: "What the actual freaking hell? Screw this."

There was a crash, followed by multiple clatters of small objects as they were seemingly flung across the room. I laughed then, and it was weird to hear something so light and carefree fall from my lips. Lately I had been channeling sad sack in the worst kind of way. I wanted to blame pregnancy hormones, and they definitely had something to do with it, but mostly it was ... other stuff.

Trying my best to minimize the waddle, I strode along the small hall and through the living area, which was deserted, and into the next room. Jessa was at her usual spot behind the absolutely breathtaking dining table, a hand-carved masterpiece that should be in a museum or something.

Seriously, I wasn't sure anyone else in Stratford understood how unique a design and shape it was. In the human world it would go for tens of thousands of dollars, easily. No human could have made it by hand. Only a supernatural would have the strength and fine dexterity skills to do what Braxton Compass had done. My twin's mate was not only a scary-as-heck dragon shifter, lethal and godlike gorgeous, but he was also an artist. Deep down. You couldn't make something so beautiful and not have artistry in your soul.

Long, inky black hair – the exact replica of my own – shot everywhere as Jessa's head flung up. She locked eyes with me. The color was a deep blue that reminded me of a perfectly-cut sapphire. One of the few differences between us was our eyes. Mine were turquoise, closer to green than blue. I made my way around to her side of the table, noticing now that she had a poor book clutched tightly in both of her hands.

She lifted it up and waved it in my face. "This is all your fault. Seriously…" She started mimicking me in a high pitched voice: "'You need to do something to calm yourself, Jessa.' So I decided to try something new."

I finally caught sight of the book cover and a torrent of laughter burst from me. Side-splitting, belly-aching laughter. I tried to catch my breath as I sank down next to her, easing my girth in behind the table. Even as the laughter died off, a huge, beaming smile never left my face. My cheeks were actually hurting.

My twin was pure comedic gold, even when she wasn't trying to be.

"Where did you get this from?" I asked, prying it out of her iron grip. Smoothing the white cover down on the adult coloring book, I flicked through the pages. Jessa had made an attempt on half a dozen of the pictures but hadn't gotten more than a few strokes of color into each one.

The title caught my attention again. "Of course you would buy a coloring book titled *The Eff Bomb*

Coloring Book – For adults who need to release some anger."

Each page contained one large curse word, with some sort of artsy or flowery design around it. I paused on an image in the middle, one which Jessa had started to outline with the now-hated color purple.

"What's a cockswabbler?" I asked, wrinkling my brow as I tried to work out if that was a real thing or made up.

As the word left my lips, I found myself looking over my shoulder, expecting my mother to magically appear and smack me up the side of the head. Lienda Lebron did not like us ladies cursing, which made life very interesting when she was around Jessa.

My sister laughed. "Dude! I think you need this book more than me. We have to update your vocab. I don't want to hear 'gosh golly gee' out of your mouth one more time."

I swatted her with the book. "I've never said golly gee in my life."

"Whatever," Jessa said. "I'm still saying this book is your fault. The coloring made you all Zen and stuff, even with a baby taking up what feels like permanent residence in your uterus and kicking the crap out of you, so I ordered one through the Guilds. I, of course, went for something more interesting than *Nature's Beauty.*"

Of course she did. The eff bomb was like her favorite word ever. It was true though, I loved coloring and drawing. I found moments of peace when I was absorbed in my art, and probably wouldn't have made it through the last few months without that creative outlet.

Jessa clearly hadn't felt the same way.

"So … seeing the pencils are now strewn across the room, I'm going to guess it wasn't the relaxing experience you were hoping for."

She growled, catching me by surprise, but at least I didn't jump anymore. After spending twenty-plus years hidden in the human world, I'd only known about this supernatural world for a few months, I was slowly getting used to all the weird. Although wrapping my head around the fact that I turned into an animal, a wolf like my sister … was hard. Seriously. Who could say that about themselves?

Jessa lurched to her feet and I followed. Both of us had to push the bench back to free our baby bellies. Even though I was a month or so further along, her rounded bump was almost the same size as mine. With two little ones in there, that wasn't a big surprise.

"I don't even understand how you can think this is anything other than stressful. Not only do I have to stay in the lines, but I have no idea what color to choose. Why did I get the hundred and twenty pencil pack? Why?" She threw her hands up. "I give up, you can keep your Zen. I'm going to go and punch the crap out of a Compass or something."

That would be her relaxing happy place.

"I'm sure we can think of another way for you to relax."

As the deep voice washed over us, everything about my sister changed. The pinched brow, the stress lines across her face, all of that vanished, to be replaced by something I could only describe as desire and joy. Joy in its purest form.

It was painful to look at, and yet I craved to see it at the same time. Life had been a lot like that lately, a warring inside of me. It was like fire. I loved the flames, the heat and the energy, but I also knew it could hurt me, could burn through the delicate layers of my skin to permanently leave a scar. Funny how the things we crave are often those which could hurt us the most.

Jessa moved then, fast, so much more graceful than she should be in her condition. Braxton was perched in the doorway. He was one of the Compass quads, famous, powerful – newly appointed leaders of the United States supernatural community.

Somehow the quads were born of hybrid parents, Jack – shifter-fey father – and Jo – vampire-sorceress mother, but each had a pure soul of the four different supernatural races. Faerie, vampire, magic user and shifter. The only one they didn't have a representative in was demi-fey. But we'd recently learned they were really just a branch of the fey, so the boys actually had all the races covered. This made them uniquely powerful. They were the pack my sister had been lucky enough to grow up in.

In the supernatural community, some packs you were born into and some packs you chose. Jessa and the quads had been best friends since they were two, and had formed their own pack. There were no ceremonies or blood exchanges like I'd have guessed, just their inner shifter, vamp, magic user, and fey accepting and bonding with the others.

And now I was one of them. I hadn't been here quite half a year, and the time had not been smooth or without drama, but somehow they accepted me and my wolf. We were pack.

Standing in the entrance behind Braxton were his brothers. Jacob with his white-blond hair and grass-green eyes was fey. Tyson with auburn hair and beautiful honeysuckle irises was wizard, a magic user. The final of their quartet, the one who was missing, was Maximus, the massive, beautiful, and lethal vampire. With dirty-blond hair, deep rich brown eyes, and tawny skin draped across tight muscles, he was built like a warrior and fought like one too. He was also the one supernatural or "supe" that I tried very hard not to think about because we shared a past, and also a soon-to-be-born baby that he knew nothing of.

Jessa reached Braxton and flung herself into his arms. He scooped her up like she weighed nothing. Which to him she probably didn't. As the two of them went into their usual greeting, involving lots of touching, and hot, hot kisses, the rest of us strode into the living room. I found myself drifting toward Tyson. The mage and I had bonded lately. Something about our shared pain gave us common ground.

He dropped down onto the couch, running a hand through his auburn-tinged hair. It was just starting to get some length back again, but I knew he was thinking about cutting it. The shorter, Mohawk style reminded him of Grace, the healer witch who he couldn't seem to get out of his mind. She'd magically cut his hair in a fit of anger and now a part of him thought of it as foreplay. Poor dude, he was the male version of me, both of us sticking our damn hands into the fire. Grace was not in Stratford at the moment, she'd had family drama. I'd guess Tyson was about a week from chasing her down. Patience was not his strongest attribute.

I settled in on his right side, Jacob giving us a wave as he hit the stairs, probably to shower and change before we left for dinner. Not that he ever looked like he needed to clean up. The fey was physical perfection; his white-blond hair never had a single strand out of place. It was unnatural and unnerving. No human would ever look like that unless they were a mannequin.

I grinned at Tyson. "So how was king school today?" He turned warm, dark honey eyes on me. It was a color I'd never seen until arriving in Stratford, both melting and mysterious. Sort of like the mage himself.

"King school," he chuckled. "Still a better title than boring-ass training to be a council leader. It's going okay. We're behind the ball from the start, so this is catch up. Today we were at Vanguard again, learning all of the securities, seeing the different wings, trying to get a handle on the next batch of criminals coming in soon." He reached over and rubbed a hand across my belly.

"How's my little niece or nephew?"

Everyone knew about the baby now; it was impossible to hide a belly this size. Family and pack also knew it was Maximus' young and no one got weird or anything about it. Which I'd never expected. Their unwavering acceptance had reduced me to tears more than once, but I'd at least waited until I was alone to explode in a pregnancy-induced ball of emotions.

"Good, just ... I really want to send him a text. I can't have this baby without him knowing. I just can't."

I didn't say his name out loud very often. It was painful, and I'd had enough of that. Tyson's hand drifted across to clutch mine. I loved the tactile nature of supernaturals. It was comforting and I sucked it up because I'd never had anything like it in my life before.

"Not a great idea. We don't want to send him over the edge, and who knows what a text like that might do. He said he was on his way back, and he's a supe of his word."

I groaned before dropping my head against the wizard's shoulder, something a few months ago I'd never have been comfortable enough to do. But once my wolf accepted them as my pack, the rest had fallen into place.

"I planned to tell him so many times right after the dragon king battle. I even stood outside his door for an hour just hoping he'd emerge. But he was in so much pain and he didn't seem to want to be anywhere near me." After losing Cardia, he'd spent time with his pack, but he'd very clearly been avoiding me with a single-mindedness that was quite insulting.

"I should have forced him to listen on that last day, when you guys were inducted into the council. Why did he just take off without even stopping to see me?" I sucked in a deep breath, trying to stuff my hurt feelings deep down where they belonged. I had no right to these emotions and I was working really hard at accepting that. Maximus owed me nothing. But he did owe our child his attention, which meant I needed him here so he could at least know before the birth.

Tyson's hand was comforting again. "You were trying to do the right thing. Give him time to grieve and assuage the pain over the loss of his mate. He's the one who took off without a word to you. This is on no one but him. He'll return soon. I know it."

The mage was probably right. He seemed to have an inside scoop to the goings-on in our universe. The gods talked to him.

"I don't think I can take it any longer," Jessa said as she sat next to me, Braxton on her other side. "I need Maximus back. Brax … get him back for me."

She turned large, pleading eyes on her mate, and I could practically see the way he was crushed under the enormity of his love for her. There was nothing he wouldn't do or get for her. I had no doubt now that his vampire brother would be back in Stratford soon.

Sinking further into the soft couch, I tried to school my features. No point letting anyone see the burning well of agony inside of me. It was stupid that every time I heard his name a sharp stab hit me in my chest before ricocheting down through my ribs. But there it was.

Every single time.

My wolf brushed against my mind and I let her wrap around me.

Mate.

For some reason she always called him mate. I'd had just about every supernatural I knew explain to me – multiple times – that there was no possible way a vampire could be my true mate. We were from different supernatural races. That was one of the first truths I'd learned upon my arrival in Stratford. True mates were within the same race. My mate would be a shifter, and Maximus' would be a vampire ... *was* a vampire. Cardia. She died in the battle against the dragon king, and was the reason Maximus had taken off.

Ugh! I would not dwell on this any longer. No more was I going to be the sad and pathetic member of this pack. It was hard though, to not feel alone. Outside in the human world I'd been nothing, forgotten, a freak, neglected by a mother who was grieving and ridiculed by humans who didn't understand the odd little things I'd done. And while I had eventually learned to hide my peculiarities – which I now understood were part of my shifter nature – the cruel taunts and feeling of loneliness had never left me. But I was not weak like that any longer. I was strong and I would not let any creature bring me down again, even a gorgeous, dirty-blond vampire.

I closed my eyes, taking a moment to inwardly connect with my unborn child, to Zen my mind, as Jessa would say.

The ebb of pain did not ease.

Dammit! Wasn't time supposed to heal wounds and stuff? The twin connection flared inside and a sense of love wrapped around me. It was so hard to explain, but the warm sensation was how I'd describe home. Together with my wolf, Jessa had given me my first true sense of family, of not being alone, and I loved her so much that my heart swelled at the pure emotion of it.

And still it was not enough.

It's going to be okay, Misch. He'll come back to us. And he'll learn to be okay with his pain. The same way you are. This child will be loved by both parents.

We didn't speak through our link much. I preferred it that way. It scared me that she could see the sadness inside my heart and soul. I worried she would think I was weak again. Jessa was the epitome of everything I'd always wanted to be, strong, sassy, beautiful, and confident. We looked almost identical, but even our face she wore better than me. Her inner confidence gave her a shine I'd never have. Which was fine. I'd learned early on looks were nothing to strive for. Kindness, intelligence, and the ability to continue caring even when everyone and thing had knocked you down, that's where my goals were.

Truth be told, I wasn't the only one who'd suffered from our parents' decisions to separate us at birth, even if they had done it to save our lives. Jessa, too, had lost her mother and sister, left with an absent, grieving father. When our parents had seen we bore the dragon mark – symbol of the long dead king who was touted to rise again – they'd known they had to separate and hide us and our marks or we'd both have been taken from them.

Despite him being a thousand years locked away, the supernatural communities had feared the king, prophesied to return with an entire army of dragon marked supes at his disposal.

Thanks to a few stupid moves from me, he did manage to escape his prison a month ago. And he most certainly had control over all of us who'd been marked, but in the end he'd been defeated by my sister and the Compasses. They'd permanently ended him, which meant all of us "marked" were now free to return to our lives.

So yes, Jessa had suffered, but she'd always had her pack, the Compass quads. And those four boys were almost the toughest supernaturals in existence. I thought Jessa was even tougher.

It's your pack now too.

She gave me that final gift before initiating the block between us again. She was better at mental barriers, having learned from her dragon. For most of her life Jessa had been a dual shifter, dragon and wolf, but had had to release her dragon's soul during the last battle. Now she was a plain old wolf shifter like me – even if nothing about my sister was ever really plain. Josephina, her dragon soul, now resided in a beautiful golden dragon body, and was queen of the beasts, living in Faerie.

I made Jessa promise she would take me to visit as soon as we could. There was no rush of course, supes lived for hundreds of years. Still, there was some human in me, and I always worried about running out of time.

A hard kick by the baby had me jumping about a foot in the air, instinctively I clutched my ribs.

"Good boy," Tyson said, shifting my hand out of the way so he could feel the kicks too. It was unbelievable to see these absolutely lethal males get all gooey over the babies Jessa and I carried.

"You don't know it's a boy," I said, my heart beating rapidly as warmth and joy flittered through my mind and into my blood.

A child was a miracle. There was no other way to describe it. And while I regretted so many decisions

I'd made since coming back into the supernatural world, I would never regret my one night with Maximus. It gave me my child, and I wondered at times if a heart could actually explode from too much love.

The baby kicked again and Tyson gave a shout: "Okay, that was a strong one. You're right, could be a little girl. We know there's no stronger being in this realm than a female. The way you carry young and feed them from your body, you're damn miracles."

From a human male this might have sounded condescending, like they were just trying to placate a silly woman, but supernatural males really meant it. They were earthier than humans, animalistic even; they cherished their females to the point that if a human female ever witnessed these bonds, they would probably die of envy.

Braxton gave a low growl then, and I could feel the heat from the dragon shifter over here. "We're blessed to have you and our new young in our lives," he said. His gaze was firmly locked on Jessa, and through the twin bond my own heart clenched at the staggering emotions of their true mateship. He had a way about him. Maybe it was the blue as blue eyes, or the hypnotic rumble of his chest, but I was never surprised when my sister was a gooey puddle at his feet.

My baby kicked me again, harder this time, and suddenly there was dance party going on inside. I shifted on the couch, trying to find a comfortable spot, or hopefully derail the party before it got started and went all night.

"How far along did the witch say you were?" Tyson was looking at my stomach now, his brows raised. "What was the gestation expected to be?"

I knew what he was asking; it felt as if this one was already ready to come out fighting. "They tested me three times, and every single time it was six months expected gestation. I'm about four and a half months, so still a bit to go."

Jessa shifted forward, curiosity lighting up her face. "I've never heard of a vamp-shifter hybrid taking six months to be born. Generally, it would be much shorter. Your baby must fall heavily toward our family line rather than Max's."

That made me think of the Compass quads themselves. They were a genetic anomaly. How could they be born of hybrid parents and each have a pure soul of the four races?

"What the heck was the gestation period for Jo?" I blurted out, hoping it wasn't an inappropriate question. I was completely void of all social graces and knowledge in this world. Totally learning the hard way, foot in mouth style.

Luckily the guys just laughed. "If you ask Mom, she'll tell you it was at least four years," Tyson said. "But she ended up going around eight months. That was the longest her body could hold the four of us, and although we were born a little early, there were no issues."

Of course not, an issue wouldn't dare show itself around these quads. Damn, they had destroyed the dragon king. They were the new council leaders. They were all gorgeous, looking like they'd been perfectly carved by the gods themselves. Around them, and my sister, I generally felt like a stupid human who had accidentally stumbled into their perfect world. I didn't fit. I didn't belong. But I would stay as long as I could. I craved their pack bond too much to leave, even if I knew the moment Maximus returned the ache in my chest would explode full force.

My newly sensitive hearing picked up Jacob coming long before he made it down the stairs. His voice rang out with a slight sense of urgency. "We need to move. They spotted Kristoff at the edge of Stratford, right on the security line. Louis just let me know. He's heading there now too."

The males were up and moving before the words even fully registered with me. Jessa was also on her feet, rounded belly just visible beneath her black cotton shirt. "If you all think you're leaving without me, think again."

Braxton froze. I could see the gears turning in his head as he searched for the words to placate his moody mate. Jessa had that half-grin on her face. She knew she'd won before he even opened his mouth.

The shifter just shook his head and scooped her up into his arms. "We have to run. I don't want you to fall behind."

Likely story. The quads carried my twin around all the time, like she was their personal queen. It was annoying and I was somewhat jealous of how much they loved her. Did these supernaturals even understand how rare this kind of unconditional love was. No competition. No jealousy. No weirdness. Just pure support and love. Assholes. Yeah, I said it. When I swore in my mind, only Jessa knew, so I was safe from Lienda.

Awkwardly pulling myself up, I started to stride toward the front door. I was going too. This was my pack and I wouldn't let them go into danger without me. I might be pregnant but I was still a wolf. And even though I'd be a lot slower than them, I'd get there eventually. The others followed me, and as we got closer to the front door I prepared myself for the argument to stay behind. That was my life, always pushed to the side.

Tyson gently gripped my arm, stopping me. Then shocked the hell out of me with, "Come on, pretty girl, I'll take you," he said, before leaning down to wrap his arms around me. "You're a little slow right now and we need to get there five minutes ago. Kristoff is a slimy bastard and he keeps slipping through our grasp."

In one smooth movement he scooped me up and tucked me into his body. I let out a muffled shriek and clutched at his thick shoulders. Unlike Jessa, I wasn't used to this being carried around business.

My twin grinned at me. "Just go with it, girl. You can't fight them. They use dimples and pure brute strength to get their own way."

I snorted. "You're just lucky I'm tired and fat. Otherwise I'd be kicking your butt, Ty ... and I'm not that slow."

Tyson just chuckled as he hugged me closer. "We're tactile guys, you're just going to have to get used to our manly ways."

That was just the thing. I didn't want to get used to it and then have it ripped away from me again. Somehow these supes were slowly infiltrating themselves into every part of my world.

And I was starting to like it. A lot.

We moved out the door so fast my head was spinning. Even though I'd put on a decent chunk of weight with this pregnancy, Tyson didn't show any strain at all as he carried me.

It was still cold, but the first signs of spring were emerging. The huge acres of forest bordering Stratford were already blooming to life. I had been loving the wolf runs we'd been having lately. Not having a murderous dragon king controlling me had really freed up my time for other fun activities.

As the security force field surrounding our town came into sight, a wiggle of nerves started in my belly. I almost let out a sigh when Louis appeared on the edge of the forest. The absolutely gorgeous sorcerer, with his light hair and arresting purple eyes, was waiting patiently for us.

I found Louis to be such an anomaly. If I'd never seen him and just heard him speak, or felt his power, I'd have expected him to look like a wizened little wizard – something about the way he knew everything, could do everything, and had an ancient power which literally made my bones ache. All things that did not fit the Calvin Klein underwear model look he had going on. He was tall, not quite as bulky as the Compasses, but definitely not lacking in the body department. Looked about twenty-eight years old, but I knew he was well over a hundred. Supes aged really well. We didn't start to look old until we were like eight hundred years or something.

Louis' power slapped across my face as we closed in on him. Together with the Compass quads, there wasn't much that could best these five. Which was a relief when I had a precious one to protect.

I still couldn't figure out what the hell Kristoff Krass wanted. He'd been the council leader for the magic users before the quads took over. Though, actually, he lost his position long before that, for trying to frame and murder the boys to keep his place of power. He was quite a piece of work.

There had been multiple sightings of the sorcerer over the past week, and now the boys were trying to deal with that as well as learn their new duties.

We'd just finished one war and I'd be damned if another landed at our feet anytime soon. But I had this weird sense that something big was coming our way, and I really hoped we were all equipped to deal with it. New motherly instincts were blazing through my soul. I would protect my child or die trying. That was the first promise I made to the baby when I found out I was pregnant, and it would be the last also.

CHAPTER THREE

Maximus Compass

I was rapidly reaching the conclusion that humans were fucking idiots.

Until recently I had never spent much time in their presence. We'd occasionally had to slip into the regular world to chase down supe criminals, but that rarely required an extended stay with the locals. It was better that way; there was something very *other* about us, and this scared the humans. They didn't like anything that couldn't be easily explained. The Guilds were the only ones who could handle knowing about our world. They were born in to it and had a lifetime of training for their role.

I'd been wandering the human streets for a week now, slowly working my way home but managing to find enough distractions that it was definitely taking me longer than expected. The excessive number of dishonorable humans was keeping me busy and fed.

During my time out of Stratford I'd saved many of this short-lived race from rape, torture, robbery, and violence. At first I'd ignored them, not wanting to get involved, but eventually the berserker rage inside of me needed somewhere to go.

Like the piece of shit humans I fed from, my nature was violent, much more so than them. I was the nightmare lurking in the shadows of their world. Until recently I'd directed those urges toward the path where it could do the most good, and hurt the least. I'd always volunteered for criminal collection duty. But now I no longer cared. I was leaving a bloody trail in my wake.

To date I hadn't killed any of the humans; that would be too easy for them. I chose to weaken and scare the life out of them, reducing them to piss-covered jeans and a fractured mind. For the rest of their lives they would be busy looking over their shoulders for me.

Not that I stuck around. Every day I moved on. Running was my release. The moment I slowed, my mind reminded me that there was no waking from the nightmare.

I started this journey high in Canada, making my way down to the east coast of America. The landmarks around me were familiar now. I was back in Connecticut, and as winter started to disperse, the earthy forests bloomed to life around me. I was about a day out of Stratford, even less if I pushed myself, but that wasn't going to happen. The moment I returned, I would no longer be able to shut down. The ripping fire which burned across my chest would be released, and I'd be consumed.

As I crossed through a small town, faces turned in my direction. I got that a lot around humans. Don't really know why. Probably because most of them were tiny-ass punks, and they feared the giant, angry male in their midst.

More likely it was to do with the fact that I looked like total crap. A shower and a change of clothes would come in handy; I'd stolen my last set a few days ago. All I had on me was a dead cell phone. The battery died days ago. Which was great at first, no way for anyone to find me, but then I started to worry. There was a reason I always harped on Jessa about keeping her phone on her. If something went wrong, there was no other way for me to reach her.

It was probably a good sign that I was worried about my pack. Meant I was starting to remember that I wasn't the only asshole in the world to have suffered a loss. Part of the grieving process was about being purely selfish. I hadn't wanted to deal with anyone else, so I took off. I'd just wanted to be in my own head, but it was starting to get damn annoying in there.

I recalled Jessa's last text. She'd mentioned the bears and a coup. Was that related to their inability to get a leader on the council? Surely they wouldn't try to take on Braxton.

If they did, that would solve a lot of problems. Challenging a dragon, you might as well fall on your own sword. Pure suicide. Especially when our Jessa was with young. My brother was going to be crazy protective over her right now.

Still … the bears had never shown much self-preservation, and us Compasses didn't have a monopoly on arrogance. I found my footsteps speeding up; my pace increased to a run. I needed to know that everything was okay with my pack. My brothers were alive; our bond gave me that much information. None of them were in pain. None of them were experiencing strong emotions. But unless we were actually joined, I didn't know more than that.

As I left that town, moving out into the less populated forested areas, I let my mind wander. As always, it went to the one place I would rather have never visited again. My mate. *Cardia*. A familiar, hot jab lanced my chest; the pain was sharp but brief, almost as if it didn't go that deep, and yet she had been my true mate. I shouldn't even be functioning, but every day it got easier to deal with her loss, which was so many kinds of screwed up. What did it say about me that I could so easily let go of the one who was my perfect half?

It said I was not worthy.

Some part of me must be defective. Broken. And because of that I had not been worthy of my gift of true mateship.

Her face was still strongly imprinted in my mind. She had been beautiful, with porcelain doll-like features and dark curls framing her heart-shaped face – the sort of looks standard for vamp females, but for some reason I always expected my mate would be strong and earthy, more natural, the way Jessa and other shifters were. Which was a hundred kinds of screwed up. I was a vampire, not a shifter. Why on occasion was that so hard to remember?

Vampire. Just like my mate. She had been so damn tiny, petite even; it had always been a worry that I'd crush her with my strength, which I'd never worried about with Jessa. She was likely to pummel me to death first. She was a nasty little vixen when she wanted to be, and like all shifters was extra tough.

Cardia was too, in her own way. Jessa and Grace had told me how vicious she'd been in that final battle. Fighting like a true warrior ... right up until that last strike of the sword.

Fuck!

I hadn't been there to save her or for her final moments. That killed me the most. She died a hero, bravely taking on an army that outnumbered ours ten to one, and she deserved to have me at her side. I didn't blame my brothers. We were a team and we had always stuck together through everything. But the loss of a mate should trump the possible loss of them. And it didn't. I knew even today, if I had to make the choice again, I'd stay with my brothers. So again, what the hell was wrong with our mate bond? It shouldn't have been like that. There should have been no thoughts of other females or other bonds.

Other females. Screw that.

I was pissing myself off with all of this maudlin bitching and moaning, even if it was only internal. Probably been spending a little too much time in my own head.

A rustle had my senses firing. I focused on my surroundings. The heartbeat was the first indication that I wasn't alone, followed by a familiar scent. My body relaxed minutely. I should have known he'd come looking for me.

Increasing my pace, faster than would be humanly possible, another surge of emotion flowed through the jagged pain in my center and I couldn't stop myself from going to full vamp speed and crossing the space between us in seconds, to tackle the figure who had been waiting a mile out for me. Strong arms caught me and I let the bond of my brothers ease through my wounded soul.

As we pulled apart, Braxton's energy kicked me in the face, which was not unusual. He'd always been strong; his dragon was an energy like no other I'd ever experienced. And now he was even stronger. Being council leader came with certain perks.

We all took some of the energy of our people, and in return we provided them with stable leadership and kept the prison towns running smoothly. The supernatural prison communities were in a bit of a shambles right now. Larkspur, the dragon king, had destroyed so many of the leaders in his bid for control. There were a lot of new faces on the councils across the globe, and most of us were learning the hard way.

As happy as I was to see him, I still had to ask: "What are you doing here, Brax?"

I hated the probing nature of his electric blue eyes as they drilled into me. He saw right into your soul. Mine was dark. It was angry. I was likely to destroy anyone who tried to pry there. My brother got a pass for now, but since my control was shot to shit, that was likely to end very soon.

Braxton's expression was hard, giving nothing away. "You need to get your ass home. Jess is upset."

That very short statement told me everything.

Jessa had turned her beautiful sapphire eyes on him and he had caved like a poorly constructed house. It was nice to know some things hadn't changed in my absence.

"I'm on my way home, brother. I don't need an escort. I know the way."

My feet were already moving. The fact that I was distressing my pack was enough to kick me into gear again, and this time I wouldn't screw around. I would make it back to Stratford today. A strong hand landed on my shoulder and I was relieved to see not an ounce of pity in Braxton's face. It would have been on then. I didn't deserve pity, and I sure as hell did not want it.

"I'll keep you company," was all he said.

The rest of our journey was quiet. I had no energy for talk, except to make sure that Jessa and her young were doing okay. Braxton assured me, with that damn proud smile on his face, that they were already giving his mate hell and they hadn't even been born yet. Flutters of something happy and light twinged the dead space in my chest. Followed by an empty, aching pain. There would be no young for me now. My mate was gone, and with that my chance for a child.

Some of my grief was set aside as I focused on the occasional odd pauses in Braxton's explanations. He would start to say something and then stop. I swear I heard him murmur Mischa's name more than once, but then he didn't elaborate, and I didn't want to ask any more. Jessa's twin was not a place I let my mind go very often, for a multitude of reasons, and none of them I was proud of.

Even with Braxton's speed slower than vamp, we still made good time, and by early afternoon were nearing the edge of the securities surrounding Stratford. I could feel the energy humming inside my chest. The connection we had to the Book of

Guidance was now a direct link to our town. Our energy reinforced the power that protected our world and protected the humans from us. I wasn't sure I'd ever felt the witch's barrier so strong. It was an impenetrable force intertwined with the energy of the five races, and Louis' sorcerer power as well.

"It's good to be home," I found myself saying as we slowed to walk the last few yards.

Braxton nodded. I could tell he'd been uneasy leaving Jessa alone even for such a short time.

I halted him before we went any further. "What's really up, Brax?"

There was something else going on, more than the bear shifters, who were yet to make a move. Apparently it had just been whispers of a coup on the wind; Jessa's text had been embellished in a bid to get me home. Which didn't surprise me at all.

My brother wasted no more time filling me in. "Kristoff has been seen multiple times in the vicinity of our town and around Vanguard. We're working to change all of the securities and vet all the guards because he still has some loyal followers, especially amongst the magic users."

My teeth slammed together as a low growl ripped from the violent predator who made up the center of my being.

"Why the hell haven't you mentioned this to me before now? You left Jessa here. That asshole could be around just waiting to use your young as leverage."

I wasn't the only one growling now. Braxton's was even more animalistic. "Don't you think I haven't considered that? She's well protected, and you leaving has caused her great emotional distress.

We let you go for as long as we could. I respect your need for space, but now you have to come back to us. The rift in our pack and our council must be sealed. It's this type of dissonance which gives Kristoff the power to slip through the cracks. We need to be strong and united against him."

"Shit!" I ran a hand through my hair, before rubbing it over my face. "Sorry. I'm really screwing things up lately."

I should have known better than to question a dragon's ability to protect his mate and young. I was lucky he hadn't attempted to rip my head off. I probably would have in his position.

Braxton gave me a knowing grin. "I'm giving you a pass because you suffered something so unimaginable. There is no way for me to even consider the possibility that there would ever be a world without my true mate in it. I don't know how you're even remotely sane. And yet I'm so grateful to have not lost you."

Somehow the intelligent bastard had read my mind. We weren't connected, so my emotions must be spilling out across my face.

"I would not wish this pain on anyone, but truthfully it's not as I expected either. There's so much I don't understand. Do we know of any supe who lost their true mate and didn't either kill themselves or go slowly insane?"

I needed to know what was going on. What was wrong with me? When Cardia had died I felt as if a part of me died also; there was an instant fissuring which started in my soul and worked its way out until the fracturing was complete. In those first days I did not know if I would survive the pain, but already time was allowing a few moments' reprieve from the hurt, and it was way too soon for that.

Braxton was doing the shrewd staring thing again and I wished he'd just hurry up and give me his thoughts. I hated being psychologically stripped bare. Supes had learned early on to stay out of my head.

My frayed temper snapped again. "What, Brax? Spit it out."

No expression change. "I have my doubts that Cardia was your true mate."

He dropped that on me and then started striding across to the barrier. It fell in an instant, allowing him inside. I was stunned for a second, anger striking hard through every cell, and as a red haze crossed my mind I went into vamped-out mode and flashed across to my brother.

My fangs were long and aching, my vision tunneled as I smashed against him. His expression told me he'd been expecting it. He didn't fight back immediately, but also wasn't surprised. My fist smashed into his jaw and I saw the feral gleam of dragon spring into his eyes.

Hell yes.

It was on now. I was going to have an outlet for my rage – better to get it out of my system before I was back in civilized society. His return hit was hard enough to crack bone. I felt my jaw jarring, teeth grinding together. I didn't have time to think about it though, laying straight back into him with another of my own crushing blows. Braxton had the dragon strength behind him, but I had my pure, blind rage.

His opinion was unwarranted. And unfair. There had been no time for anyone to get to know her. I barely fucking knew her. But that didn't allow him the right to disrespect our bond.

"You only fight me because you know I speak truth," Braxton grit out as he elbowed me sharply across the jaw.

Beyond words, I jumped to my feet and kneed him straight into his side, cracking more than one rib in the process. *Arrogant shifter, thinks he knows everything.* Gold was bleeding into his eyes now and I knew the dragon was hovering just beneath the surface. Bring it on. I had enough aggression that we could be fighting this out for a month.

My head snapped back as he landed a solid blow; my cheek throbbed and I was pretty sure my jaw was dislocated. Still, that didn't stop me from smashing him in the gut, and swinging around to clip him in the right side, breaking another few ribs.

Braxton was an unmatched fighter; he was not coming at me full force yet. But I had many years of training and knew how to hold my own with any supe. Eventually, though, as my anger faded out, the sharp ring of truth in his statement settled into my mind, taking root in a way that told me I would have to consider his words. Otherwise the thoughts would drive me insane.

Both of us were sprawled on the ground, breathing heavy. My body ached in about twenty different places, and even with advanced healing and blood I'd be feeling this tomorrow.

Words tumbled out: "How is it possible that there were so many signs of the bond? What other explanation could there be? We were true mates."

Braxton seemed to consider his next words carefully. "Having felt a true mate bond now, I believe you were missing something essential. Even with those other signs. When you talked to me about the coldness between you ... the way you didn't need to touch her ... the way you didn't like many of the fundamental parts of her personality. There is no way the fates would have gifted you a mate so incompatible to you."

I had spoken in some length to Braxton on the issues Cardia and I faced during our very short mateship. At first everything had been as expected. A strong attraction. A blood compatibility. But then this weird space, which had always been between us, started to grow, little negatives which colored the relationship. It was too damn soon for the honeymoon period to wear off. That could take decades for supernatural mates. If it ever happened at all.

Still, I had to offer some sort of explanation. "Maybe our bond was different because it's vampire and not shifter."

There was no denying that a certain level of ruthlessness existed in my race. Practical and methodical we were. Designed to be warriors. To fight without remorse. We were one of the more battle ready of the races.

Braxton laughed, and then groaned. I'd definitely nailed his ribs. He deserved it though. "We've seen plenty of vampire mate bonds, Max. It's as strong as for shifters."

I'd been grasping. We both knew it. "It's too late to find out now. Cardia's dead, and the dead reveal no secrets."

Braxton lifted his head and fixed a hard glare on me. "The fact that you can even mention your mate's name and the word dead in the same sentence, tells you everything, bro."

Clenching both of my fists, the shaking in my arms intensified. "I'm so fucked up. I shouldn't even be here, I shouldn't be able to exist without Cardia, and yet the pain eases more every day. I want answers."

Neither of us moved then, both staring into the forests around us. The leaves above us were thick enough that the area was heavily shaded; the undergrowth was also thick. A scent drifted across the wind and my body instantly reacted. *Damn.* I wasn't emotionally prepared to deal with this.

I couldn't stop myself from turning to find her, Mischa, frozen on the edge of the forest, her eyes darting across the scene of our fight. The area around us was ripped and plowed as we'd pummeled each other into the ground.

Her scent was familiar and my beast inside roared to life. This was not the first time this had happened, and just like the other time I pushed the instinct down. The vampire part of my soul didn't control me. We had a symbiotic relationship, we were as one, but my mind was stronger than my base instincts. To aid in this, I cut off my sense of smell, locking it down so I could keep a clear head.

With a shake of her head, Mischa started to move. Her footsteps were heavy as she pounded closer; she was stomping. Okay, clearly she was pissed about something, and that was not a part of her personality I was familiar with. I'd always known she had a fire burning deep in her essence, one that hadn't emerged yet. At least not in my presence.

Maybe today was the day. I was strangely looking forward to whatever words were about to come out of her mouth.

Braxton and I pulled ourselves up to sit, which gave me a front row seat to Mischa in all her angry glory. *What the...?* Everything inside of me froze as the petite female stormed across the clearing to reach us. Was she ... what the actual fuck? Was she pregnant?

I released my senses to roam free again, and as I sucked in deeply I scented the slightly different note of her essence. Without thought I was on my feet, the energy roaring to life as the beast inside started to lose its mind, thrashing against the heavy cage which kept the predator locked down.

I expected Mischa to freeze as I started to stalk toward her. No doubt my eyes were as black as pitch, and the heavy throb of my fangs indicated they were at full extension. I was fully vamped out.

But she didn't. She continued marching toward us, sidestepping me in an instant so she could ream Braxton a new one.

"Braxton Compass, what the heck are you doing fighting with your brother? Jess is waiting for you at the house." Her voice lowered then. "She's run out of cake." The very real panic in Braxton's eyes would have had me laughing, except I was no longer in any sort of place for laughter.

The dragon shifter's eyes flicked back toward me and he took a step closer to Mischa, crowding sort of protectively around her. "It's not the best idea for me to leave you with Max. He's not in control."

My brother wasn't wrong. I was hanging on by a thread. And while I respected his need to keep his mate's sister safe, everything inside of me was screaming that that was my job.

Mine.

This was a mental battle I'd been having with myself since Mischa had first appeared in Stratford. The connection between us had been instant and it had been strong. Her similarity to Jessa, did have me wondering for a short time, if that was the reason for the bond. I'd even tried to convince myself of that, but I knew it was something more. But what was it? What the hell was going on with me? At times I felt stronger emotions toward Mischa than I had to the vampire who'd been my true mate ... supposedly.

Unable to stop myself, I moved with super speed to her side, reaching out to touch her. At the last minute I managed to refrain. "Who do I need to kill?" My voice was at the lowest of registers, right before the vampire side of me took control. She hadn't been fertile during our time together, which meant... "Whose baby is this, Mischa? Who dared to touch you?"

My words were coming out wrong. She was not mine, she was free to be with any of the supernatural races. It's just that I'd never seen her with anyone before I left, and she was clearly heavily pregnant. It could be a few months for a vampire hybrid or even longer for the other races. She'd only been in Stratford for five months though, and in that time we'd been a little busy dealing with the dragon king and his bullshit.

It better not have been rape, because death would be way too kind for that supe. In fact, he would wish he killed himself by the time I was done with him.

I lost the battle with my hands then, and somehow I was cupping her face. She was a tiny thing, a foot shorter than me, slim but curvy. Her eyes were the color of oceans and I often found myself wanting to stare into the mesmerizing depths.

I was just opening my mouth, to demand more strongly this time, when she reached up and her soft hands grasped mine. Heat shot around my body, through my dead heart, and had my stomach roiling. Before I could figure out what the hell that was, she wrenched my hands off her face and took a step back from me.

What the hell? She'd never done anything like that before. She'd always been so gentle and sweet, seeking me out. Unlike most of the races, she'd been raised with humans, and had never acted like a normal shifter.

After we slept together I'd had many regrets. Mischa had been desperately trying to find her place in our world, and as my pack mate's twin, and a virgin, I should never have touched her. Our night together had been ... a mistake. Of sorts.

I'd handled the days after in true asshole fashion, not knowing a better way. I had hoped that by distancing myself from her, she would come to understand that a long-term relationship wasn't possible between us.

Then I'd met Cardia at the sanctuary and everything changed. There had been no choice but for me to fully turn my back on Mischa. Complete cold shoulder. I'd had to protect her from Cardia. I'd known very early on that the vampiress was possessive.

Case in point with Jessa. I'd taken a stand with our relationship and my true mate had not handled it well. A time would have come when she'd have retaliated. Jessa could hold her own, but Mischa was not a fighter. I'd wanted her far from Cardia's radar.

Mischa and Braxton were currently having some sort of silent conversation, and it was pissing me off to the point where my fangs were so fully extended that my gums actually ached.

"Talk to me!" My glower landed on Braxton. "You lied to me, Brax. I asked how everyone was and you never mentioned Mischa was pregnant. Not once."

The pauses made sense now though.

Surprisingly it was Mischa who spoke up again, fire blazing through in her voice and flickering in those ocean eyes. "Don't blame Braxton. I wanted to be the one to tell you. I tried right after the council leadership ceremony, but you took off so fast. You just ... left."

For the first time a note of vulnerability crept into her tone. It was gone in an instant, her face hardening again, but I had heard it. The truth was I had avoided saying goodbye to Mischa. That another female was even close to my mind or heart when I had lost my true mate ... it was not a fact I could deal with.

"So tell me now. Everything."

My patience was gone, and even though I knew I'd already pushed hard enough, I couldn't stop from growling her name to hurry her along.

She bristled at the demand in my voice and I never in a million years expected her to say what she did next.

"I'm over four months pregnant. The baby is yours."

CHAPTER FOUR

Mischa Lebron

The past twenty minutes were like something out of the *Twilight Zone*. What the hell was happening?

I'd been out walking in the forest, something I tried to do every day, as I found it calming for both me and the baby, when I heard the shouts. I'd recognized the bellow and dragon energy of Braxton, and for some reason found myself running through the trees to see what was going on with him. I really should have known the missing Compass quad would be there too. That tugging sensation in my gut only ever happened around Maximus, but I'd been completely blindsided to round the corner and find him locked in a man-battle like no other.

Holy sweet mother of mercy.

Seriously, if these two idiots hadn't been trying to pulverize each other into fine grains of sand, I'd have been tempted to pull up a chair, snack on some candy, and watch the show.

I must have caught the tail end of supe-wars, because after a few more grappling moves, both of them ended up sprawled on the ground. It was then that reality really hit me hard. Hard enough that my knees threatened to drop my huge butt to the ground.

Maximus was back. He had finally returned home.

Breathing deeply, I allowed myself one moment of pain, one moment to breathe in the sight and scent of the massive vampire. Yes, I was a freak who could scent other beings.

Why did he have to be so perfect? So goddamned perfect in every way—well, except for his abandoning asshole personality, that was. But physically there was not a single thing I could fault on Maximus. On any of the quads, really, but while Braxton was absolutely godlike, I preferred Maximus' stronger features. He was a little rougher, with a broad, masculine face, built and shaped like a huge, Viking warrior.

Apparently I was into the Viking type of dude. Who would have thought it? I'd always expected I would fall for someone arty. *Good one, Mischa.*

I was still frozen to the spot when his head whipped around and he locked me in those dark eyes. It took me a few extra deep breaths but I managed to pull myself together. I was going to try very hard to act like this was no big deal. Actually, it was perfect timing because I didn't want to wait another second for him to know about his baby. I couldn't wait another second.

I started stomping toward them, keeping my focus strong on my angry energy so that none of my soft and painful Maximus feelings would crowd back in.

His gaze was predatory, and it took every iota of my inner strength to keep striding forward, to not freeze under his now-black eyes and ferocious expression. Why was he so angry? Did he already know about the baby?

In one swift and smooth motion he was on his feet, moving toward me. As each step closed the distance between us, the ache in my chest increased. My stomach swirled uneasily and I knew my current stress was not great for the baby. Which is why I chose to side-step around his large form and head for Braxton, desperately clinging to my pretense of not caring. To save face, I scrambled for something urgent to tell the dragon shifter.

Braxton's dark blue eyes followed me, his concern was barely concealed. Every now and then his eyes would dart back to his brother. I wanted to ask them what the hell they were fighting about, but instead decided to act like it was no big deal. And for these supes, it kinda wasn't.

Reaching the dragon shifter, I quickly scolded him for fighting because Jessa would expect that of me, before switching topics to something very pressing. "Jessa is out of cake," I murmured. Which was our code for "Jessa is out of cake, get her some freaking cake, she's actually going to kill someone if she doesn't get some cake."

A tendril of what looked like panic fluttered across his dark eyes. I could see he was torn about leaving straight away to find his mate, but in the end he crowded closer to me and said, "It's not the best idea for me to leave you with Max. He's not in control."

So I wasn't the only one who noticed that the Viking vamp was currently in a state of mega-pissed-offness. Before I could think up anything else as a distraction, the furious supe super-speeded my way, towering over me. I lost my breath and suddenly I couldn't ignore Maximus Compass any longer. His broad shoulders filled the forest, his presence sucked all remaining oxygen from around me. I worked extra hard to keep a calm face.

Maximus' hands twitched at his side as he finally growled out, "Who do I need to kill? Whose baby is this, Mischa? Who dared to touch you?"

That low voice did something to my brain, like spasmed it out, so it took me a few seconds to actually register those words. So he definitely hadn't known about the baby until he saw me. And he was angry about it. Oh, and when did he think I had time to be getting it on with someone else? Men ... seriously!

But if he thought it was someone else's baby, well ... that didn't make any sense. That should have made him happy. I was getting the impression that it hadn't crossed his mind even once that this could be his child. Great, this was going to be a really pleasant conversation.

Before I could calm my thoughts enough to compose a gentle way of breaking it to him, he reached out and cupped my face in his huge hands, covering up my cheeks and encasing me in warmth and energy.

No, no, no, no! I could not let him pull me in again. I had been without his attention for so long now that the slightest touch had me drowning in soft, gooey emotions. *No!* I would not go through that again. I'd barely survived last time, and everyone had suffered for my weakness.

It was so hard, but I managed to reach up and knock his hands away, freeing myself. Something flickered across those blacked-out vamp eyes then. I found myself shifting to see Braxton, wondering if he had any idea of what I should be doing or saying to make this situation better, but he was as unreadable as his brother.

"Talk to me!" Maximus drew both of our attentions, but his gaze was focused on his brother. "You lied to me, Brax. I asked how everyone was and you never mentioned Mischa was pregnant. Not once."

Wrong. So very wrong. I let the anger free again, jabbing toward the vamp. "Don't blame Braxton. I wanted to be the one to tell you. I tried right after the council leadership ceremony, but you took off so fast. You just ... left."

Shit. Some pain leaked out in that last part. Time to lock it down again.

"So tell me now. Everything!"

Suddenly I was the sole focus of those obsidian eyes, glittering with emotions as they captured my gaze. Captured and held.

With great effort I again freed myself from him, drawing on the strength I had been working hard for. Strength and independence. He had left me, more than once, and I had learned not to trust him.

"Mischa," he said, warning in his tone.

Right! Okay, asshole. You want to know everything, you're going to get everything.

"I'm over four months pregnant. The baby is yours."

He stilled. In fact he was so still that if I hadn't known he was a living, breathing supe, I would have expected the massive warrior was a statue, bronzed and perfectly preserved by a Renaissance artist. I wanted to glance at Braxton again. Hopefully this time he'd give some indication of what I should be doing.

I had just dropped a massive bombshell on the grieving vampire, something I'd been trying to find the time to say for months, and I wasn't sure what the right protocol was now.

The uncomfortable silence grew, and I'd just reached the point where I had to say something when Maximus started to growl, these low, ripping growls which started in his chest and ricocheted outwards until most of his body was shaking. I'd never seen him like this before, almost as if he was blurring around the edges as his body tried to shudder apart. Unable to stop myself, I took a step closer to him, one hand raised as if I could calm him with my touch. Yep, I was an idiot. If anything, that would probably have made it worse.

I never got to find out. Before I could connect with the growling, transitioning, weird vision of a vampire, Braxton snagged me around the waist and had me up and in his arms in seconds. In the blink of an eye we were moving, and he didn't stop until we were right on the edge of Stratford.

"What's happening?" I asked breathlessly, pounding on his chest to let me down. I struggled until eventually he set me on my feet, and then swiveled around and planted himself firmly in front of me.

"I'm going to shift," he said. "Get back."

My head was spinning with questions and fears, but I didn't hesitate to get out of his way. Squished by giant lizard was not my preferred way to go. In a flash of motion and a distinct spark of energy, the six and half feet of male was suddenly standing on four massive and muscled, black and blue scaled legs. His gigantic body blocked my line of sight, so I had no idea what was going on.

"Mischa!" Jessa's shout came from a few hundred yards away, but she managed to make it to my side in seconds. "What's happening? Why's Brax all dragon-beast?"

I didn't answer straight away. I was trying to edge my way around the huge creature blocking the path. Was Maximus heading in this direction? Was he the one Braxton feared?

Every time I moved, the dragon moved too. And each time he twisted that long neck around to throw squinty yellow-eyed glares in my direction.

"Misch…" Jessa was going growly now.

"Can't you, like, read each other's minds and stuff now you're mated?" I didn't really have answers for her. Well, any more than Maximus is back.

Max is home? I hadn't even realized that she was in my head, but maybe that was easier for her than trying to get into the dragon's head.

Yep, Braxton has me blocked out. He's focusing on a threat. She paused for a second, putting two and two together. *Max is the threat? What the fuckery?*

Uh oh. Now she was going all mama bear for one of her quads, and she had an especially soft spot for Maximus. Those two had a tight bond. The way he'd stuck by her even when he found his true mate had shown me how much strength and loyalty he had—

not toward me of course, but for those he loved he would do anything, move mountains and sacrifice his happiness. He was a male of worth and would be a wonderful father.

Jessa let out another curse, and then before I could stop her she reinstated the block between us and took off. It was ridiculous how fast she was still, even pregnant. Unable to stop myself, I followed. There was no way I was letting her take on the threat … or Maximus on her own. Braxton's roars echoed after us, but neither of us glanced back.

"Jess!" I shouted. "What the hell are you doing? Max is all vamped out or something, and he's not in a good place."

I heard her derisive little laugh, but she didn't slow.

There were heavy thumping steps behind us. Only the trees were stopping Braxton from taking to the air. He was much faster when he flew. Somehow Jessa had known where we were; she'd probably followed our scents. I still sucked the big one at differentiating individual scent trails, especially trying to figure out if they were new or old, but my twin was an expert.

Truth be told, almost all shifters, even those yet to reach the maturity of their first change, were better at this stuff than me. It was going to take me forever to catch up with my race, but I was determined that eventually I'd be as knowledgeable, skilled, and strong as everyone else.

As the torn-up clearing came into sight, Jessa ground to a halt and lifted her nose to scent the air, before turning to glare at the rapidly advancing dragon. She had clearly figured out what had happened here. Not surprising; she knew these boys better than anyone. I also stopped, my head darting around. Maximus was no longer where we'd left him.

Where had he gotten to?

Just as I had that thought, hard bands wrapped across my shoulders and midriff and I was snatched up. I shrieked for a second before his scent caught up to me. I wasn't being kidnapped by Kristoff the crazy evil sorcerer. Nope, it was Maximus, the crazy-ass vampire.

As he took off, using that speed which was dizzying, I caught one final glance of horror on my twin's face. She took a step forward as if to follow, but her dragon got to her first, blocking the path. Then we were gone. The force-field around the town dropped briefly and I felt none of the magic or energy as we crossed to the other side.

As Maximus ran, clutching me close to his chest, I wanted to tilt my head back and see his expression. At the moment, though, keeping the contents of my stomach down was taking at least ninety percent of my concentration. I'd been extra sensitive to food and rapid movement for my entire pregnancy.

Still, there was enough of my brain left to notice that despite his strong, almost desperate grip, he was holding me gently. There was no anger in his arms; the true soul of Maximus always shone through, even if he was fully vamped.

At the speed we were moving, I wondered where he planned on taking me. Seriously, we'd soon be crossing out of Connecticut at this rate.

"Max," I said softly; he would hear me even if I whispered. "Just slow down. We need to talk about it. You can ask me anything. I'll explain it all to you."

Forcing those words out was enough to have my stomach rebelling again, and I had to shut down so I could breathe very deeply. Every part of me hoping and praying that I wasn't going to throw up my lunch.

With my luck it would go all over both of us, and if he didn't stop running soon we were going to find out. I gagged and covered my mouth. A second, more wrenching spasm rocked through me, and thankfully Maximus chose that moment to slow down and come to a stop. I was gently deposited to the ground, and immediately I hunched over, heaving as I fought the nausea. There was a whoosh of air, and I was alone for a moment, before suddenly his warmth and scent wrapped around me again.

I felt a trickle of cool air as Maximus brushed my hair back from my neck, then something damp pressed against my forehead. My eyes closed at the pure bliss; the cold was enough to tame my pregnancy-induced heaving fit. I lifted my head, seeking the vampire, who was crouched close to my side, holding me in one arm and using his other to run the damp cloth down my heated cheeks to my neck.

"I'm sorry, Mischa." His low words were deep, gravelly. His eyes were still blacker than black, his features almost luminescent as the energy of his kind held him in its thrall.

I straightened, wiping at my mouth. I'd managed to not vomit but still had that bile taste coating my tongue. Gross.

"There's a river just on the other side of these trees," Maximus said. "If you're okay with walking, the water is safe for you to drink."

I nodded. "I'd kill for some water right now." His knowledge of the nearby river explained where he'd gone to wet the rag, not to mention there was now a ragged tear on the bottom of his dark-blue shirt. That's where the cloth had come from.

He wasn't touching me now, and unease was filtering back through us. This horrible tension seemed to be a fundamental part of us. Only those first few days of our time together had been fun and flirty. Then we had sex and everything changed. If I knew sex was going to cause me this much trouble, I wouldn't have bothered. Okay, that was a lie. I actually kinda loved every second of it. Whichever male came next as a possible mate in my life was going to have to live up to Maximus ... and his shoes would be pretty darn hard to fill.

Following him closely, I could smell the dampness and hear water thrashing so loudly we must be approaching what I could only assume was a massive, torrent filled lake.

Nope.

When we pushed through the last of the trees, I found a waist-deep, filled-with-rocks, pretty, burbling brook. There I went forgetting about my supersonic supe hearing again. To keep me safe, my wolf had been locked down most of my life. With her release I'd gained her additional senses, and still kinda sucked at controlling them.

Relieved to be stepping away from our tension-filled space, I increased my pace to drop down on the edge of the creek. Leaning forward, I cupped my hands into the clear water and lifted it to my hot face, removing the last of the nausea-sweat coating me.

Pregnancy was really doing a number on me. At least the witch seemed to think I wouldn't be in this condition for that much longer, which was a definite bonus to being a supe. Poor humans had to go through nine to ten months of this, and I'd only have six. Of course, if my baby had been half fey ... well, let's just say by fifteen months I'd probably be ripping the child out myself.

I'm only kidding, bubba. You stay in there as long as you need.

I patted my stomach; it was really without thought now, second nature to touch my child. But then I remembered Maximus and my head shot up. He was watching me closely, still doing that glowing, vibrating, growling thing.

His growls were low this time, almost unnoticeable unless I paid close attention. I rose, brushing my hands along my pants to dry them. Instinct cut through me and control over my actions fled. My wolf brushed against my soul and rose up to settle within me. I knew she would be peeking out from my eyes. I'd spent many an hour in front of the mirror when I had first shifted, teaching myself how to bring her to the surface without actually changing. I loved to see the animalistic glow of her in my eyes, the slight alteration in my features as the supernatural side of me became dominant.

Most of the time it was difficult to not think of myself as human. I'd been with them my entire life and I usually felt human. But right now I had never felt less like the old Mischa.

There was a swirling of black in the vampire's eyes as they followed me across to him. I wasn't marching, more of a stalking stride. Stopping right before him, I held both of my arms wide. I was opening myself up to him, allowing him to step closer.

"What do you need to know, Max?" My voice was more growly than usual; that was my wolf's influence. "What do you need from me?"

It wasn't totally my fault that he didn't know about the baby before now. He had been a grade-A asshole to me. Ignored me. Left without saying goodbye. He never even checked with me once when the dragon king was all up in my head. He couldn't have made it more clear if he'd tried that he didn't give a damn about me, but I still felt guilt that he was finding out at this late stage. Especially when he had to be hurting so badly because of Cardia.

Speaking of...

"I'm so sorry about your mate..." I let the low anguish in my tone seep out. "No matter what happened between us, I never wanted you to lose your love. The pain ... I can't even imagine."

I only had my pain of losing Maximus to go on, and since true mate bonds were so much more than our little thing ... well, I had no idea how he was functioning.

He still wasn't speaking, which made me uneasy. What was I supposed to do? I had no idea, no precedent to go on here. Before I had to think too hard on it, he stepped forward. My arms were still spread wide, so he ended up pretty much pressed against me. Well, against my belly. He towered way over me, so I tilted my head right back to see his face, and when I did my heart pretty much stopped. His perfect masculine features were a wash of emotion, his cheeks slightly flushed as his head dropped down, his chin almost hitting his chest.

He was absolutely killing me here. I could scent tears, sorrow, and so much more from him. Finally, I couldn't stop myself from reaching forward, but before I could touch him he surprised me by dropping to his knees. His black eyes met mine for a second, and I could see he was asking for permission.

Clenching my hands into hard fists, I used the pain of nails cutting into my palms to halt my own tears, before inclining my head in a single nod.

Slowly, almost reverently, he lifted his hands and placed them on either side of my belly. His large palms were hot, and instantly spread warmth through me. You'd think with the massive increase in padding around me I'd be a lot warmer, but I'd been feeling the cold really badly during my pregnancy.

Maximus still had to bend his neck to rest his head close to the baby. I wondered if he was listening for the heartbeat. His vampire hearing would pick it up easily.

We remained like this for many moments. My chest was aching as his tender and silent moment with our baby started cracking the protective shields I'd erected around my heart. I could not go there again, be that vulnerable.

I started babbling: "I never found out the sex. I want it to be a surprise. Jessa is having one of each and she's already anticipating the drama her two little ones will get into."

His eyes met mine, and I thought for a second something like amusement flickered across those dark depths.

"Thank you," he said to me. The vibration of his body had eased; his vamped-out features were fading. "You've given me the greatest gift, something I never thought would be mine, and I owe you a thousand apologies."

I blinked a few times, trying to wrap my mind around those words. I had never expected ... he was saying everything I'd been hoping, praying, and waiting to hear.

But still ... there was something flat in his voice. Don't get me wrong, I could tell he was overjoyed— it was obvious—but I was guessing it was hard to be really happy when it was me and not Cardia carrying his young.

As if sensing my distress, the baby started to move then. Strong limbs kicked out and nausea trickled across my lower belly when the baby rolled over. Maximus' hands flexed against me; his eyebrows rose high as his eyes followed the movement of skin rippling across my abdomen.

"So strong," he murmured, and I caught the trickle of a single tear as it tracked down his cheek. I couldn't stop myself from reaching out and brushing the wetness from his skin. It was the first time I'd voluntarily touched him, and it hurt as badly as I expected. It was so unfair. Why did my body crave him? Why did my hands seem to know him so well when I'd only held him for such a brief time?

If you asked me, it was bullshit.

CHAPTER FIVE

Maximus Compass

The last few months had brought a whirlwind of change. Life-changing events shouldn't happen every month, they should be spread out over years so that one's goddamn heart doesn't actually stop beating.

When Mischa dropped the baby news on me, the predator inside ripped free in a way I'd never experienced before. This wasn't the first time I'd lost control of my vampire side. It had happened a few times before, especially in those early years of teenage hormones and newly discovered powers. But this was something so much larger. There was nothing I could compare the emotion to, not even meeting my true mate, or losing her.

Which was fucking sad when you really thought about it.

When Braxton had taken off with Mischa – to guard her from my loss of control – it did nothing but piss me off. He was protecting her, but she was not his to protect. Mischa was carrying my child, and I would be the one to place my body before any danger which sought to touch her. I would protect her and our baby with my last dying breath, and the fact that my own brother had thought I was a threat to her ... well, I was going to kick his ass again ... when I managed to pry myself away.

My child was not even born yet and already held a clenched fist around my heart. I was owned by a little supe, and my life would never be the same.

As my hands covered Mischa's tiny bump, I could hear and feel the strong and rapid thrumming of the heartbeat, like a million miniature galloping horses. The tiny fighter continued to kick and roll under my hands, as if sensing I was close by and wanting my attention.

You have it, little one, now and forever.

A muffled sob wrenched my attention up, and I found myself entranced by those ocean-green eyes again. They were misty now, emotions washing tendrils of blue and yellow through them. Need and something so much more clenched deep in my chest, and I knew then that I was lost.

Mischa had truly given me a gift. My shattered heart was again beating in a strangely rhythmic manner. Her news had breathed life back into my world, but I needed to know how. How had this miracle happened?

I had so many questions, but one thing I definitely didn't need to know was why she hadn't told me earlier. I'd made sure that it was never easy for her to be alone with me. There was never a moment to confess something this huge. The fact that I hadn't known the moment she did was solely on me.

Reluctantly removing my hands, which was so much harder than I'd expected, I got back to my feet. Not wanting to tower over her while she told her story, and worrying that she might need to rest her feet, I took her hand and led her across to some small boulders lining the creek. They were large and flat. Perfect to sit on.

The moment we sat, I pulled my hands back from her and rested them against my thighs. Then, like a stabbing lance, my emotions rose up again, the vampire fighting for dominance. Too much had happened lately and my control seemed to be getting even worse.

Except when I was touching her. For some reason, physical contact with Mischa calmed the beast. It hadn't always been like that, though. Was this new bond I could feel between us because of the child growing inside of her?

Sucking in deeply, the cool, fresh air hitting my lungs hard, I started with the most important thing I had to say: "I owe you a massive apology. I haven't been here for you at a time when you needed me the most. All of this must have been difficult and confusing, especially while trying to deal with Larkspur's mind control. I just ... shit, there's nothing I can really offer but my sincere sorrow. I will do better, Mischa. I will be a better supe for you and our child."

She made a noise like a strangled gasp. "I ... I have waited so long to talk to you about this, but ... I can't quite believe you're taking it so well. I thought you would be angry with me. Maybe even think I was lying about it being yours."

Aw, my poor human-raised supe. "If you were lying, everyone would already know. We can scent the truth." I had found it a little odd that the baby was scenting as pure shifter blood, but it didn't bother me. If Jo Compass had taught me anything, it's that you never knew what mixed-race matings would give you in the genetic lottery.

Mischa was all big eyes and flushed cheeks. She seemed completely staggered by my attitude. She couldn't possibly understand the joy singing through my veins. Supes love children, and while it's not difficult for us to produce them, it is generally harder than it seems to be for humans.

"It wasn't your fertile time, Mischa, so how did this happen?" This was the reason I hadn't initially thought the baby could be mine, the fertile periods for shifters were very clear.

She dropped her eyes, reaching out and running her hand over the smooth stone she sat upon. I could see the way she centered herself, gathered thoughts before speaking. She was so unlike Jessa, whose confidence was unparalleled. My oldest friend would not think before speaking, she just let her emotions fall free. Somehow it made Mischa's words more appealing, like she had carefully selected them just for me.

"When my wolf side was suppressed..." she finally said, "it screwed up my body, hormones, and fertility. When I thought I was human, I never had a ... fertile ... period or anything. Mom told me not to worry, I was just a late bloomer. Of course, by my early twenties I knew there was something wrong, but since I figured I was probably never going to have children anyway, I never bothered to ask her about it again."

Why the hell wouldn't she have children? The question burned across my mind, but I would not interrupt her during her story.

"Then when I arrived at Stratford and found out all the big family secrets, everything made sense. I wasn't human. When my wolf side was unlocked, Mom explained to me about fertile times and how to recognize them. Then when we were together, you mentioned that you couldn't sense any fertility, so I never gave it a second thought."

It was the truth. There had been no scent or sign that she was even close to her time to conceive a child.

"Basically, the unlocking of my wolf side threw my entire body into some sort of weird stage of created-fertility, trying to realign itself with the phases I should have been following all along. I literally created my own, virtually undetectable fertility ... different to the normal shifter phase ... but clearly still enough for us to conceive."

I silently thanked the gods. Maybe the fates didn't hate me after all. "I need to know everything, Mischa. How did you find out? Was anyone there with you?"

My guilt was again crushing me that she might have been alone to receive and deal with this life-changing news. If only I hadn't met Cardia at the sanctuary, then Mischa would have come to me.

I had to shake my head at the realization that I'd have preferred not to meet my true mate in lieu of knowing of my child months ago. Braxton had to be right. That was not normal.

Mischa was explaining things quick and precisely. "I started to get sick, this aching pang in my stomach which really hit hard when we reached the Romanian sanctuary. Eventually I went to a healer and he ended up dropping the bombshell on me. I made him check twice. He was also the one who figured out how I ended up pregnant when I had still not had a noticeable fertile period."

Her fingers stilled along the smooth rocks, and finally her eyes rose to meet mine. I could see fires burning deep in their depths. "You had Cardia by then, and Jess was missing. I didn't know what to do, and then the dragon king's daughters, the twins, started hanging around me. They were so ... persuasive. I was an idiot. I should have known better than to let them manipulate my thoughts and emotions. I'm so very sorry for the part I played in Larkspur's rebirth. Everything which led to that ... final battle."

She'd already apologized to me once about Cardia, and instead of accepting her heartfelt sorrow I was kind of wishing she'd stop mentioning it. The darkness inside was starting to wind around my memories of Cardia. Starting to taint the bond even further.

Pushing this aside, I decided to address the other part of Mischa's apology. Larkspur's daughters and their evil ways.

When we'd had to run to the supernatural sanctuary, to protect her and her sister from being found as dragon marked supes, Mischa had fallen in with the dragon king's daughters. Manipulative bitches, they messed with her head, and got her to help them free the king.

It wasn't really her fault though. We should have been looking out for her. She knew nothing of our world. She was naïve and easily targeted. If anyone was to blame, it was me for rejecting her so brutally, and our pack for getting so caught up in other bullshit that we failed to hear her cries for help. I'd been wanting to tell her this for a long time:

"It's not your fault, Mischa. The supernatural world is kill or be killed. You didn't grow up here and that makes you vulnerable. You're just too innately soft and trusting. There's true goodness inside of you. The fact that others took advantage of that, well, the fault lies squarely with them—and with us for not being there for you."

I had never been angry with her about this, even when others were looking for a place to leave their blame.

Her face crumpled just slightly before she pulled herself together again. "I want you to know that I planned on telling you first about the baby. I never breathed a word of it until the day before the final battle. You still hadn't come near me, and with the stress of Larkspur's control ... well, I broke down with Jess and confessed everything. Please don't think that everyone knew about it behind your back and was talking about you or anything..." She took a deep, shuddering breath. "Of course, once the belly popped out there was no hiding it, but before that I kept it quiet."

It was interesting the way she phrased those words. Something told me Mischa had spent a lot of her life in the dark, having others know more about her life than she did. It clearly bothered her.

"I don't blame you, Mischa. I accept full responsibility for what happened."

She seemed to calm then, finally uncurling her legs and stretching them out. Following her lead, I extended my much longer legs out across the rocks before me. I let her words mull through my head. She had been so alone. Well, no longer. I had no idea what life was going to bring us in the next little while, but Mischa would not have to doubt me again.

The stillness of nature enveloped us, and even though I could have sat there in relative peace for days, I knew it was not safe to keep Mischa outside the protective barrier any longer. Especially if there was anarchy afoot with both the bear shifters and Kristoff.

I rose silently, preparing to reach across and help her to her feet, but she was already up and moving before I could. My vampire didn't like that. I pushed the beast down as I followed her back toward the forest.

On the edge of the tree line I reached down and placed a hand on her biceps to halt her, before bending to scoop her into my arms. Before I could, though, she slammed a flat palm against my chest. Her strength and fiery expression brought a smile to my lips.

"I have feet and legs. I do not need to be carried around. I'm not Jessa."

This little wolf was finding her fangs.

Under normal circumstances, I would feel the need to defend my best friend, but I knew Mischa had not meant it as an insult. She was trying to differentiate herself from her twin, and she, like everyone else in the supe world, probably thought I was in love with Jessa. I wasn't, not anymore. Not ever really. My pack mate was the most infuriating, amazing, sarcastic, pain in the ass, and I wouldn't want one second of life without her, but she didn't stir my blood the same way Cardia had. Not even the same way Mischa did ... *does*.

Shit, it was all so damn confusing.

I realized I'd never really told Mischa any of that. She deserved to know, especially now.

"I need you to know that I've never confused you with Jessa. Not really. Even when my emotions were a bit tangled between the two of you, I saw you, Misch. Only you. The timing was not the best for us, but under other, more normal circumstances, I think we could have had a shot at a chosen mateship."

I was only speaking the truth, a truth I'd had many hours to contemplate.

She stared for many moments, then the slightest smile graced her lips. "Thank you for telling me that. I believe that too ... but it's too late now," she said, not unkindly. "So much has happened, and there's too much baggage. But I would be a liar to say that I'm not grateful to hear that our time together was not about you and Jess."

I shook my head. "I see similarities between the pair of you, but you're both very different supes. Not just your upbringing, but the fundamental parts of your personalities. You're both amazing shifters, but..." I let the briefest of smiles escape then. "One thing neither of you do have is long legs or vampire speed, so for now, if we're going to make it back to Stratford before nightfall, you'll need to accept my help."

She gave me stony eyes for a second and I could see her actively trying to figure out a way to get around me carrying her. Eventually, though, she gave a final glance down at her belly and let out a whoosh of air.

"Dammit! Okay. Thank you."

I didn't hesitate, having all the permission I needed to reach down and scoop her into my arms. Her slight weight was nothing as I held her close to my chest. I could hear the baby's heartbeat again, and what sounded like tiny hiccups. *A damn miracle.* I was the luckiest vampire alive.

Okay, yes, I had lost my true mate. But even that pain was dulled by the roaring joy brought about by the sound of my child's heart.

Mischa was silent for the first half of the journey back to Stratford. Eventually she started to wiggle around, lifting her head to see me. I could feel the heaviness of her stare. I knew something unpleasant was coming in the next conversation.

"Why are you not more broken up about Cardia?"

Fuck. Unpleasant, heavy, and impossible to answer.

"Ty said you'd be completely different, but … you're not." She paused for a moment. "Actually, you are different, because you're being nice to me … how you were when I first came to Stratford. I mean … I bring you news that you're going to have a baby, something I'm sure you expected to do with Cardia, and … dammit…"

She never cursed normally, and combined with her babbling it was clear she was both flustered and embarrassed. I could feel the heat of her skin as she fought for words.

"I'm making a mess of this conversation. Curiosity got the better of me, and I hope I didn't upset you."

She fell silent, and I could sense her withdrawing back into her more reticent personality. Which I did not like at all. Shit, I had to try to find the right words again, but Cardia was a sensitive point for me. Mostly because I had no fucking idea what the hell was going on there.

"Misch, I don't know what to tell you. A baby is a wonder and gift no matter what circumstances brought it about. Yes, I did lose my mate, and I have been trying to dig myself out of darkness ever since. Your news seems to be the very thing for me to start clawing my way back to the light."

My arms tightened even further, hugging her slight form closer to me. "Cardia and I were ... complicated. Braxton said something to me about the true mate bond that I didn't like. That's why we were fighting. He believes ... he believes she wasn't really my true mate, that she couldn't be because of the strange nature of our relationship ... some of the distance between us."

Only the faerie gods themselves would know why I had decided to share this information with Mischa. It had always been like that though. From her first night in Stratford when I'd walked her home, we'd talked about everything as if we'd known each other forever. That was the magic this wolf shifter held, and I had no explanation for it.

Her expression was carefully blank. "How could that be possible? True mates have a bond, right? You can feel each other and stuff."

"Yes, and the connection did appear when I fed from her. It was like this sharp jab in my neck, and then I could sense ... feel her emotions. Still, I'd be a liar if I didn't say that the bond wasn't what I expected from a true mateship. There should have been more attraction or love or something ... I didn't question it that much, expecting it would grow with time."

Mischa shifted around and I started to slow, lowering my head so our eyes could meet. I wanted to focus fully on this conversation.

"The connection never deepened between you?"

I didn't really know how to answer that. Truth was, the connection never did go to the place I expected. Cardia and I shared a bed, shared thoughts and conversations, but ... there was a coldness in my mate which I didn't care for. Even when I had to go into Faerie to search for Jessa, I didn't mourn leaving her. I recognized that much more fully now. At the time I'd thought I was being practical, but now that I had a child on the way I knew nothing but the direst of emergencies would tear me from Mischa's side, from protecting her. My vampire had claimed this little wolf shifter and our baby as pack, and we protected pack.

"Damn ... I never thought of her as pack," I murmured. "That's what was wrong. My brothers, Jess, and you are all pack or nest mates to my vampire, but he never accepted her."

Mischa coughed then, and I could see the red tingeing her cheeks again. "You think of me as a pack mate?"

Before I could answer she said, "I haven't seen many true mates, but judging off Jess and Brax and my parents, it seems like there was something seriously wrong in the bond between you and Cardia. Is there any way to find out why?"

Damn, looked like Braxton might be right. I didn't like the thought that my life and emotions had been messed with. Was Cardia my true mate and something had caused the rift? Or was the mate bond somehow manufactured so I'd believe her to be my mate? Why would that have happened? What was the end game in Cardia infiltrating my life?

"Could it have been about Larkspur? Or his daughters?" Mischa said, somehow cleverly picking up where my thoughts were going. "Could they have used Cardia as a 'man on the inside?' Larkspur's daughters did know a lot about us. They used that information to get me to agree to their plan. At the time I never realized, but looking back I see that they knew exactly what emotional buttons to press."

I ground to a halt, my entire body going into lockdown. The growls rocked me again, but I let them come this time as the rage bubbled up like an erupting volcano. "Are you saying that maybe this was all to make sure you were alone so they could use and abuse, manipulate and almost kill you, knowing you wouldn't have anyone on your side to protect you? That Cardia was a plant to keep me occupied while all this shit went down?"

I was yelling at this point, which was stupid, but I couldn't control myself. If Mischa had died in the Romanian prison, our child would have also. A child I'd never have known of. The very thought that I could have lost them both that day, was too much for me to handle.

Mischa wiggled out of my arms, and even though I didn't want to I let her back to her feet. "I don't know, Max. It seems very extreme just to make sure I was in a vulnerable position. Why didn't they do the same for the other quads?"

My extended fangs had my words lisping again. I needed blood and less rage. My vampire was not so easily subdued right now. "Because they knew I was the one you were closest to. You relied on me for guidance when Jess was busy with Braxton and all of her other dragon marked troubles."

Mischa fell silent. I could see the trembling of her limbs, hear the rapid beat of her heart as she fought for control. Unable to stop myself, I wrapped my arms around her, pulling her into me. My size engulfed her, but for some reason we fit together perfectly. Cardia had been just too tiny; there had been no easy way for us to hug. But Mischa … she was perfect.

"We'll figure this out," I murmured. "I'm going to get to the bottom of what the hell happened to me in the sanctuary. Cardia had nest mate vamps there. They might be able to give me some background or history." I'd never found out that much personal stuff about her, she was so reticent with information. I never pushed her because I didn't really care to know. I had no idea where she originated except she'd been in the sanctuary most of her life because of the mark.

Mischa's trembles eased as I held her. The fierce expression was back on her face when she pulled away. "Max, she wasn't affected by the dragon king's call. I know we thought it was because of her bond with you and your calling to defeat the king, but what if she was never dragon marked? That mark could have been a tattoo, or like magically stuck on her." Her brows rose and those depthless eyes went opaque. "That can happen, right? Magical tattoos and stuff?"

I nodded. "Yes, that can definitely happen. The mark would have been the easiest part for her to fake. How she got through the sanctuary doors is a much bigger question."

My heart lurched. A feeling of disloyalty was strong and potent within my mind and body. Questioning Cardia was a betrayal of our bond, but at the same time I'd be an idiot to not question the issues that had been present in our relationship. Easy to ignore at the time, especially with so much going on, but now ... well, I was going to find out everything.

I took a second to ground myself, using the stillness of nature, the scent of the forest, the call of animals around me. I wasn't sure if I felt better or worse. The fact that the mate bond might have been falsely manipulated meant I wasn't just a cold, unfeeling bastard toward my mate, but it also meant some asshole had messed with my life, and my pack. They had caused untold grief. I could have missed the birth of my child. If Jessa hadn't insisted I return, and if I hadn't had responsibilities to my brothers and our town, I doubt I would have returned home for a long time.

Mischa made a muffled noise, almost like she was clearing her throat, and my attention zoomed straight to her. But she wasn't looking at me, she was staring into the dense, bushy forest.

"Did you hear something?" she murmured.

Immediately I unleashed my vampire. I'd had the beast so locked down that my senses were dulled. I should have known better when we were outside the town's protections.

As I slowly circled, taking in the entire area, I reached out and pulled Mischa to my side. The slow steady thud of hearts beating and blood pumping started to filter through the air. She was right. More than one supe was closing in on us.

"Hold on," I said as I snatched her up and took off. My speed was hindered only slightly by the additional weight – and the very large worry that too much jostling was not good for the baby. Shifters were tough, even when pregnant, but I would take no risks.

"I can shift," she whispered up to me, her voice only slightly trembling. 'That way if I have to fight I can."

I gave a violent shake of my head. "No! No way will you be fighting in your condition."

The breath whooshed out of me as she somehow managed to kick me in the gut. I recovered almost immediately, but hey … impressive shot.

Her voice thrummed with anger as she let loose on me. "Not trying to channel my twin here, but in regards to my condition, I'm pregnant, not dying, and you have no right to issue orders or demands. I'll never blindly follow anyone's orders ever again, and since I'm still very much in possession of a brain, you can explain yourself without demanding and we might even be on the same page."

I knew it wasn't in my best interest to laugh, but I was definitely enjoying this new side of Mischa. "My plan is to keep you and our baby safe. I'm the idiot who lost my mind and decided to bring you outside of the town's protections. I can't stand the thought that you two might be in danger…"

I cut myself off before more messed up thoughts fell out of my mouth. Every time I talked to Mischa, I ended up telling her so much more than I planned.

What the hell was this chick in possession of, some sort of magical faerie dust that had me spilling my innermost emotions? Definitely something going on there, but I had no time to deal with that. Now I needed to kill any motherfucker who thought they could threaten Mischa and my child.

CHAPTER SIX

Mischa Lebron

There have been a few moments in life which have defined me. The first was when I was three and almost killed two boys in the playground. They were five and six years old and had been bullying a little girl and her younger brother. Poor kids had been trying to build an epic castle, and I was wandering across the yard to help them out when all hell broke loose. The two boys, who I later found out were brothers, Mark and Mitchell Jones, were poor kids who had an alcoholic father and a prostitute for a mother. Still, at the very naïve age of three, I knew nothing of these matters, so when they started smashing the sandcastle, kicking sand into the faces of the other kids and shoving them around, I saw red.

If I'd been observing my three-year-old actions from an adult perspective, I'd have had no problem telling I wasn't human. I ran faster than was humanly possible and dived across to pummel both of the boys into the ground. If Lienda hadn't been close by, I had no doubt my red rage would have prevented me from stopping before I seriously injured them. It was lucky she was there, and additionally lucky that not many others were around the park that early.

We moved the next day, and I got the biggest kick to the butt for acting on instinct, which confused me at the time – what three-year-old even knows about instinct? – and exposing us to the humans – another phrase which confused me. Still, that was the first time I started to understand that I was a freak, that I didn't think or act the same as the people around me. It was also the first time my mom was really disappointed in me, and I didn't even understand why. I now knew she'd been trying to keep me safe, but the truth was, her lecture tore me down and was the first time I started to question who I was. To hate who I was.

No parent should teach their children to deny their true self. Because of that moment I would spend the next nineteen years trying to mold myself to fit in with humans, and since I was not a human, all I really did was lose small parts of my soul, until there was nothing much left but the shell of a supe.

Some of my soul returned when I found out the truth of who I was, when I found out about the supernatural world. When I found my sister. That was when all of the messed up thoughts and events started to make sense. More pieces of soul clicked into place when I fell pregnant, because the pure rightness and love was so all encompassing that it changed me fundamentally. And now there was one more thing that had changed me, that I never anticipated happening.

Maximus Compass.

As he ran at vampire speed through the forest and lands of Connecticut, both of us probably being chased by psychos who wanted to kill us and wear our heads as a hat or some crap, I'd never felt happier or more content. His pure joy and acceptance of our baby, well, it was so much more than I'd expected. It was the first time I felt that I had someone in my corner. A friend even. I knew raising a baby was going to be tough – it takes a village and all that, or so the humans say. In my opinion, Maximus was going to be a pretty darn good village.

"You okay?" His low voice jolted me and I focused on our surroundings again. I was really not good at this stealth and subterfuge thing. "I'm not shaking you around too much?"

Right. He was concerned for the baby, which was to be expected. All of the Compasses had turned into crazy protective monsters over me and Jessa the moment they found out about our babies.

"I'm perfectly fine. Me and bubs are tough."

I tried to lighten the mood, but it was clear that the rigid lines of tension which had Maximus' face looking like it was carved from granite were not going to disappear until we were back in Stratford.

"Don't worry, Misch, I'll never let anything happen to you. There are a few of them following us, but they are going to regret that very soon."

At that moment supes burst out of the trees to our right and charged straight for us. I expected Maximus to go mental then, until I noticed one of them was a dragon ... who happened to be carrying my twin on his back. Jessa. She looked like the queen of the dragons. Which was pretty fitting actually, since Josephina, the dragon from her soul, was now the queen of all wild dragons.

Maximus powered across to his brothers and I was gently deposited to the ground beside my sister. Braxton started shifting back, Tyson standing by to clothe him. My twin took two steps forward and threw herself into Maximus' arms; the two of them began whispering furiously. I waited for my normal jealousy to rear its ugly head. I hated to envy anyone, because we all knew that people fought battles you could not see, but the closeness of Jessa and her pack, well, it was a sore point for me.

But the jealousy never came. I felt only a sense of happiness and contentment at their love and acceptance, to see the pack bonds solidifying. Maybe because now I felt like a part of their world, their pack. It didn't hurt that Jessa was solidly mated and it was a true bond. Maximus wouldn't stand a chance even if he wanted one. And according to him, he didn't. Which blew my mind and eased that part of my soul which had always felt used by him.

Tyson reached out and hugged me hard. My heart gave a wrench, which happened every time someone showed me this sort of affection, a hug for no reason other than being happy to see me. "Good to see you and my nephew in one piece, wolf girl."

Pulling back, I shoved him a little. "I keep telling you, it could be a girl."

Maximus was suddenly at my side then. "Boy or girl, it doesn't matter."

Holy shit. I felt a delicate sort of smile lift my lips, emulating all the soft emotions swirling around inside of me.

Tyson hugged his brother then too. "So glad to see you back, bro. We've missed you."

Tyson threw me a questioning glance, eyebrows raised. I knew immediately what he was asking. Why was Maximus looking so happy and not … devastated and broken? We'd have to tell them all about the Cardia theory later and see what they thought on it. Braxton clearly had some opinions, since he'd been the first to ever mention it, but he wasn't the only smart one in this bunch. All of their insights would be useful.

Braxton stilled then, and all of us froze as well. The dragon had the best senses of any of us, but as he slowly scanned the surroundings, he didn't seem to pick up on anything.

Eventually he turned back to us. "I heard your call, Max. What's going on?"

"Mischa and I were being pursued by at least four supes. I detected shifter and magic user. I was making ground on them, but didn't want to risk them being stronger than me on my own. Not with the baby to protect."

"We should join, take them on at our strongest," Jacob suggested.

The fey was often right about these sort of things – I thought he was a bit of a fortune teller myself – so I wasn't surprised when no one argued.

I hurried to Jessa's side and we stood back to back, keeping an eye on the forest around us. The quads reached out and linked to each other, power swirling in heavy arcs around them; they were connecting through their special quad bond.

"I can't believe Braxton let you come," I said to Jessa.

A snort of laughter left her. "Let ... oh no, baby girl, I have much to teach you. The key to any solid mateship is to curb that "letting me" bullshit early on. Braxton knows I'm strong, capable, and smart, and he's coming to realize that his over-protectiveness is going to result in a lack of sex and a swift boot in the ass."

It was my turn to snort. "Lack of sex ... yeah, right."

I could feel the silent chuckles as Jessa fought to contain her laughter. "Yeah, you have a point. That punishes no one but me. Still, there are plenty of other ways I can make life very uncomfortable for my sexy-ass mate and he knows it."

He most definitely did. But I also knew that Braxton was very good at picking his battles, and he would fight her when he really needed to. That's why they worked so well. Jessa was the epitome of the old adage: if you gave her an inch, she would take three zillion miles. Braxton doled the inches out in small increments, and reeled her back in when she got out of control. The perfect balance really.

Conversation was lost then as the quads finished their joining, energy wrapping around them in visible strands. Braxton wasn't in his beast-man fusion state, which totally reminded me of oldschool werewolf movies where they shifted into a man-wolf, except Braxton's was dragon spec. He seemed to be able to choose now whether he went into the fusion body. As the quads' power grew, so did their control.

I had to clench my fists at my side to stop from moving. The pain of my nails pressing into my palms was just enough to keep a clear head. For some reason, when Maximus was joined to his brothers, the connection I felt to him increased exponentially, like I had to physically restrain myself from the need to touch him. I'd noticed it when I'd seen them join before the battle with Larkspur.

A battle I'd been part of longer than anyone realized. Thankfully I'd managed to stop myself from attacking any of our side, even with the king's voice in my head trying to control me. I had been stronger than Larkspur's call. My entire life people had been forcing me into a fake mold and I had refused to let the dragon king do the same. Thankfully, when things had gotten really bad, Jonathon had found me and knocked me unconscious. Which had brought blessed relief.

Jessa's low voice startled me. "Are you feeling the connection, Misch? When the boys join, the mate bond thing kicks in so hard. It is taking every single piece of restraint I possess to not go over there and start licking my mate."

I saw Braxton grin and knew he could hear our conversation. Then Maximus turned and nailed me hard with his black gaze. The vampire was riding across his skin, and he was so much larger than normal. Holy shit. Really? Like he needed any extra help in the physically dominating and hot-as-hell thing.

"Misch!"

My twin startled me again. Damn, I had forgotten all about keeping an eye on our surroundings. In my current frazzled state, the bad guys could have snuck up and stabbed me, no problem. Of course, they probably wouldn't have made it that far with the way the vampire had his eyes locked on me. Well, not me. Our baby. But still, I got the protection for a while. I was the baby's home for another month at least.

"Mischa ... you there?" Jessa was tapping her foot now and I realized I still hadn't answered her.

"Yes, I'm here. And no, I don't know what you're talking about."

She returned my glare with one of her own. "Yes you do. You know exactly what I'm talking about. What's going on with you and Max?"

I shook out my hair, reaching up to push it behind my ears. I recently had it cut, and the shorter, shoulder length was taking some getting used to. "Nothing is going on with us except that we're having a baby. That's our bond."

Jessa turned back to stare at the quads, who were fanning out around us, waiting for the ambush to arrive. "Baby my ass, that's not the way a man looks at his baby mama, unless that baby mama is also his girl. So I'll ask you again, twin sister, what is going on with you two?"

With a huff, knowing she wouldn't give up, I leaned in close. The boys were prowling around us, scanning the perimeter and not paying attention. I kept my voice low as I told her everything which had happened between Maximus and me. How he'd accepted our child without question, how it felt like some of the aching sadness in his dark, espresso-colored eyes had eased. How the bond with Cardia might not have been a true one.

"Interesting," she said after a few moments. "Never liked that vampire bitch anyway. She was shady. Still, I'm definitely seeing more in that stare than simply wanting to keep your baby safe. I've known these boys my entire life, and something major is churning in Max's head."

Jessa was reading too much into this. Of course his emotions were strong, he'd just found out he was going to be a father, and he recently lost his mate. His fake true mate. Or whatever.

Either way his thoughts were going to be messed up. The truth was I probably, sort of, almost definitely, loved Maximus Compass. But I would never accept a relationship with someone who was only in it for our child, or because it was convenient. If the past few months had taught me anything, it was that I needed to stand on my own two feet, that I should never accept anything other than true love, devotion, and passion from the supe I chose to spend my life with. True mateship didn't interest me so much. I wanted to choose. And I wanted them to choose me.

The quads, who were still fanned out around us, about twenty yards from where we stood, started to spread out further. When they were a good distance away, Maximus swung his head around and leveled a long look in my direction. He gave me the old "wait right there" hand gesture, and followed his brothers as they continued to hunt down those who had been following us. They must be close again.

My hand dropped to my belly and I sent as many comforting thoughts as I could toward my baby.

We stood there in silence for a few beats, before Jessa said: "Braxton's picked up their trail. Four of them. The boys are gonna take the little assholes down and then come right back."

I nodded, figuring as much. My sister started to pace, before tilting her head to the side. "Can you hear that?"

She started to slowly move then, heading in the direction of the thickest greenery around us. Having no idea what she was talking about, I stuck close to her. After a minute I finally began to understand what had caught her attention. It was a whirring noise, almost like an engine, low, blending into the forest sounds around us. What was it doing out here in the middle of this unpopulated landscape?

I grasped onto Jessa. "I don't think we should go any further." My instincts were screaming at me to get out of here, even if I had to throw Jessa over my shoulder. I must have been channeling Braxton or something.

Our eyes locked and the bond kicked in hard between us. It was so much more difficult to keep the blocks up when we were touching.

We can't let the boys go off and fight them without our help. Jessa's voice was firm. *This might be some sort of trap for them.*

What help will we be to them if we're kidnapped, gagged, and tied down in the back of a vehicle?

She shook her head at me, something dark in her blue eyes.

We're not human, and we'll not go without a fight.

I tried one last time to reason with her: *We don't even know what we're walking in on.*

We'll just have a sneaky peek.

That was the fundamental difference between me and my twin. She went in without thought. I was more cautious. It wasn't fear which held me back, it was an overly developed sense of logic. It just didn't make sense for us, two pregnant shifters, to run into the dense forest toward an unknown threat. That noise could be a vehicle, or a large piece of machinery. Not to mention the boys expected us to stay where we were. They were going to lose it when they came back and we were gone. It was irresponsible to run off on them like that.

I spoke out loud this time. "I understand what you're saying, I'll always fight when we're directly attacked, but in this instance we're actively looking for trouble. It's not smart."

Jessa sighed. "Way too much human in you, Misch. We're part animal, designed to act on instinct. It's been honed for thousands of years. Don't ignore your instincts."

She took off then, darting through the trees. Um, hello, my instincts were saying to stay right here, in relative safety.

With a shake of my head I followed her. Braxton was totally going to kill her. She'd better enjoy her time outside Stratford, because soon she was going to be on heavy lockdown.

Don't ignore your instincts...

Seriously, the last time I'd followed my instincts I fell for a vamp and got knocked up. Instinct could kiss my butt. The grass whipped around me in a dusty array of seeds and winter-browned growth. New greenery was just starting to push its way up. Spring. My absolute favorite time of the year. Let's just hope Jessa didn't get me killed. I'd like to be around to enjoy it.

My twin's dark hair disappeared briefly amongst the first set of trees. Keeping my waddling to a minimum, I managed to gain some ground on her, and as the darkness of the canopy closed around me, she came into view again.

Running while this pregnant was neither practical or elegant. I thrashed through the bush with the same grace as a herd of elephants, but I was pretty impressed with my speed. The engine sound was louder now, a deep thrumming ricocheting off the trees, which were creating a large, naturally acoustic stadium. The closer we got to the noise, the less it sounded like a vehicle. In fact, despite the smooth and seamless nature of the hum, I could hear clanking, and mechanical whirling, almost like it was a large saw mill or something with a conveyer belt...

My thoughts died off as Jessa ground to a halt. "What the actual..."

"Fuck?" Jessa said.

I hurried to her side, and together we spent a few tense seconds trying to discern what the hell this was.

"Hansel and Gretel, right?" Jessa's voice was no louder than a whisper. "I'm not totally up on human fairy tales, but there was one about a house made of candy."

I snaked out and gripped onto my sister's hand. "Yes, the old witch lured the children in, then fattened them up so she could eat them."

Jessa's head shot around to face me, her blue eyes wide, and glassy. "Witches don't eat children."

I shrugged. "Well, that was the story, and I don't think she was a witch like you know from the supernatural community. She was a human version of a witch, so she was evil and stuff."

How the hell was this possible? Here, in the middle of this perfectly normal forest, was a house straight out of the storybooks. Single level, not overly large, styled in colors of pastel rainbows – pastel rainbows which were made totally of candy, cake, and sweets. Peppermint stick railings on the wraparound porch. Gum drops, Twizzlers, goobers and more. Buttercream icing was perfectly swirled on the roof tiles, and none of it dripped or anything. Not only was the place covered with every sort of sweet imaginable – trust me, my wolf senses were having a field day with the scents – but each candy was so perfectly positioned across the structure that there had to be a ton of magic holding it all together. It was also the source of the mechanical whirring noise.

Jessa shifted forward and I tightened my grip on her hand. "Do you think it's a good idea to go any closer? The house sounds like it's going to transform or something."

She tilted her head back to me. "This is Supe land, where our Guilds come to drop off goods, where our criminal search teams travel through to get in and out. This house should not be here. I don't even care that I haven't had cake in days and the roof seems to be made of slabs of chocolate cake, with buttercream swirls and flaked chips of real, German-made cacao flakes…"

Her voice got all breathy at the end. Someone needed to get her chocolate fix. "Are you sure it's not your cake addiction talking right now? Because if we both end up in a cage while a witch feels our fingers to see if we're fat enough, I'm going to be really upset with you."

Jessa's eyes fell down to my large stomach and I followed to hers. Both of us cracked up then, our laughter mostly silent.

Still, as we sobered, both of us placed a hand on our bellies. "Maybe I should wait for Braxton this time," Jessa said. "I'm not saying that we need men to do things for us, but with our precious cargo on board, a little backup wouldn't go astray."

I nodded. "Good plan, sister. I'm totally down with that."

Of course, before we could turn and make our way back to the clearing to find the guys, a huge gust of wind started churning around us. As my hair whipped across my face, I squinted into the unnatural and newly formed whirl of air. *It was coming from the house.* Holy hell. That explained the mechanical whirring noises we were hearing. The house was creating its own weather or something, and Jessa and I were in a crap-ton of trouble. There was no way we could cross the heavy wind barrier that had gusted up to surround us, we would be swept up and thrown to our death.

Jessa and I squished ourselves closer together. "Any brilliant ideas?" she shouted to me.

I nodded. "Yes, go back in time and kill you in the womb."

Jessa cracked up then, holding her stomach while she tried not to fall down. "I think I love the new, asshole version of you. It's so much better than the pod person you were in the sanctuary."

I circled around, trying to see if there was a weakness in the wind. "I was under a lot of stress and did some stupid stuff. I'm not proud of myself, but you, my sister, just leap every time before you look."

Jessa shrugged, and I could see that she didn't disagree with that statement, but didn't really think it was a bad thing either. And generally it wasn't.

"You just have to remember that you don't have a dragon to fall back on any longer."

Jessa's face fell and I felt terrible for bringing up her loss. Josephina had left a massive hole in my sister's heart and soul, and she was definitely still hurting. But I needed her to stay alive, even if I had to drill it into her. Despite my earlier jest about killing her in the womb, I couldn't live in a world she wasn't in. I loved her more than almost anyone else in my world. Except my baby.

Which was the emotional manipulation I hit her with next: "Plus you have two little dragon babies to think about. And yes, knowing you and Braxton, your children are definitely going to be all-powerful, natural dragon babies which could take on the world ... but just in case they aren't, you need to be more careful."

Jessa started to growl, but she also reached across and hugged me. "You're probably right, sister." She pulled back a little to meet my eye. "And you're going to make an amazing mom. I haven't told you that enough. I'm so proud of you. Your strength is admirable."

Don't cry. I ordered my tear ducts to dry the hell up. We were in the middle of a situation here; this was no time to fall apart. I pulled Jessa back in for one last fierce hug, and then both of us focused fully on our surroundings.

"Should we just take the risk and see if we can dive through the barrier?" Jessa said as we inched our way closer to the right side of the wind tunnel. As we stepped closer the wind whipped across our bodies and I could feel the strength of it. "Or should we go into the cake house and see what we find?"

The wind cut us off on all angles except for the direction of the house. Which didn't seem like a great thing. "I'm sure we both realize now that this is a trap to lure stupid supes or humans in with the candy and then blow up the tornado. Now we have no option but to go into this quaint, surely not dangerous at all, perfect cottage."

My sarcasm was on point.

Jessa sighed, just a little exhalation, but I could feel her annoyance. "I'm not great with patience, and despite the fact that I've called through the bond for Braxton, he's still not here."

"Maybe this wind thing is more than just a physical barrier. Maybe it's also a magical one that's blocking your call?"

My twin straightened and took a few steps closer to the whirling vortex around us. Her hands drifted along the edge, the way a mime's would during a performance.

"It's odd," she finally said, without turning away. "Generally I can sense magic with ease, and while there's something threaded through this wind, it's not like any magic I've known before."

Great. Weird, unknown magic. Just what we needed. As Jessa continued creeping along the edge of the wind, her hands brushing up and down in a sweeping manner, I followed closely behind. Like Jessa, I had always been able to detect magic.

In the human world I'd never understood why these weird, almost static electricity-like sparks would trigger between me and certain humans. Now I knew why, of course, and also why those sparks had filled my blood with energy. Magic. So foreign to my understanding, but at the same time starting to feel pretty normal.

Jessa's pace picked up and we were soon standing in front of the house. She had that "cake glazed look" again as she stared up at it. She was totally trying to figure out how to get some of the icing off the roof.

"We shouldn't go inside," I said, nudging her to bring her back to reality. "Every instinct I have is telling me it's a bad idea to go in there. People go in there and never return."

"What are you basing this information on?"

I was probably grasping, but something about this scene triggered a memory. "Mom has always watched the news, every night without fail. Now out of habit I find myself flicking it on. While you were in Faerie, we had a lot of human news stories about hikers going missing in this state, and other weird things with animals. No one in Stratford seemed to care. The supes had much more important things to worry about with Larkspur, but now that I see this here, it's all starting to make sense to me."

"We don't interfere in human problems unless there's a supernatural element," Jessa mused. "Normally, though, something odd this close to Stratford, on our outer territory, would definitely be investigated. The whole Larky thing left everything a mess. No leaders. War across the councils. This slipped through the cracks somehow."

That bothered her. A lot. Surprisingly, I felt the same strong sense of anger and annoyance. I was really starting to feel as if Stratford, and the supernatural community, were my true home and family. I didn't like that someone was trying to take advantage of the recent conflict, and I kind of wanted to rip their heads off and shove them up their own butts.

"Even if this is targeted mainly at humans, it's clearly still supernatural in nature. So we need to investigate it, right?" For the first time I was the one to step closer to the building. "We can't let them prey on humans, or others. What if it's Kristoff or the bear shifters and they're using them as sacrifices or something."

Jessa's head shot around to me. I could see the thoughts firing through her mind also. "Ever since Giselda went on that extended visit to Italy – which kind of bothered me at the time but I was actually really happy she left – I've been thinking that there was something extra weird up with her."

Giselda was my sister's arch-enemy, a witch who was the daughter of Kristoff. What if his daughter was the one helping him with whatever plan he was trying to enact?

"Giselda might never have left America either," I said. "Despite her getting the all-clear, she's probably helping her father." The witches had used some sort of spell to clear her of anything to do with Kristoff and his crimes, but that wasn't totally foolproof.

Jessa growled, picking up my last thoughts. "If anyone knows how to get around those truth spells, it's the Krass family. There was a reason they refused a shifter be in the room. They wanted only magic users dealing with the issue. And since Giselda never technically committed a crime, she still had the right to refuse other races be present."

I was slowly learning how our world worked. I should have been taught from birth, but circumstances being what they were ... I was way behind. I was taking the most basic of classes, and some private lessons to try and hurry my progress, but was still pretty ignorant to the ins and outs.

From what I knew, supes didn't have that many "real" laws. The races seemed to keep track of their members, and make sure they didn't go around causing too much chaos. For the larger crimes, then the Book of Guidance passed judgment, and criminals could end up in one of the supe prisons. There was no death sentence unless you fought in the field, but with our long lives you might wish you had been put to death after hundreds of years locked in a prison.

The howl of the wind increased and I found myself spinning around, my back to the candy house. Jessa and I had been so busy talking that we'd missed the sweeping wind closing in on us. It was so close now that if I took a single step forward I'd have been swept up into it.

"Any ideas?" I said, as we both slid back as close as we could to the house. My heels were against the front step; if I moved back any further I'd been up through the peppermint railings and onto the chocolate deck.

Before she could answer, I noticed movement on the other side of the wind wall. Shadows moved into view, large and distinctive.

"Braxton," I heard my twin say with an exhalation of air. "We stay put until the boys figure out how to break through this."

Of course, that was a brilliant plan. Except for the fact that the house must have heard her and decided it was not okay with that. The wind exploded around us. My feet left the ground and we were swept up into the gale. I reached out and grasped onto Jessa's hand, covering my stomach with my other as I fought to protect my child from whatever was going to happen.

The front door of the house slammed open, and I swear as we were sucked into the unknown beyond, multiple roars ripped through the wind. The Compass shadows disappeared when the front door slammed behind us, enclosing me and Jessa in darkness.

CHAPTER SEVEN

Maximus Compass

My head was a mess. My heart was a mess. But my vampire instincts never let me down and neither did my brothers. I was heading south, chasing down our prey; the boys were spread out across the forest. The distance between us was great but I could sense them strongly through our bond. The quad bond. It was also through this that I kept tabs on Mischa, via Braxton and Jessa.

The dragon shifter's attention never strayed far from his girl, which was exactly how a mate bond should be.

The twins hadn't exactly remained where we left them, but the area around them was still clear of danger. Which was a relief, allowing me to immerse myself fully in the chase. My vampire side was amped, the bloodlust riding me hard. I had not fed properly in a long time, and the faint life in human blood was dull and tasteless compared to supes'.

Unlike other vamps, I could go a long time without feeding, but the time was nearing. I would have to find a donor, or settle for bottled blood. The thought of feeding from a female supe just wasn't sitting well with me. Humans had been different, they were not my kind, but when vampires fed from female supes, there was something intrinsically sensual about it.

So it looked like it was bottled blood for me. Almost as bad as human.

Scents crashed into me as I closed the distance between me and my prey – one of the four supes who had been stupid enough to try and stalk my steps earlier. I had zero tolerance for any being who thought they could threaten my pack. And with Jessa and Mischa pregnant ... well, let's just say my brothers and I would be asking questions later.

We protected what was ours.

Mine's a shifter. Tyson's magical essence was strong. His words cut off as he confronted the male. I could see through his eyes if I wanted, but there was no need. *Shifter bear,* Tyson finished.

He would call for us if he needed help, so I pulled my focus back to the one I was tracking. A flash of black caught my eye, clearly not part of the natural landscape around me. Asshole was going down, and once I found out who sent him, he was going to find himself in Vanguard, where the guards might pay extra close attention to him.

My senses were firing hard, and I followed the scent I had locked into my brain. I could pick this supe out in a crowd any day, but I still had no idea of their race. The muddiness of it suggested demi-fey.

I kicked up my speed another few notches and the black came into sight again. It was a cloak shrouding a small, hunched form. The figure moved fast, almost at the same superspeed as me, which ruled out ninety percent of the demi-fey.

After another minute, I was starting to get the picture of what I chased. Harpy. These bird-women had leathery skin, beak-like noses, and a penchant for war and violence. What the hell was she doing near Stratford? Actually, what was she doing on Earth? I'd never seen one in the human realm – especially not outside of the prison system. They mostly stayed in Faerie where their unusual looks and vicious nature was less noticeable. Jessa and Braxton had had a recent run in with them, and I knew if my brother caught up with this demi-fey first, she probably wouldn't make it to Vanguard.

The figure hunched over further before ducking beneath some small bushes. There was no easy way for me to follow that path, but I could see where those bushes ended. I dashed around the side just as she darted out, and grabbed the back of her cloak.

The material was smooth, silky even. Not what I'd expected from the coarse-looking thread. Definitely a Faerie garment, which made it that much easier to slip through my fingers.

"Shit!"

My curse had her speeding up again. This was not my day. I needed about a hundred hours to sleep, feed, and time to catch up with my family and appreciate the gift of Mischa and the child she carried. I also had to look into this Cardia fake mate and fake dragon marked thing. I did not need a goddamn harpy leading me on a chase through the wilderness.

A twinge of unease crept along my spine then, and almost in the same instant I felt the spiciness of

Braxton's worry in my blood. Surely he hadn't run into any trouble with his prey? Not even worth worrying about, which meant his concern was ... Jessa. There was no other explanation.

We'd left Mischa and Jessa back in the clearing, secure in the knowledge that the four of us had our pursuers on the run. But what if we'd missed one? What if this was all a trap to leave the girls vulnerable?

Braxton. Are the girls okay? He had me locked from his mind now; my footsteps slowed as I waited for his reply. The harpy was disappearing again, but that was the least of my worries. Braxton's deep tones came back at me hard. *Maximus, fall back. Jess is blocked from me.*

I didn't hear anything more, I was already gone. The world blurred around me as I ran; the entire time I prayed to the gods, to the fey, to anyone who would listen. I could not just find out about the pregnancy only to lose Mischa and my child so soon.

I could feel my brothers close behind but I was going to get to the clearing first. Breaking free from the trees, I zeroed in on where we'd left the girls. It was empty. As I ground to a halt, I forced myself to slow my breathing. I needed to get my shit together so my senses could work to their full potential. As the blood pounding in my veins eased, I was able to scent the path the girls had taken. The trail was strong; they'd only just recently left.

I charged into the forest, Braxton right behind me. He was in human form, the forest too dense in places for his dragon. There was an odd thrashing sound in the direction we were heading, almost like a tropical storm, but it was still clear skies above us.

"Can you feel Jessa?" I asked when Braxton reached my side.

"Yes," he said, that one word brimming with fury. "She's worried. She hasn't actually called for me yet, but I can tell she's in trouble."

Whomever had touched them was going to die. Plenty of places to hide a body out here. Wouldn't be a problem. "I've got their trail. No time to wait for the others, they can catch up."

Braxton didn't say any more. Locked on with laser focus, both of us crashed through the shrubbery and dense foliage. The light, foresty scent of Jessa was strong. She always reminded me of new life, swirling winds, and the strength of nature. It was almost as if her scent were part mother nature, part sexy nymph. Mischa, on the other hand, had some elements of Jessa's earthiness, but with a slightly sweeter undertone – floral even. Hers was the real deep, rich aroma of the first blossoms of spring, and I could follow that scent across the world if I had to.

The path we strode showed clear signs of damage from others who'd used it before us. Many more than just the twins had followed this trail. It was well-used, leading us right into the densest part of this pocket of forest, toward the mix of storm and machinery noises.

"What the fuck?" I cursed as we dashed into a clearing.

Braxton was already growling, both of us grinding to a halt. The storm noise made sense now. The entire clearing was filled with a massive tornado, twenty feet high and thick enough to almost obscure the objects it surrounded.

"This is magically created," Braxton said. "So what the hell is it doing all the way out here? There are no magic users in this area."

None registered to our town anyway, which meant this was probably dark in nature.

As we stepped closer I could just make out the shape of a small house nestled in amongst the trees, and standing before it seemed to be the twins. Or at least twin-shaped shadows.

"Have you ever seen anything like this before?"

Braxton swiveled to meet my gaze. "Never."

Great. I stepped as close as I could, trying not to flip the hell out. Just the knowledge that something which was clearly dangerous and magical in nature was separating me from Mischa ... I was on the edge of losing it.

"It's not attacking them," I said, my eyes darting at vampire speed to try and discern everything from the scene. "But I think the house is made of ... candy ... which is all kinds of screwed up. Is the house holding them hostage?"

Braxton snarled, very dragon-like, and when I turned toward him I could see the yellow splashed across his eyes; his features were getting that lizard look about them. Most of the quad bond was disabled at the moment, just enough connection remained so Tyson and Jacob could find us, but I still picked up the animalistic nature of his mind.

Braxton's words were guttural. "The boys are almost here. I'm going to drop the rest of our bond and shift."

I stepped back. In a flash Braxton was naked and then he was dragon. Stepping to his side, I waited for him to charge the wind barrier. If anyone could break through the magic of this unnatural tornado, it was the dragon. And he wasn't going in without me.

"Max!"

Jacob's shout let me know he was almost there, Tyson right behind him. Which was good; I wanted us at full strength. We'd take no chances with the girls or their babies.

My baby. Fuck. Heads were going to roll when I got to the other side. The dragon launched itself toward the wind, but just before his snout crashed through, a filtering of magic washed over the area, slamming into the four of us, knocking us back a few yards.

What the hell? Magic rarely acted so strongly against us like that, especially not the dragon.

Braxton was already moving again, Tyson and I close to his right, Jacob on his left.

"That was dark magic," Tyson rumbled. That explained the strength. "Someone is casting a spell using demon energy."

The wizard raised his hands, and as he started to murmur under his breath, I felt his own potent brand of energy zip away.

"Can you tell where it's coming from?" I asked.

Braxton had paused. One wrong move with dark magic and we might make the situation a lot worse for everyone. Demons were not to be messed with. It was only their inability to live on Earth without a host that gave us any advantage against them.

Tyson took a few minutes to answer, by which time Braxton's rumbles and fiery breath had increased exponentially. Finally the wizard said: "The darkness originated in that house. Strong sorcery, mixed of so many energies, but ... fuck ... I'm getting a whiff of the Krass family."

Those words were an accelerant to the fire inside of Braxton. The dragon tilted his head back, roaring and letting his huge plume of flames spring free. He then took off at a crazed run.

Tyson continued speaking as we followed the beast: "I've had enough classes with that asshole to know the signature of his craft. Arrogant sorcerer hasn't even bothered to hide his trace."

Braxton was just about to dive through the wind barrier again – nothing was going to stop him this time – when the heavy energy in the area increased and the barrier started tightening in on the girls, moving faster than we could reach it, even with vampire and dragon speed.

That didn't stop us from trying though.

My hand had just scraped along the edge of the wind when there was an imploding pop noise, and in a blink the gusts scooped up the twin shadows and then they were gone. Within two heartbeats there was nothing left in the clearing.

Even the house was gone.

Everything inside of me turned to pure darkness, my fangs shooting free; my rational side disappeared under the craving of the vampire. I could hear Braxton roaring beside me, and I knew Tyson and Jacob were equally as angry. All of us lost ourselves for a few moments, a trademark of males when they feel true fear. Fear is not an emotion we Compasses are well equipped to handle, and I for one wanted to tear this forest to pieces until it revealed my pack mates.

I scraped together as much of my sanity as I could. The deep exhaustion which had been plaguing me for days was forgotten as adrenalin coursed through me.

My focus was on Tyson. "Can you trace that magic?"

He nodded. "Yep, already on it."

I left him to it, knowing he needed to concentrate. Braxton was flapping his wings, so I stepped across and touched a hand to his flank.

Are you going above to scout?

We all had strong mind blocks, but could send messages mentally using touch. Braxton's mind could be hard to reach when he was in dragon form, but this time he was open to me.

Yes, and if I find something, I'll signal you with flames.

With a nod I stepped back and let him do his thing. The canopy wasn't thick above us, a few swipes of dragon claw and he was through. Then he was gone, the rhythmic swishing of his wings fading.

Tyson was still muttering away. Jacob had his hands pressed against the trees, communicating with the nature gods, trying to find the disturbance in the land. We had used these techniques a lot over the past twelve months when we were trying to find Vanguard, so this was all second nature to us. Of course, we never were successful, always looking in the wrong place. We couldn't let that happen to the twins. That just was not an option.

I strode into the clearing and across to where that house had been only moments before. Besides the cleared, round zone, there was no evidence that a building had stood here at all. The grass was not flat; there were even some small wildflowers peeking up through the tall green grass. If I hadn't seen it with my own eyes and still felt the prevalent tendrils of heavy magic, I would not have believed a building had stood there.

"You got anything, Ty?" The bite in my voice was enough that even my brother flinched, and he was a tough asshole.

"The magic woven here is complex and it's old. Someone has been doing this for a long time." He dropped his hands and a resigned look crossed his face. "I think we're going to need Louis' help on this one. Dark magic is hard to navigate. I don't have the experience."

In normal circumstances I'd find it amusing how annoyed Tyson was that Louis was a stronger magic user than him, but right now I cared about nothing but finding the girls.

"Can you contact him from outside the barrier?"

Tyson nodded. "Yep, already sent him a message. Since our power and his are all linked to the securities around Stratford, I have a direct mental link to his magical energy."

Which meant I probably did also, but vampires weren't huge on mental links. I'd leave that to the others. We fell silent then, waiting for Louis. The sorcerer knew more than any other supe in Stratford, and he had better know something in this case too. Otherwise we were screwed.

The sound of Braxton's dragon had faded away now. He'd be powering around the forest, trying to spot that house again or sense the strange magic. I continued scanning and moving around. There had to be something here, some sort of clue as to what we were up against.

Jacob's murmur drew my attention, and as he moved away from the trees and back toward us, he spoke rapidly: "The forest is keeping its secrets for now but the magic used here calls to me. We're looking at demon energy, fey, and a very strong sorcerer."

Shit. "After years of being told that Faerie is a dead land, it seems to be involved in a lot of the drama in our lives recently."

Tyson ran a hand through his hair, standing it up on end. "Yep, it feels as if this dragon marked thing set off some sort of ricochet across the realms. Unleashed new magics. Woke those ancients who were sleeping. Now we have to deal with the fallout."

My vampire roared to life. "Mischa better not be part of that fallout. We have to save the girls."

Tyson stared hard at me, doing a similar sort of probing thing that was usually Braxton's MO.

"What?" I snarled.

The wizard just shook his head and let the smallest of annoying smiles grace his lips. "Nothing, just find it interesting that the first name you mentioned was Mischa and not Jess."

I shot forward and grabbed the front of his shirt. I dragged him toward me and he didn't fight. Nope, just continued grinning at me, which made me want to slam my fist into his face.

"Mischa is pregnant with my baby. She is mine to protect. I *will* kill any motherfucker who puts a single hand on her."

The red haze in my head was making it hard for coherent thought. Instinct had kicked in and I was now in predator mode. I loved Jessa, I had no doubts of that. I would die for her in a heartbeat, but for some reason Mischa was wrapped around my vampire soul. The protective instincts I felt toward her were like no other. I could not stand the thought that she could be anywhere right now, and fuck knows what was happening with her.

Part of me wondered if this insane need to protect her would fade when the baby was born. I hadn't felt this strongly when we were together before. Which logically suggested it was our child connecting us. But another, larger part, was really hoping these emotions toward Mischa stuck around.

Yeah, I was screwed.

Tyson still didn't have the intelligence to be afraid of my current mood. "Max, calm down, man. We'll find them. They're our pack. Whoever took our girls is going down."

The words *our girls* echoed through my mind, and as they registered I was slammed with an extra boost to the fury already coursing through my body.

I was losing my goddamn mind. Why the hell would that upset me so much?

Tyson was my brother. I should be happy he cared about the pack. I should be happy that he was here to keep an eye out for them when I was weak and could not stay. Instead I resented that he knew of Mischa and the baby before me. I resented that their relationship had deepened and moved to a true and comfortable level of trust and acceptance. They'd hugged like old friends before.

I had noticed.

It was not my place to say anything, but the vampire inside of me did not feel the same way.

Before I could act on these emotions, strong energy crashed against my mental shields. Louis. That bastard was too powerful for his own good. His damned sorcery followed him around like an entourage.

My brothers and I stepped closer together, an instinctive move when faced with that much raw power. Lucky for us, the sorcerer was on our side. If that ever changed we would have a hell of a lot to worry about. I didn't fear anyone in this world, I was secure in my power, and my strong pack, but there were a small handful of supes who gave me concern. Louis was the top of that list.

He wasted no time on small talk. "What happened?"

Tyson strode to his side and for once managed to keep his visible annoyance toward Louis to a minimum. He reached out a hand. "It will be easier if I show you."

The magic users clasped hands for a second; there was no evidence of energy flowing between them. I couldn't even feel a change in their normal levels of smash-you-in-the-face magic.

Louis didn't speak his spells out loud anymore, he was able to manipulate magical energy with his thoughts and intentions. Although I noticed he would still verbal cast on occasion. Probably an old habit.

Louis' face went from benign to pissed off in seconds. With this change in expression came the first trickles of a loss of magical control. My vampire reared up as his strong magic wove around the clearing. Tyson pulled away from him then, and turning to me and Jacob mouthed, "Brace yourself," which gave us just enough time to shut down our own energy before Louis exploded.

His power buffeted out with the force akin to a nuclear bomb. I almost hit the ground as it passed through me and continued outward. I managed to remain on my feet, but it was not without some effort.

Well, damn. Had Louis actually been containing some of his energy over the years? That had been true power. What had his abilities been like when he led the council? The boost from his followers must have shot his sorcery to an almost uncontrollable level.

I was struggling at times to control my new influx. Probably why my vampire kept getting away from me. And I had nothing on the sorcerer in base power.

Maybe in a few years we'd equal him, but we were young. Only time would see our powers increase and allow us to be as formidable as Louis. Although, when we joined in our quad bond, we came very close. Nonetheless, not a pissing contest I needed to be part of.

Tyson on the other hand…

Louis had not moved since shooting out his energy. I tried to be patient, but that ran out pretty fast. I strode closer to the sorcerer. Wading through his energy was like trying to swim through honey. It took so much more effort than it should have just to cross a few yards. As I closed in on him, I forced myself not to stare at his hypnotic purple eyes, swirling in a dizzying motion as he focused outward, searching, trying to figure out what had happened here.

By the time I was at his side, his energy was starting to die down, which allowed me to leash my predator side enough to speak. "What did you find, Louis? Where are the girls?"

The question came out hard and with a level of growl I wasn't exactly proud of. I didn't like to lose control; it spoke of weakness within. I needed to deal with that soon. But for now there was no choice but to go with the anger and pain. It kept me functioning.

"I'm glad you've finally learned of your young," Louis said, no inflection at all in his tone; he could have been discussing the weather. "How is it that the girls managed to get taken under the four of your watches?"

Great, now the sorcerer was going to reprimand us like children. "You've made your point, we screwed up. But I'd rather you spent your time helping us. We can hash out our mistakes at a later time."

Louis snorted then, and some of his normal joviality bled back into his features. "I'll make sure to bring it up again soon. In regards to the twins, they have been taken into another dimension. It's lucky you called for me so quickly. The essence fades even now. In another few minutes I would not have been able to trace them. They would have been lost to us."

Tyson crossed his arms, keeping his distance from the sorcerer. "What dimension? Faerie?"

Louis shook his head. "No, for once it's not Faerie stealing from us. It's far worse than slumbering gods and dragon rulers. This time the girls are in the land between. The Great Divide."

The beast inside roared again, my fists clenched hard. That explained the demon taint. They resided there, trapped in a small section of the land between.

This was bad. It was not an easy task to traverse between that realm and Earth, hence why the demons were stashed there. Not to mention the dead lands housed countless souls that had not or could not move on to the next life. Humans called it purgatory, but to supes it was hell.

CHAPTER EIGHT

Mischa Lebron

Jessa and I huddled as close as we could. The darkness was so complete that the only way I knew it was my sister next to me was our twin bond. From the moment the wind barrier had whooshed us through the cottage doorway, we'd known nothing but darkness and soul-crushing fear.

And Jessa's cursing. Which was oddly comforting.

I felt her shift forward then to grab onto the bars of our tiny cell. We were in a six-by-six-foot box, the distinct scent of damp and mold in the air. Thankfully no other being seemed to be in the box with us, but I was getting the sense that we weren't alone in this room. We hadn't heard any others but I knew they were out there.

Jessa's yells broke the silence again, which had me practically jumping out of my skin.

"You piece of shit, asshole mutha-douche-canoes better open this cage up and let us out immediately. Do you know who you're messing with? You just kidnapped the mate of a dragon. A dragon! I cannot wait until he gets here and rips your scrawny head from your body."

It didn't surprise me that she was using Braxton as a scare tactic. He was scary. Like the scariest supe we knew. Though I knew it bothered Jessa that she had to resort to such things. She was lethal on her own, but right now she no longer had her own dragon and was pregnant, and therefore slightly vulnerable. Her independent nature was taking a back seat to the need to protect her children. I was independent too, but in a different way, a lone wolf kinda way. Never had a pack before and did okay. Now that I had a pack, things should be even easier, right?

Meh, probably not. I had learned early on not to expect the knight to ride in and rescue me. In my world a true knight was even more mythical than shifters. Still, there was a part of me deep down, that felt the bonds of my pack, and it brought me a sense of comfort.

Jessa huffed heavily as she fell back against me. Our connection flared strongly and I lowered the mind blocks. *Can you scent anything about this place?* she asked me.

I closed my eyes and breathed deeply, forcing all thoughts and fears away, seeking to understand the space we'd been dropped in. I let the artist side of my brain paint pictures for me around the small cage in the center, Jessa and I enclosed within.

Okay, that's un-freakin'-believable. You just, like, painted with your mind, and I can see it. Her excitement jolted me out of my concentration and I had to take a few more centered breaths to get back to the Zen place.

I let my senses free, my wolf rising from within a swirl of wild energy. She joined with me and we tried to discern even one distinct thing from our surroundings. More images appeared in my painting, but they were murky. There was the slightest hint of sulfur in the air, and a sense of heat that was strong but sort of ... distant. Like we were on the sun, but there was a shield around us stopping it from incinerating us. I could feel that the world outside of this cage was bad, but how bad was yet to be determined.

Could we be in Faerie? I asked Jessa. *Because there's no way we're still in that candy house. It was tiny and I can tell this place is large.*

I'd never been to the magical land, but knew plenty about it from my twin's journey through it. I knew that her Josephina, queen of the dragons, was there somewhere. Not to mention the floating-illusion castle which had been Larkspur's lair.

Yep, it was definitely a portal to somewhere else. A magical doorway. Are we in Faerie? I really have no idea. Doesn't feel like Faerie. The magic there is strong and easily recognizable, but maybe someone has this cage locked down. Shielded. Maybe they're hiding the world from us and us from the world.

Which is going to make it hard for the Compasses to find us, I surmised.

Jess laughed then. It echoed, and in that moment the image in my head increased ten times. This place was huge. I knew it, even though there was no real evidence to back up my feeling.

They'll find us, Misch. Our pack never leaves a supe behind. I know you aren't used to someone having your back, but you'll always have us now.

I loved the sentiment, but knew there'd always be a part of me expecting it to be torn away. You couldn't rely fully on others. It was the sure-fire way to be let down hard. I did appreciate her comfort though, and decided to be as truthful as I could.

I trust you guys more than I've ever trusted anybody. I'm honored to be part of the pack.

This pack had as much of my trust as I was willing to give. Probably eighty percent. And I only trusted them that much because they weren't humans. Supes did things differently than humans. Their word meant something, and pack bonds were real and tangible, like magic in a way. There was a level of devotion between pack mates which could not be replicated in the human world. But still, I would be keeping a part of myself safe. For me and my child.

Do you hear that? Jessa said, breaking me out of my thoughts. I focused again on our surroundings.

It took me a few tense, breathless seconds, but finally I heard a low scraping sound. Something was definitely moving around, still some distance from us, but closing in.

I tried to keep the fear out of my mental voice. *What do we do? Is there a plan?*

I wasn't the same as Jessa. Things did scare me. Bravery was something I really had to work on. Preferably some other day, when I wasn't stuck in a weird magical cage, inside a weird candy house, in the dark of an unknown land. We were just like the stupid humans in the fairy tales, lured in by chocolate cake and peppermint sticks.

Jessa shifted closer to me. She was practically sitting in my lap now. Which was not at all awkward with both of our baby bellies.

Don't let them separate us. Fight with the techniques we have been practicing. Even pregnant, you know the areas to aim for. We want the four strike zones, so make each hit count.

Right. Despite my frazzled mind, I had no trouble recalling our lessons. The four strike zones: nose, throat, gut, groin. Jessa had been teaching me basic self-defense and fight moves, and she said those were the best places to aim for maximum impact. Especially for someone like me who had very little training.

I knew that even on a female assailant, kicking them straight between the legs would hurt them enough for me to possibly get away. During training, Jessa had phrased it as a "straight shot to the lady balls."

The scraping was getting closer … and slightly louder … and Jessa and I shifted so we were both crouching. I took extra care not to make a single noise as I hauled my extra-padded butt up. Of course we had to get kidnapped when I was the equivalent of eight or nine months pregnant.

Shit!

My mental shout must have been loud enough to shock Jessa. She jumped next to me, and then wrapped her arm tightly around me.

What? she said with urgency. *Did something happen? Is it the baby?*

What if they want our kids? I almost couldn't say those heinous words, even in mental speak, but it would be stupid not to consider it. We were pregnant to the Compasses. They were powerful and feared. *Especially yours, Jess. You could be carrying the dragon babies to rule all supes or whatever.*

My twin felt frozen at my side, but I could tell from her jumble of thoughts that this worry had already crossed her mind. She'd kept it from me so I wouldn't freak out.

All we can do now, Misch, is fight for our lives. We don't let them take us easily. We protect our babies and we hold out long enough for the boys to find us. Her voice got all fierce then. *Whatever they do to you, hold on for the boys. They will come for us and every single asshole in this place will suffer.*

I never got to answer her. The scraping distracted us again. It sounded so close now, and I was mentally preparing myself to fight, when lights blazed all around us. Unnatural illumination filled every crevice of the building, as bright as the middle of Times Square in New York City. My mom and I had ended up there one night, near Christmas actually, and I remembered the pure energy and excitement that had thrummed through the city. The way the night was almost as bright as day with the advertisements.

This was what the lighting here reminded me of. Fluorescent. Fake. Designed to showcase us in these cages using bright, unforgiving light.

For the first time we could see the enormous room we were in, long and narrow. From what I could see, there were similar cages to ours running up and down on either side of a walkway.

Jess and I both moved closer to the bars of our prison, straining to see what was right at the end of this path. It was really far away ... but it sort of looked like there was a raised podium with a bunch of chairs scattered around it.

"Mischa…" Jess said, her voice low as she trailed off.

I jerked my head around to meet her gaze and saw she was looking at the cage across from us. Following her line of sight, I was shocked to see a large pair of red eyes staring back at me.

"What is that?" I blurted, louder than I intended. The creature didn't react to my rudeness, which was when I understood that these cages were soundproofed in some way, even with the open-bar designs – magically blocked so we couldn't hear the other prisoners. But we could still hear movement outside of the cages. Or whatever was making that whirring noise.

Jess tilted her head to the side, such a curious animal sort of gesture that it made her seem so foreign for that brief moment. "I've never seen anything like that in real life, but my guess is that's a hellhound."

I swallowed hard and tried to calm my heart rate as I examined the beast. It was relatively canine in shape, not to mention huge, sleek, and leathery in appearance, like a dog whose skin had been dehydrated. Its body and head were oddly shaped but definitely still recognizable, with an elongated face and a jaw filled with razor sharp teeth, more than one row packing its muzzle. Red eyes were locked in on Jessa and me, and its stare was unnerving. Pure focus. No humanity at all. It was like staring into the eyes of death and knowing there was no way to stop it coming for you.

"Okay, so I think we can speak normally," Jessa said. "The cages appear to have a sound deadening spell on them. It allows some noise in but nothing out."

I nodded. "Yep, that's what I think too."

"You have any ideas what we're stuck in the middle of here?"

I didn't answer immediately, choosing instead to give her my best "what the hell?" face. Why was she so calm? My sister, who couldn't even color in a picture without cursing and throwing it across the room, was suddenly yoga shifter on Zen juice. My crazy sister appeared to find violent-kidnapping-hellhound situations calming. Should have expected that.

Jessa was still waiting for my answer. "Well, by the looks of it, there are a lot of us being held in these cages. Presumably all of us walked through some sort of fairytale story and ended up here. Could it be a fight club situation? They put us in the ring and we have to fight to the death, and fey or other supes bet on it?"

I'd heard about this sort of thing in the human world, illegal betting rings, fight clubs. They'd done it with animals – dogs mostly – and also humans. If that was the case, and I had to fight the hellhound, I was dead. I had very minimal training, and that thing looked deadly. It still hadn't taken its freaky red eyes off us.

"You could be right," Jessa said, unfortunately agreeing with me. "I can see two ogres, a black-coat centaur – nasty bastards those ones. Not to mention harpies and what looks a lot like a cell filled with pixies. And that's just in the cages surrounding us."

I managed to draw my eyes from the hellhound – he'd totally had all my focus – and paid closer attention to the few other cages visible around us. Each held one or more inhabitant. Some were close to the bars like us, others didn't appear to have moved at all, remaining prone in their prisons. They looked like they'd been there for a long time, and hadn't reacted as we had to the artificial lighting.

Jessa drew my attention again. "A few years ago we had some issues with supes disappearing. I mean, it's not that unusual for different members of the races to take off, do their own thing, even assimilate into the human world for some time, but these cases were different. These were supes that people would miss. I don't think the councils ever got to the bottom of that one, and for a time we had no more trouble, but there are plenty of families out there missing loved ones who want them back." Troubled blue eyes locked on mine. "What do you think the odds are that this had something to do with that?"

"Just like the missing humans," I said, my voice hoarse. "It could all be connected. How long ago was the missing supe thing happening?"

"About five years."

Well, great. So we could be stuck here for years. No freaking way was I having a baby on this dirty concrete-looking floor. No way.

Jessa must have seen my expression, because she gave a dry laugh. "I wouldn't worry about being stuck *here* for that long, Misch. Something tells me the spaces here are very valuable, and the occupants are only around long enough until the next one arrives to take their place."

Uh, none of that sounded good. My mini panic attack was interrupted by the sounds of chattering, and then that same scraping noise we had heard earlier. Both of our heads swung in the direction of the podium, and as I focused there I let out a low curse.

Holy crazy cat lady.

The podium was filled with figures. We were too far away to tell if they were supe or human, but still ... how in the space of only a few minutes had hundreds of people settled in around the raised platform? Upon the stage was a single male. He looked human from this distance, but something about him seemed a bit off.

"What's in his hand?" Jessa side-whispered to me. "Is that some sort of stick ... a staff?"

I leaned forward, squinting best I could. The artificial lighting was playing havoc with my wolf vision, so I had to rely on the advanced non-supe side of me instead. The man stood right in the center, feet spread, gripping a long, white, almost glowing piece of wood. He shifted it across to his left side and the scraping sounded again.

"Whatever the stick is, it's what is making the scraping sound," I murmured.

Jessa groaned. "That's what I was worrying about."

Okay, she had two seconds to share or I was going to pretend I was the evil twin and start beating her to death.

Picking up on those emotions through our bond, she gave a chuckle. "There are a few mystical objects in the supernatural world, things which have power beyond our understanding, and most of which have been lost over time. We study them in our history classes, but I've never seen one of the ten power pieces before." She paused to clear her throat or something.

Hurry up!

"One was the staff of Gradiella. One of the fey gods created it. This staff was said to be able to call to a supe's soul, to control, to merge powers. No one really knows. These objects have not been seen for tens of thousands of years, but from all the pictures I've seen it looks a lot like what he's holding. The most telling description was this weird sound it made, like it was alive, a whirring as it wove magic."

Okay, we were screwed.

Jessa didn't look as worried as me, but she was uneasy. "I can't feel the power from here. These cages don't just block sound, but also magical resonance."

She slammed both of her hands against the bars. We'd both tried this a few times since ending up in here, even calling on our wolves, but so far there wasn't even the tiniest shift in the metal. It was reinforced to withstand trolls and ogres, no way could we break through. And yet we still had to try. The Compasses might be rubbing off on us.

"Times like these I really miss Josephina," she growled. "I took her strength for granted. No way would these cages hold a dragon. Nothing can hold a dragon."

The whirring and scraping started up again, and this time we were watching closely enough to see the male on stage waving the staff around. He lifted it above his head and the sound amplified tenfold.

It started to echo through our cell, and I was about ten seconds from slapping my hands over my ears when something far worse distracted me. Cells started flying down the center row – like literally the entire six feet by six feet box, bars and occupants included – two at a time, starting from the end farthest from the podium. Jessa and I stared bug-eyed as a set of unicorns and another water-filled cage of mermaids dashed past.

My heart clenched as I caught sight of the supes' faces. Even with their foreign features I could tell they were afraid.

"Holy shit," Jessa was murmuring under her breath. "Come on, Compasses."

If this was a fight club, or something far worse, it was clear that these horrible beings had been doing this for a long time. The boys were not going to have an easy time finding this place. We just had to hope they got here before it was too late.

The two boxes which had zoomed past us were deposited on the podium, one on either side of the man with the staff. Jessa and I weren't the only ones glued to the front of our prisons trying to see what was going on. Most of the other cages occupants were too. I was pressed so tightly against the bars my belly was getting a little squished, but luckily baby Compass wasn't giving me hell for it.

My attention flicked back to the cage in front of us. Okay, everyone was staring at the platform except the hellhound. It was still eyeing me like I was dinner for tonight. Get in line, buddy. I returned my gaze to the staff guy. The cages on the stage were now open and the inhabitants were standing before the crowd. Let me just say, the mermaids did not look impressed to be on dry land. It seemed only a force of magic was keeping them upright.

Staff guy started to talk. We could hear every word loud and clear.

"Welcome, and thank you all for coming to our sale. We have some truly spectacular offerings tonight. None of you will leave here disappointed. Warning: do not bid beyond your means, we offer no second chances. You will make payment or you will forfeit your life."

He slammed his staff down and the floor shook. Even all the way under our cage.

It looked as if the inhabitants of the seats around the stage were shifting slightly, but I still couldn't get a clear view of whether they were human or supe or ... other.

Staff guy continued: "First on the sale block we have two unicorns from the Land of Illusion and Bespelling in Faerie. Prized for many magical properties, the dust and residue of their horns are key components in many dark magics. Their hides will keep you hidden and protected, and their blood will rejuvenate and heal. We're going to sell them separately. Let the bidding begin."

"It's a supe smuggling ring," I whispered to Jessa, tendrils of freak-the-hell-out clear in my voice. "They're going to purchase us like slaves and then do whatever the hell they want with us all."

She didn't answer but I could feel her agony and fury. There was nothing we could do but stand and watch, waiting for our turn to end up on stage.

One by one, cages flew past us and the inhabitants were sold to the absolutely despicable excuses for human or supe in the audience. The price of purchase ranged from dragon toenails to a spell for eternal youth. Apparently that spell was worth a fortune in the human world, which made it very valuable to the staff-wielding asshole selling off supes.

I had no idea what the little cloaked being sitting very close to the platform was, but he now owned a unicorn, two ogres, three pixies, a witch from the original bloodline of Norta, half a mermaid – apparently they could just slice her right down the middle and go halfsies on her heart – and a bunch of other supernatural creatures.

From what we'd seen the majority of the cages held demi-fey, but there was certainly a mix of the other races also. Including a rare white tiger shifter, who had a thatch of white-blond hair and eyes which were such a piercing shade of light blue that I could see them all the way from my cage. He went to a female standing in the shadows. Two guesses what she wanted the stunning male for. There had also been two human lots. They were sold just the same as the supes, and went for one of the highest prices so far.

"How is this happening?" I murmured. "How are they getting away with this?"

Jess had been very silent, but I could feel the vibrations shaking her entire figure. Her fury was barely contained.

"I'm going to kill every single asshole in here," she said slowly through clenched teeth. "One way or another, this will be stopped. We just have to figure out a way around that staff's control."

That was easier said than done. It didn't matter which creature, race member, or other, stepped out of those cages, they seemed to be completely under the mercy of the staff's control. Then, once they were sold, magical bands were strapped onto their wrists, or legs, or whatever appendage they had handy, and they were immediately immobilized, ready to be transported by their new owner.

Owner. Okay, I was totally with Jessa. We were killing them all.

Who knew I had such a bloodthirsty side? Probably my wolf's influence. She was practically howling inside of me; my stomach churned as dread filled my gut. Luckily I was past the worst of the morning sickness and could control my gag reflex, or Jessa and I would find this prison even less comfortable.

Two more cages flew past us and I missed the inhabitants this time because I was too busy noticing that there were only two more cages on the right side of us. Pretty soon we were going to be up there on the stage. Shit ... us and the hellhound.

"Lot two hundred and sixty-six: a pair of love birds from the Alaskan region. These mythical and rarely seen pairs mate for life. Their wings contain essence which will brew a true-love potion. These will sell together, as to separate them means instant death. Bidding will start at ... thirty pints of sorcerer blood, from the mage at the front..."

While the furious bidding ensued for the love birds, which were seriously two of the cutest fairytale-looking creatures I'd ever seen, Jessa and I started to whisper out a plan.

"I think if we stay connected to each other, it's going to be harder for him to control us," she said. "There's strength in a twin bond, not to mention we both carry Compass babies. If anything is going to give us the ability to withstand the control, it's the power of the quads. They're like born of the freakin' gods or something."

I nodded a few times, a slice of me hoping for the best, but more of me expecting that things were going to go to hell really fast.

Truth was, we could not let ourselves fall into the grasp of any of that crowd out there. They were here for terrible reasons, and the creatures that they purchased were all going to suffer horribly at their hands. It would be better to die than to let that happen.

But we also had our babies to think of. So there was no choice but to fight until our very last breath.

The bidding finished up on the love birds. Next was an arctic yeti. Standing well over ten feet tall, pure white with fur that looked as soft as a lamb, the poor thing just stood there blinking large, obsidian eyes. I couldn't see the details clearly, but I was sensing panic and confusion and fear.

I found myself growling then, and it was so wolf-like that I had to be impressed. I'd never managed the very deep rumbling growl like that before. Jessa did it almost daily. Especially if her breakfast wasn't ready when she sat down.

"If we get out of here, Jess," I said through clenched teeth as my anger took control, "we do not stop until we figure out who is behind this and we kill them. Then we track down every single one of these assholes here who thinks it's okay to buy living creatures like they're nothing more than objects, and we make them all pay."

Jessa blinked exaggeratingly slow for a few moments, before the hugest grin I'd ever seen crossed her face. "Firstly, great job with the cursing. Secondly, you and I are on the exact same page about how this is all going to go down."

We were cut off by the rattling of the cages next to us, before they flew past. The poor supes inside were next on the chopping block, which meant we were only minutes from our turn on the stage.

Jessa and I waited in silence, our hands linked. The seconds seemed to pass by so fast. Then, as our cage started to shake and detach itself from the row, I reached out and grabbed onto the bars with my free hand. Crap! It was time. Despite the fact I was prepared to do everything in my power to free us from this mess, I still couldn't halt my final thought.

Maximus Compass, if you're coming for us, now is the time to get here.

CHAPTER NINE

Maximus Compass

I was going to kill Louis. Or at least give it a damn good shot. What the hell was taking him so long? The sorcerer was currently doing something meditative as he tried to figure out how to get to the land between. The red haze, which seemed to be a permanent part of my vision now, crashed down again, and I was about to lunge toward the magic user when the heavy whooshing of Braxton's wings distracted me.

We all turned toward the dragon, waiting for him to descend back down through the gap in the tree line.

Tyson's normally laidback, happy tone had been replaced by something angry and dark. "Do you think he found anything?"

"No, he'll not have found anything, because they're not here on Earth any longer," Louis said, getting to his feet.

"Well, did you find something then, oh great one." Tyson's tone was mocking, and even more growly than before.

"You can call me Louis. Great One is so formal," Louis said without missing a beat. "And yes, actually, I have picked up on the same energy. It's across the country though, so we're going to have to take a step-through, and we need to hurry the hell up."

My eyes shot to Braxton, who had landed and was in the process of shifting back. "Clothe the man and let's move our asses."

Jacob's hand landed on my shoulder, and I could feel the soothing energy of his fey power as it tried to calm the beast. His essence was all elements, nature, and ancient gods, but I was not in the mood.

"What's up with you, Max?" Jacob said as I knocked his arm down. "I mean, I know the girls are gone, but we don't know anything bad has happened yet. Usually you're the calm one keeping Braxton from losing his shit. Now we have to hope Ty and I can manage the two of you."

Good luck with that. Braxton and I were both stronger physically and energy-wise than our younger brothers. Not by much, but just enough that Jacob and Tyson would be in trouble if they had to contain both of us.

"Lucky I'm here then, isn't it?" Louis was back to being annoying and cheerful, although I could still sense that undercurrent of fierce supe he'd tapped into before. He was worried about the girls, especially Jessa. He had claimed her as family, and that meant something very real in our world.

His purple-hued gaze locked in on me. "I think I can handle a few mated males losing their minds."

A sort of blankness descended over the red rage and I remembered for the first time in forever that Cardia was dead. Shit. Had I even reacted this strongly when she died? Despite Louis' assertion about mated males, Mischa was not my mate ... and yet my vampire was murderous, absolutely inconsolable in its rage. We craved to find her. We needed to make sure she was safe, and not just because of the child. No ... because of her.

I was so fucked up.

Tyson magically clothed Braxton, and by the time the pair got to us Louis already had the swirling portal ready to go.

Braxton's voice was guttural: "Did you find them, sorcerer?" Even though he was no longer wearing scales and claws, his eyes were still blazing yellow.

A few months ago, when the dragon king stole Jessa out from under him, he'd lost his soul. What was left became a pure killing machine, and it was only through the quad bond that we managed to pull him back from that insanity. I wondered if I would even bother this time, or if I would simply join him in the killing.

"I haven't found the girls yet, they're not on this realm." Braxton didn't look surprised, which meant he'd already figured that. "But the transportation magic used had a distinct, dark magic feel to it. I've locked in on a similar vibe, somewhere around Sequoia National Park in California."

The dragon shifter didn't say another word, he just stepped into the portal, and the rest of us followed. The journey was short. As we exited the step through into a woodland of massive trees, warmth hit me hard. Definitely west coast weather here.

I stood shoulder to shoulder with Braxton, and for once I think both of us were in the same mental space – completely losing our minds. His anger was palpable and it elevated mine. Neither of us were able to stand still as we waited for everyone to make it through and for Louis to close down the doorway. Luckily, he started to move immediately, practically running as he led us across a mile or so of forest. Braxton and I kept pace on either side of the sorcerer. Our main priority was to keep him safe while he was following the energy. We'd be screwed without his guidance, and the girls were relying on us.

"It's much stronger here," Louis muttered. "The energy. It's all part of the spell to make it difficult for other magic users to pinpoint the location … but they need to get up earlier than this if they want to try and hide magic from me."

Braxton was growling again. The sound died off as we crossed a small trickling brook and found ourselves staring at a clearing in the forest. Normally I'd think the sight before us was completely insane to find in the middle of protected national parklands. Except of course we'd just come from the candy house from hell, so it was all starting to seem normal.

"For fuck … is that real?" Tyson said, his eyebrows raised, mouth open. "Are they the three little pigs' houses?"

I looked to Louis. The sorcerer was doing that shrewd gaze thing as he tried to figure out what the hell was going on. Finally, he gave a strangled laughed. "It's freaking genius. It really is."

"What the hell is genius about this … scene?" I snarled. "And how is this supposed to help us find the girls?"

Three tiny houses. The points of their roofs stood no higher than my waist. The first was made of straw, the second was made of sticks, and the final, you guessed it, was made of brick. In our world, kids weren't big on human stories, but some of their "fairy tales" were really stories passed down by supes, just modified for humans. Have you ever actually read the Brothers Grimm? Dark stuff, and not all of it made up.

Louis took a few steps closer to the straw house. "What better way to lure powerful creatures than using the magic of fairy tales."

The magic of fa—what was the mage talking about?

Braxton, who was still in full yellow-eyes mode, let out a bellowing roar. "Explain yourself now and get us to the girls. They need us. I'll not wait a moment longer."

Louis dropped all pretense of joviality and went into scary, badass sorcerer mode. His voice was low; power twanged across the air on each syllable. "Fairy tales are powered by the energy of humans and supes. Every time a story is read, every time a child believes in it, there's a certain power to the tale. Someone has tapped into this, has sent out a spell which will recreate the fairy tales using the energy contained within each story. They then lure in unsuspecting humans and supes. Don't you feel it, the way it's drawing us in? Don't you want to step forward and touch the houses?"

Now that he mentioned it, there was a power struggle going on inside of me. I wanted to be closer to the little houses, and it was more than innate curiosity. It was a spell, subtle and slow moving, insidious enough that I wouldn't have noticed anything until I was snared. That's why Louis had not moved any closer. He'd known that to step into its boundary would initiate the spell and he'd be unable to escape.

"So how do we break the spell?" Jacob said. "It's not natural, the forest does not like it. We need to end this now."

Louis' grin was back, but it wasn't nice. It was hard and scary. "Oh, that's easy enough. We go and introduce ourselves in person. Easiest way to get to The Great Divide."

Okay, so much for not stepping into it. He crossed the space and the rest of us stayed close to his side. Just like with the girls, a massive wind blew up around us, and the whirling vortex started to usher us closer to the houses. I didn't bother to wait for it to suck us in though. If Louis said this was the way to Mischa, there was no more time to waste.

Of course I had no idea how I was supposed to fit inside a house which stood only at the height of my waist. Or even which of the three houses to choose.

With no time to debate any further, I ran straight at the middle house, prepared to emulate the big bad wolf and smash it down. Just before I hit it though, the vision changed, and as my hand touched the side of the stick wall, the entire scene vanished, changing into a cage.

My sprint did not halt, and with Louis and my brothers right behind me, the five of us dashed straight into the box. The moment the last of us crossed the threshold, there was a whirring, followed by the crash of the entrance closing.

Louis was still looking all fascinated sorcerer, examining our prison. "Generally the magical illusion would hold much longer than that. Definitely until the lured was inside of the house. But we're too strong. Maximus smashed the spell. All that's left is the portal. We should be on our way now to the land between. I'm just hoping we don't register as a threat. If that happens there's a possibility the prison will reject us and dump us out halfway."

We should have gone in one at a time. We were some of the most powerful supes in our entire world. Add Louis in there and nothing could stop us. If there was some sort of magical security system on this place, we could very well find ourselves floating in the abyss. Which I did not have time for.

The whirring grew louder and darkness descended around us, so all encompassing that if I hadn't been able to feel my brothers crushed against me I wouldn't have known anyone else was there with me.

My heart clenched and I had to fight through the pain in my chest. Since losing Cardia I'd tried not to be in darkness. When my eyes had nothing to focus on, my brain started to demand attention – the pain started to demand attention. And I did not have the energy to give into it.

This time, though, all I could see was Mischa, with her soft green eyes and rounded belly that held my child. The image was so strong. Why could I see her as if she were standing right before me, and yet when I tried to recall my true mate there was barely a shadow, no detail, almost as if she was fading away from my brain and soul, which, if she'd been a true mate, was damn impossible?

Braxton's, and now my theory, was starting to feel right. When we got the twins back I was going to focus on finding all the answers. If it turned out Cardia was not my true mate, that someone had falsely created the bond for whatever reason, I would not stop until I broke every single facet of the spell and rid myself of any lingering emotional attachment.

To be dealt with later though. My focus was elsewhere right now. I clutched at the bars before me, my body primed and ready to attack the moment we arrived. I felt the unbreakable strength of the material housing us. They were used to transporting those of power and physical prowess. Were we going to be strong enough to break free?

As if he'd had the same thoughts, Braxton initiated our quad bond; there was a flare of light as our power merged. The space was really too small to house our newly beefed up, bonded bodies, but somehow we fit. Louis was no doubt feeling very uncomfortable.

In the brief bursts of light, it seemed as if we were traveling through a wormhole. Dark endlessness surrounded our cage as it hurtled through time and space.

My brothers were looking grim, Louis not so much. The sorcerer hid his true emotions very well. I wouldn't want to face him in a poker game, or cross him in a trial. Master of secrecy, he held himself rigidly. But one day that would shatter. No one could contain the level of supernatural power he held indefinitely. He'd crack, and as long as I wasn't the focus of his explosion, I'd be happy to sit back and enjoy the show. It would be like no other.

As our quad power settled down, the light above us started to wane, and soon we were back in darkness. But this time there was no need to worry. I had plenty of voices in my head to keep me company. And annoy the hell out of me.

Jacob started on me again: *Max, I've never seen your vamp side quite so in control.*

This time it was hard for me to escape the probing nature of my fey brother. I could hear his concern.

I did not want his concern.

I'm angry. So goddamned angry that I can barely continue to function without wanting to tear the world into a million pieces. Someone took my girl and my child. No one touches what is mine.

I hadn't expected to let so much of my inner fury free, but there was nowhere else for it to go. I trusted my brothers above all others; they would never use my weakness against me. Braxton adjusted his stance; through our connection, blasts of his fear and anger continued fueling my own. Joined like this I could feel that Tyson and Jacob weren't that far behind us in the pissed-off-level. They loved Mischa and Jessa too. They had slightly less to lose, but in a pack we were all family. We all had everything to lose.

We'll not lose them, Braxton managed to rasp out. *If it's the last fucking thing I do, I'll shake this goddamn land until it gives me my mate back.*

For the first time I got glimpses of what it had been like for him when Larkspur took Jessa to Faerie. The same sort of emotions were swarming through me too, like there was a bubbling pit of hatred inside of me, like I could lose the last facet of humanity which I had clung to when Cardia died. If I lost Mischa and our child, there was nothing I could cling to, nothing that would stop me from going rogue.

What is Mischa to you, brother?

Tyson was uncharacteristically serious. I realized that the bond I'd witnessed between them was stronger than I'd thought. Clearly it had developed in the time I'd been gone from here, in the time I'd cut her out of my life with ferocious and cruel intent. I was too messed up to give Tyson any other answer than the one which was thrumming through me.

She's mine. She's everything.

I felt the confusion, theirs and my own.

Someone messed with us, with you, Max. Jacob was tuned in to everything, always speaking to the gods and nature. He knew shit. *There's no way Cardia was your true mate, so how the hell did she end up at the sanctuary? How did she form the bond with you?*

I was breathing deeply, aware that if I couldn't keep it together I would probably hurt my brothers. We were too close. There was nowhere for me to release. Braxton's hand slammed onto my shoulder and I knew he was promising me that he would step in if I lost it. He would protect the others.

That thought calmed me. Just enough for rational thought.

As soon as we rescue the girls, I'm going to investigate my bond with Cardia. You're all right, it was not a normal true mate connection. I need answers. I need to know who screwed around with my life.

Ask Louis, Tyson said. *I might detest the cocky dick, but he is powerful. And old as shit. He probably has the best knowledge of whether this is even possible.*

Damn. He was right. I hadn't been utilizing my best source of information. Of course the moment I opened my mouth to ask him, our cage reached its destination, slamming to a halt in a place which was damp and had next to no scent.

We've arrived, boys. Time to introduce ourselves.

Tyson sounded a little too happy. He was really looking forward to releasing his inner anger on whatever stupid assholes had decided to touch our pack mates.

They were all going to die. The thought brightened my day.

Wherever we had landed was cloaked in a magical darkness. There was rarely any place truly without light or shadow unless magic was involved. This didn't bother Louis though. The sorcerer just flicked his fingers and some sort of bulbous light appeared above our heads. Its beams cut through the darkness, and despite the small size, managed to spread a decent amount of light in all directions.

I could see our cage clearly now. It had a solid roof and floor, and all four sides were floor-to-ceiling bars, thick and heavy duty. Magically reinforced for sure.

Braxton reached out and gripped the bars. Through our bond I could feel him connecting to his dragon. The beast was ferocious, almost completely untamed as it searched for its mate. The strength which coursed through my brother was enviable. I did not have the same within me, but the vampire was not without its own benefits. No one else moved. We could assist him without laying a single finger on the cage. I sent my energy along the bond; Tyson and Jacob did the same. The dragon thrashed within the inner cage Braxton had imposed around him, and I felt his control slipping as more and more power flooded through his body.

Jessa, I mentally reminded him. With a roar, Braxton wrenched on the side of the cage. Once, and then again. I heard the screeching of metal and that burning metallic scent of a spell being destroyed. With one final yank, the side of the cage was completely torn free and flung out into the darkness. It landed against another cage, which I'd only just noticed was across from ours.

In fact, as I stepped free of the box, I realized that this entire place was filled with cages. Eyes started to follow our movements. Every single barred box held a prisoner. There were so many demi-fey: gargoyles, trolls, imps, centaurs; and also supes like us: magic users, vampires, shifters, and fey. There might have even been some humans there, or at least supes with very little magical energy.

As the magical light moved across the large building, more faces were reflected back at us. There were hundreds. I moved across to a vampire two cells down from ours. He was gaunt, emaciated to the point where a swift breeze would have knocked him down. Our cells worked double-time to keep us in perfect health, but without a regular influx of new blood, our bodies started to turn on itself, sucking the very life from us.

"How long have you been here?" I asked him, as his flat, dark eyes locked onto mine.

He blinked a few times, opened his mouth to answer, but no sound came out. Weird. I reached forward to the bars, and found my hand bouncing off it, about a foot from the cage.

"There's spells on the outside of these prisons," Louis said, his voice low and brittle. "Noise can go in but nothing comes out. You also can't touch the bars from the outside."

"What the hell is this place? Why are they holding all of these supes?" Tyson asked, wandering along the row.

Louis took a moment to answer, and it sounded as if he was trying to keep his emotions in check. "I believe it's a smuggling ring, supe auction of sorts. Lure them in, cage them up, and then once all the cages are filled, host a huge auction event and offer them up to bidders."

A damn smuggling ring! "We need to find the girls immediately," I all but roared.

Louis shook his head. "They're not in this room. I have already scanned. I have no idea the time difference here. For all we know they could have been sold months ago."

Braxton was beyond listening to him now. All of us dived out of the way when he lost control and burst into a massive black and blue dragon. His bulk crushed the cages on either side of him, and the dragon magic completely circumvented whatever spells lined these prisons.

For many minutes Braxton raged along the row and smashed free the prisoners, Louis' light following along with him. Supes spilled out into the path we were on, each of them emerging in a burst of rage. Looks like we had found ourselves some allies.

"Let's find the assholes who stuck us in here," Jacob roared, his white-blond hair flying behind him as his fey energy lit him from within. "They must pay for this. This must be stopped so no more of us are sacrificed."

This was also our best chance of finding Mischa and Jessa. Whomever was running this thing had information. The supes around me were shouting and beating on the wreckage of the cages near them. I let my vampire free, and as my gums ached and fangs released, I knew it was going to be difficult to return to my more civilized side when this was all over. Of course, if I didn't find Mischa, that wasn't going to be a concern.

Braxton's shift to dragon had broken our quad connection, but that was okay, I could still sense my brothers. All of us were charging along the path with a bunch of enraged supes and one pissed-off dragon. We pushed past all the smashed cages, heading in one direction and hoping it was the right way. The place was still dark beyond Louis' light, but then more of the magic users sent out their own lights, leaving very little darkness for anybody to hide within.

At the end of this path was a platform, probably where the prisoners were paraded across to be purchased. We smashed through the chairs and up onto the elevated area. Not everyone was going to fit on here; there was at least a hundred of us now, but there was a doorway on the other side. We all kept moving. Louis didn't hesitate, blasting out with his energy and slamming the door open. Lights flooded through the opening, and once I made it through I could see another stage.

With a roar I pushed my way to the front, determined to be the first on the other side. Braxton's dragon came through next. Neither of us waited for the others. We were on a mission.

The light on this side was blinding. It took me ten seconds to adjust and take in the scene. We had stepped into a back area with cement floors and a damp scent. It was small, this area, and appeared to be a lower level. Braxton and I moved as fast as we could toward the other end.

"Shit," I growled.

On the other side of this path was a massive warehouse, which I could tell immediately was a mirror image of the one we'd just left, right down to the elevated stage we were at the back of. The only difference ... this side of the area was right in the midst of a supe sale.

And Jessa was standing on the stage.

The MC for this event hadn't noticed us yet. He was too busy touting all of Jessa's values.

"...one of the dragon marked – still wears the mark even. Was house to an actual dragon and has contacts in Faerie. Believed to be carrying twins, naturally conceived dragons who will hold dominion over the supe races. This is an extra special lot tonight, and there are very few of you here who can afford the price. As you saw before, she is a phenomenal fighter and would make a great member of your personal security. Her sister set a record just before at eighteen rare fey stones. Let's see how much better we can do with this one."

If he said anything more I missed it. There was nothing in my head but white noise and death. Mischa was gone. She had already been sold.

Braxton was moving but I was faster than him. I reached the stage and my hand was around the announcer's throat before he could even blink. Jessa's eyes were huge; so much anger simmered through them I could almost see the liquid fire. She didn't move toward me, her body looked to be frozen in position.

It was then I noticed the hooked staff which the soon-to-be-dead supe was carrying. My fingers flexed around his throat as I reached to wrench it from him. But the moment it touched me I was frozen to the spot.

A voice was suddenly in my head. *Well, what do we have here? You think to come into my house and threaten me … you're going to make a fine sale item.*

Control was gone from my body. I could see, feel, and hear, but movement was beyond me. My vampire lay dormant, under the control of the staff pressed against my chest. The supe, who I was getting a sorcerer vibe from, ripped himself from me and let loose with a chuckle, probably trying to break the tension which had spread across the crowd of dead fuckers down in the audience.

The moment I was freed from here, I was going after every single one of them. This was illegal and completely screwed up. You did not traffic in supes, and since they weren't on Earth, where the laws of supernaturals stated that all get a trial and end up in prison, I could easily kill them and face no consequences.

In The Great Divide, you do the crime, you get your head ripped off.

The quad bond flared to life then. Jacob and Tyson were on the stage with us now. Braxton, who had been a little slower due to a bunch of guards attacking him, was close by. I could see from the corner of my eye a multitude of body parts scattered around him. Those guards hadn't stood a chance against the might of a dragon claw.

As Braxton reached my side, our quad bond settled in strongly, and with the swell of my power control returned to my body. The dragon magic, which weaved through all of us, was circumventing the staffs control.

I wasted no time. I smashed the staff-wielder in the jaw – a magic user, and not even a particularly strong one. In the same movement I yanked the staff right out of his hands. The moment I did, the moment I held it, ancient power ripped across me and it was only the strength of my brothers that kept me from losing my mind completely.

Knowledge rushed through me and I understood now what I held. *The staff of Gradiella*. This was an ancient and lost magical object. How had this low-level wizard gained control of it?

Once the power of the staff was in my hands, everything else fell into place. The supes who had followed us from the other storeroom rounded up everyone involved in the trafficking ring, all the old and powerful males and females here to buy and sell slaves or obtain race members to use for potions and curses. Not to mention those who just enjoyed torture and sick perversions.

They were all going to die.

Walking along the row of them, each on their knees, waiting for our verdict, I used the staff's power. One by one I touched it to them, and the moment I did I could see into their minds. I could see the truth.

A few moments later, I returned to the stage. "They're all guilty."

I didn't look away as the previously caged supes roared and then swiftly delivered justice in its most brutal form. The power of the staff kept those sentenced to death locked down long enough for them to have no chance at fighting back. Their deaths freed all purchased supernaturals, they emerged from the shadows, magically binding cuffs falling from their bodies.

I ached to see Mischa step free from the wings, but there was no sign of her at all.

"Justice is served," Louis said.

For the most part it was, but this ring went so much deeper ... things I'd seen in their minds. I crossed to Louis and in a hurried few sentences filled him in on what I'd found in the minds of the depraved.

"They meet up monthly for these auctions. It has been going on for many years. The ones we just sentenced to death were all regular clientele, although a few are missing today. If we search their properties we'll find many missing supes."

I knew where each of them kept their slaves. I'd seen it all in the dark depths of their minds. Louis wove some magic around my words so that he could listen to them again at any time for reference. There was a lot of information involved.

"I'll call on the councils," he said, grimly. "We'll track each and every single one of them. Now that I have the magic essence of those fairytale portals, I can make sure they're all destroyed."

It didn't seem like enough, but at least we had a place to start unraveling this all. "Where did they get this staff from?" I held it out, before almost dropping it when it started to shrink. Eventually it was nothing more than a stick which I could easily slip in my back pocket. I would keep it for now, until we figured out what to do with it.

Louis shook his head. "I don't know. The Staff of Gradiella has not been part of our history for a long time. I heard it ended up in the demon realm, but if that's the case, how did it fall into these hands?"

Great question. Also a scary one. I'd never known a supe to mess with demon energy. It was too easy to lose yourself to the darkness. Once you were demon touched, it was next to impossible to come back.

"It's probably why the smuggling took place here," Tyson said as he came up to our side. "The demons are benefitting from this somehow, stealing the energy, or maybe taking a cut of the purchase price."

Made sense. Demons loved power and energy. Always looking for a way to break out of this dimension and destroy the other realms.

There was movement on the stage as Jessa slammed her fist into the face of the staff wielder. He was the only one still alive; we needed him to tell us where Mischa was, who had purchased her. My fear was barely contained. I couldn't believe I'd missed her by seconds. Seconds.

Braxton was at Jessa's side, back in human form. I was pretty sure he hadn't taken his hands off her for even a moment since finding her here. I could see the pain and desperation bleeding across his features. He'd been in warrior mode before, but now that he had her, he was about to shatter apart.

I knew. I understood. My heart soared to see that Jessa was okay, but Mischa was still missing.

"It was Kristoff," Jessa said to me when I crossed to her. "He purchased Mischa and then disappeared in a rush. He was completely whacked out, worse than I've ever seen him, and according to this little slimeball..." She kicked the magic user on the floor. "He's one of the organizers of this smuggling circuit."

Goddamn it. This was bad. I needed to get to Mischa now, because that sorcerer was going to make her suffer. Anything to punish our pack. He hated the fact we had "stolen" his power and position on the council.

In a fit of rage I dropped my head back and a roar ripped from deep in my chest. I couldn't stand the thought that Mischa was in his hands. We had to get her back. There was no other option.

CHAPTER TEN

Mischa Lebron

The cuts littering my arms and legs were already healing, but the pure anger simmering inside of me was not going anywhere. I had to physically hold on to my wolf's soul. She was trying to force the change on me, but we'd already done that once, and the chains which held me didn't change too. Half my body had been crushed. I couldn't let my wolf free again, even though I'd have loved to escape from my human body for a short time. And claws and razor sharp teeth wouldn't hurt as weapons against the sorcerer standing over me.

Kristoff.

The asshole who had tried to frame and imprison the boys ... my boys. Had tried to kill my sister in Vanguard. I had never hated anyone with quite the passion I now hated this ... dick. Yep, I said it. He really deserved to die, and I just hoped I lived long enough to see it happen.

No, scratch that. I was definitely going to live through this. I would do what Jessa asked of me earlier. I would hold on to the hope that I'd either fight my way out of here or one of my pack would find me. Then we could punish him together.

As he took a step away to get more supplies or something, my mind drifted back to the last few hours. My heart clenched at the thought of where Jessa might be right now. I really hoped the boys had made it there before she was taken. I'd thought, in the last moment when Kristoff has stolen me away, that I'd felt Maximus' presence. Probably just wishful thinking.

I breathed deeply, images smashing through my mind. When we'd first been released from the cage back at the supe sale, Jessa and I had stuck to our initial plan. We'd kept our twin bond strong and fought the staff's hold. For a second it had worked, but then we'd been jumped by guards – who must have been invisible or something, because they literally appeared out of thin air.

We'd fought as hard as we could, and the staff-wielding douchebag had stood to the side, watching closely, clearly enjoying the show. Unfortunately, we were overwhelmed by their sheer numbers. Plus we were a little hindered by our pregnant bellies.

I had managed to smack one in the balls though, and another in the temple. He'd been knocked unconscious, which was a proud moment for me. Jessa took down about ten. My sister was a fighting machine, even carrying twins.

Once we were subdued again, I'd been first on the chopping block. Kristoff had appeared out of nowhere. I knew by the glassy fear in Jessa's eyes that him being there was a very bad thing for me, but there had been nothing either of us could do. He'd taken me through some sort of black wormhole, apparently the easiest way to get out of the realm, and deposited me in his evil lair.

Then the torture had begun.

We were a few hours into it now and I was starting to wonder how much longer I could hold out.

My head shot up as he crossed the chamber toward me again. I fought against the hold of his magical cuffs, but I was beyond exhausted. I'd been up for God knows how many hours. No food or drink. I was worried about the baby. Kristoff could do anything he wanted to me, but hurting me hurt my child and that was not okay.

"I have to leave you for a short time. I need some more supplies, which I think will work very well in igniting your bond and bringing the Compasses to me. Just in case you manage to finagle your way out of those chains, I'm moving you to the dungeon."

Shit. I had to fight him now. It was my best chance. I wished I had more strength left, but I'd find it somehow. Kristoff reached down and unhooked a set of keys from his belt. There were at least a dozen clinking there, lots of them looking like ancient, ornate pieces. Selecting a small bronze one with a clover style end, he slipped it into the side of my chains and released me from the chair. I still had cuffs on my hands but I was no longer tied down.

I slumped lower, eyelids half closed, as if all energy had deserted me. I was hoping Kristoff would reach for me. As my body slid further down, the sorcerer leaned across me and gathered up the sleeve of my shirt into his closed fist, and as he moved to lift me up I swung my other arm back and slammed the side of my hand into his face. Instead of using my fist, I hit him with the metal of the cuff, a weapon he had unknowingly provided me with.

He let out a shout, and at the same time pain slammed into my own face and I couldn't prevent a small shriek from escaping.

My face throbbed as my body was magically yanked out of the chair. "Stupid shifter," he spat at me, wiping a hand across his face, "your race is all brawn and no brains. Those magical cuffs you wear do more than secure you to the chair. They link your life essence to mine. If I die, you die. If I hurt, you will feel every ounce of it. And lucky for me it only goes one direction, so I can torture you for the rest of my life and never feel a single slice."

With a cackle, he slammed his hand into my temple, and I barely held on to consciousness as he continued floating me out of that room and into another.

By the time the disorientation had cleared, I was in a cell. Story of my life lately. This one was at least twelve feet on either side, had a small bench, and a bucket in the corner. No doubt the delightful amenities. Pregnant shifters had to pee as frequently as pregnant humans, so I quickly made use of that. Once I was finished I sank against the wall, leaning my head back to try and assuage the pounding in my temples.

Kristoff had thought of everything. Clearly he knew the Compasses were going to try and kill him. Maybe he was even hoping they would, and that I would die also.

"Hello."

The soft voice had my eyes slamming open and my body up off the bench. I hadn't even for a second thought I wasn't here alone, but that had definitely been a voice.

I crossed the space to the front of my cage, and gripping onto the bars tried to see in the dimly-lit room. It was cold down here, dark, with only some high-up sconces that held burning flames to cast a little light.

"Hello," the female spoke again, weaker this time, and I could sense that it was taking a lot of effort for her.

"Hello," I replied, feeling like an idiot. "I'm sorry, I can't see you. Are you in a prison cell also?"

There was a brief coughing, and movement like she was shifting around. "Yes, I have been down here for ... I don't even know how long. The sorcerer purchased me after I was drawn into Little Red Riding Hood's house. Damn Huntsman."

Little Red Riding Hood? Ours had been Hansel and Gretel. My theory that they were using fairytale stories as the draw seemed to be right. Perfect thing to lure in anyone who came across it. Of course we'd be curious. Who wouldn't if they came across a real life fairytale in the forest?

The soft feminine voice continued: "After I followed the axe-carrying hottie, I was stuck in this weird auction house. Kristoff purchased me. Has kept me here ever since. He drains my blood and has these cuffs on my wrists so I can't hurt him."

Despite the touches of humor, there was still so much sadness in her melodic voice. My heart was literally aching as I listened to her stumble and search for words.

"What race are you from?" I asked her. There was a pause, and I wondered whether she was going to answer or if she'd passed out or something.

Her words floated across the basement again. "The human race. Why? What race are you from?"

"You're human?"

There was a groan, and more shifting. I could see some movement in the darkness now. She was across the way from me, toward the far end. I caught only glimpses of golden hair and a slender frame.

"Yep, hundred percent grass-fed human." There was a pause, and I think I was supposed to laugh but my mind was too crazed. "Sorry," she continued. "Vegetarian joke. I've been down here so long I'm starting to think I've lost my ability to socialize. You're the first person I've had a chance to talk with in forever."

She was definitely a human. Supes did not talk the same way as humans, and it was easy to recognize the difference now. But what did Kristoff want with a human? What power did she offer him?

"My name is Mischa," I said, "I'm not a human and neither is Kristoff. He's a sorcerer, magic user, and I'm a wolf shifter."

She already knew he was a sorcerer, she'd said so before, but maybe she didn't quite realize what that meant. There was maybe ten seconds of dead silence before words burst from her. She sounded stronger: "I knew it. I knew he wasn't just a human playing witch. There were too many weird things, but how can all of this be true? You can shift into a wolf? Like a werewolf?"

"Yes, sort of the same thing. In my world there are five supernatural races, and each of them has a different ability or affinity. There are many types of shifters. Wolf, bear, fox, tiger, and so on."

I wasn't supposed to tell humans about our world, but this chick had already been exposed in a huge way. She deserved to know what she was up against.

"I have a pack of very powerful supes. They'll be coming for me." My faith was still strong. "Do whatever you can to hold on, I *won't* leave you here."

A strangled chuckle escaped her. "Strange that just today I had pretty much given up hope. I have fought and tried to escape, and prayed to no avail. I decided to just give up, let Kristoff finish me off, and finally be at peace. Then you arrived … like a beacon of hope."

Emotions started to choke me then and I held tightly to the bars as I fought down the tears. Hope. I had never been hope for anyone.

"What's your name?" I asked when I finally got my emotions controlled.

Her voice was fading again, and I could see that she'd slumped down at the bars. "It's Justice. Justice Anne Winter."

So human. First, middle and last name. So much more important than it was for supes. They used pack or last names, but it didn't mean much.

"Well, it's very nice to meet you, Justice. And like your namesake, we are going to make Kristoff pay for this. I promise you."

There was no reply, but I could hear her quiet sobs as she struggled up off the floor.

For the next few hours, between her need to rest, Justice and I chatted, talking about everything and nothing. I loved her little bursts of humor; they were dry and witty, and I realized that I actually liked her. I'd never had human friends. Not really. There'd always been something to keep us apart, but this one was a keeper. I just had to make sure we both got out of here alive.

I felt the moment Kristoff returned to his lair. An insidious darkness crept in around me and I could feel the bad mojo. "He's back," Justice said, her voice low and dead now. "He will be coming for one of us soon."

Yes, he would be, and I was determined that it be me. Justice was human, fragile. There was only so much more of this abuse she could take. She had to be so strong just to survive this long, but I could feel the weakness slowly breaking her.

Steps got louder as Kristoff descended into the freezing pit. All too soon his ugly, pointy face came into view.

"Looks like you're ready for phase two of my plan, little wolf," he said, his manic grin in place. The cell doors clicked open and I walked out without any assistance. "Glad to see you now understand the futility of fighting me. I leave nothing to chance. Nothing!"

And the crazy was back. I flicked one glance back down into the dungeon, silently telling Justice to remain silent. There was nothing she could do to help me now.

Of course, like all humans, she didn't like to listen to orders. "Leave her alone, you ugly asshole!"

Her shout was firm, and I didn't like the way Kristoff's eyes narrowed toward her.

"Glad to see you two made friends down here. Maybe your spirits will keep each other company when you both depart this world … soon." The promise of our deaths lingered in the air.

The sorcerer laughed, and flicked out his fingers toward her cage. I reacted immediately, jumping into his side and knocking into him. He let out a yell before backhanding me across the face. I hit the ground, rolling to protect my stomach, before maneuvering to get into a position where I could kick at him.

My aim was off due to a baby belly being in the way, but I still managed to partially slam him right in his junk. Which, yep, hurt me too, but since I wasn't a dude, the pain was far less than his. And totally worth it.

Eyes watering, he gasped a few times before crushing a hand around my throat and lifting me by the neck. "If you fight me again, I'll kill her. I'll kill her slowly and painfully right in front of you."

I could tell he was serious. Except to suck in a few deep breaths, I didn't move at all as he lowered me back down. My throat was throbbing.

Justice was still screaming as we left the room, begging him to let me go. She was fighting for me, a stranger she barely knew, and I would do the same for her. I would take whatever punishment he dished out to make sure she wasn't hurt.

Back in the main torture room, Kristoff chained me to the chair again before turning back to the bench across the other side of the chamber. It held a scattering of paraphernalia, ornate jars and a few small boxes. He was still limping and I took great joy in the fact that my kick had hurt him. Small victories.

When he turned around again, the ugly freak was holding a small, ornately carved chalice. It was a deep, rich purple, with gold inlay, and had the dull patina of an object which was very old. As he closed the distance between us, I could scent something dark and oily held within it. Everything inside of me shied away from the contents. This was going to be much worse than the countless slashes he'd inflicted earlier today.

"I need the Compasses to come for you, and the previous pain wasn't doing the job. I need something ... more permanent." His voice was slightly high. "Once they sense you, there will be nothing to stop them. If there's one thing I can rely on when it comes to that powerful pack of posers, it's their loyalty." His unblinking eyes regarded me for a moment. "I would have preferred to purchase Jessa from my traveling band of Merry Men. She has a tighter bond to the Compasses, but I didn't have the time to wait for her. My presence had to stay undetected."

Traveling band of Merry Men must have been the smuggling ring. And did he say his? As in he was behind that setup? Well, at least when he died that would get two things off my to-do list.

He was still babbling away and I was starting to wonder if Kristoff had enjoyed a drink or two. Guy seemed to be half wasted as he swayed around the room. "You're almost as good as Jessa anyway. You carry one of their young. They'll feel the pain."

Back to the weird mutters at the floor. Still, his words were more than a little disturbing. Especially the part about the pain. Even though they were healed now, I could still feel those magical slashes. Did he think they had not been painful? Holy heck. How much worse was this new thing going to be?

Hold on, precious baby. I mentally sent out calming thoughts, preparing myself to not flinch, to not let whatever pain I'd feel filter into the bond with my child.

I could do this. I was strong enough.

Kristoff tilted the chalice over my leg and let the darkness trickle over the sides. I had been right about the oiliness. There was a strong viscosity within the fluid; it hung almost suspended in a large drop, before gravity finally won.

Do not show pain. Do not feel it.

I started to chant in my mind, which I had done many times over the years as a child. My differences led to lots of bullying, lots of running and hiding from the cruelty of others. As they would punch and kick me, throw things and smash food into my face, I would go to a place inside my mind where they couldn't reach me, where the pain didn't reach me.

I hadn't had to go to that place for a long time, but I would now. Only this time, as the first burning bite of oil dropped onto my thigh, I found myself not in my mind but with my child.

Hello, little one. My mental voice went all deep and warm and I could feel the love pouring out of me. And shockingly, the same warmth was returned to me from my baby, my beautiful, perfect, precious child.

The oil splashed me again, and a part of my body connected to my pain sensors knew that this pain was akin to slowly being burned alive. Piece by piece my skin shriveled away, but I had distanced myself to keep my mind safe. Or maybe my mind was completely shattered now. Either way, I would not give up this moment with my child for anything.

Your mommy loves you very much, sweetheart. And so does your daddy. He's going to come for us, and until he does I'll keep fighting for you. I'll always fight for you. You'll never be alone.

That was the real truth of it. I had always been alone. Even when Lienda was around, she was absent. Her devastation at the loss of her true mate had meant she was little more than a shell. She had retreated into herself, working eighty hours a week and barely acknowledging I was alive. The mother I'd seen over the last few months was completely different. That mother was warm, and loving, and kind, a ferocious protector and a shoulder to cry on.

A blinding shot of realization hit me then and I understood the truth behind my actions in the sanctuary, and in those moments after. When Maximus had been stolen from me I had acted like Lienda, like a person who had lost their true mate and would do anything to get them back.

I could acknowledge that Lienda had sacrificed greatly for mine and Jessa's safety, that she had given up twenty-plus years of life with her mate while her soul slowly shriveled away, but she should have been stronger for her child, the way I had needed her to be. Now that I had a child of my own, I would never let my weakness hurt her.

As I wrapped myself around the tiny energy at my center, I felt with great certainty that it was a girl. I was going to have a daughter. This joy was short-lived though, as the sorcerer chose this moment to go completely crazy.

"React, damn you!" Some of my inner calm was lost as spittle smashed across my face.

Kristoff flung the oil to the side, and in a flash slapped me hard across the face. The crack echoed loudly, and as my vision went blurry, dots dancing before my eyes, I lost my tenuous ability to hide internally.

The right side of my face was numb now, that sort of numbness which preluded a serious injury, where you knew that once the pain finally registered it was probably going to kill you. Of course, I could take comfort in the fact that no matter how badly damaged my face was, there was no pain which could compare to the agony scorching my left leg.

Once the black dots stopped spinning before my eyes, I was able to really see the damage being inflicted on my body. My left thigh was completely destroyed, the skin burned and bleeding, red and weeping. The pain was like nothing I could describe; I had no precedent for it, and truly I wondered if the anguish would kill me.

In the true nature of burns, the oil continued burrowing down into my skin, like a red-hot poker slowly piercing through flesh and muscle.

Screams were in my throat; I had to swallow them down multiple times. I couldn't stop from thrashing against my chains, hoping movement might offer the slightest relief to the burning. Sitting felt like the worse thing I could be doing.

"Lemmego, bastherd," I attempted to shout, but the moment I opened my mouth there was a blinding jolt of agony to my brain. Great, so my jaw was probably fractured too. As another stabbing pain lanced through my jaw and temple, I upgraded the injury from a fracture to completely shattered.

"Nice to see you've returned to me," Kristoff said, appearing to be once again in control of himself.

Crazy got temporarily shelved, making way for the regal sorcerer. Somehow even his hair appeared neater, his clothes less shabby. Had he glamoured himself or something. "Apologies for the *Lunarti oil*. I try not to use this sort of dark magic often, but since your mate bond is not formed, the pain had to be intense."

"Wht mat bwond?" My garbled words were a mess, but he seemed to understand.

"It surprises me that your idiotic pack members haven't figured it out yet, especially after the whole Cardia death debacle."

I felt the skin on my face stretch, pain lancing me again. My eyes widened and lips parted. How did he know about Cardia?

The sorcerer grinned, and strode across the room to retrieve a chair. He placed it before me and sat down. "Let's have a little chat. There are many things you don't know, and not even your upbringing with human apes is an excuse for that."

His whole personality changed again. Now we had the genial council leader. My head was spinning at his rapid shifts in personality.

He got right to the point. "You see, I liked my old life a lot. My position on the council gave me certain privileges that I was not ready to give up. I had a great thing going on with the traveling band of Merry Men. I was one of the originals to start the smugglers. I even came up with the idea that we should tap into the energy of fairytale magic. It's strong, powered by the belief of millions of humans.

"At first my plan was simple. There's an old law that if there are no suitable members available to take over council leadership, then the original members continue to lead another term. Another twenty-five years. I had the quads all but locked in Vanguard, but then Louis stepped in. That damn sorcerer barely left his home for decades, and he chose that moment to return to the world."

I knew I loved Louis for a reason. He had impeccable timing.

"He defended the Compass punks and everything blew up. So then I turned my attention to Larkspur, the dragon king. I decided to take advantage of all the chaos in our world, knowing that once he was free, I could step in and help him rebuild the supernatural world."

I swayed then, the pain weakening my body. I continued to listen though. I needed to know all of this, needed to hear all the ways he had tried to hurt people I loved.

"Cardia was my daughter. She's Giselda's half-sister."

What the actual heck? Seriously! I really needed my jaw to be usable so I could scream at him. My shifter healing was extra slow at the moment, especially with my leg. The burning was deepening and I could see muscle and tendon now. Something told me the true horror in the oil was that it never stopped torturing. Blood filled my mouth as I bit into my tongue, trying to hold back another scream. The sorcerer was watching me closely, so I held my face immobile.

Eventually, though, I had to take his dangled bait. "How did you fake the mate bond?"

Most of my words came out clearly. He smiled this weird creepy grin which transformed his face. Kind of like that doll who used to come to life and stab people. A few drops of sweat ran into my eyes; perspiration covered me as my body burned. Kristoff's creepy smile faded away at my continued silence, and then with a loud exhalation he continued.

"From the moment you arrived in Stratford I knew you were my key to taking down the Compasses." He sneered the last part. "When my original plan fell through, I knew I was going to lose my leadership, so I sought another source of power. The dragon king. Information of the prison break outs was world-wide, and I knew the sanctuary was the best place to start. I sent Cardia there, using a friend of mine to get her inside. She became my spy in there. We learned of Larkspur's twins, how they were freeing the marked, and that they needed you and your sister to open the doorway. Cardia also started to pave the way for us to be part of the king's army. His plan to rebuild the supernatural world under his rule was okay with me. I would be happy stepping in as second to all his power. He would need some trusted members to rule with him. I was to be one of those members."

He was going into crazy mode again, some of the sheen wearing off on his glamour. He brushed back his now unruly hair. "When the Four came looking for you, I had Cardia speak with Quale. He was the one who could convince Louis that the safest place for you was in the sanctuary. The twins would reward us greatly for getting you all there. Plus, we had a plan to make sure you'd co-operate also, which they were very grateful for. You see, I've always seen the true mate bond between you and Maximus, and with your naivety of our world I knew that if I took him away from you, your devastation would allow an emotional manipulation by the king's twins. You'd jump right in to help them."

And jump like a damn idiot I had.

"So I raced across to the sanctuary and spelled my daughter. I had blood from Maximus, and with his blood I could create a binding. It's a dark spell which shatters a soul and allows a manufactured mate connection to form. That's why he suffers in her death. His soul was broken, lost, without direction. But there was no true mate bond there. You're his true mate."

I scoffed. He was lying … he had to be. But, dammit, a lot of his words made sense. If Cardia was a plant, that explained why she wasn't affected by the call of the king, why she'd always treated Maximus with a cold disdain. I'd heard them when they were alone, and it had not always been pleasant. There had been a distance between them.

She wasn't his true mate. I was. I let those words mull around my cloudy mind. I wanted to believe them, for a multitude of reasons. For one, it helped explain the whole sanctuary thing, where I'd lost my mind. If he was my true mate, then my actions were more than crazy pregnancy-induced hormones, it was my soul screaming over the loss of a mate. But there was one thing which blew the entire argument out of the water. I swayed forward in my chair. The chains were the only things keeping me up now.

"I'm a shifter, and Max is a vampire. There's no way for us to be true mates."

That was the true issue, the one which had been breaking my heart for months now and left me in my current state of knocked-up-ness. I'd refused to accept it before, and look where it got me.

Kristoff gave me a look of derision and sympathy, both of which I wanted to shove down his throat. "You poor, stupid, simple child. The Compasses are many things which have never been seen before. Despite Max's close bindings to the vampire world, the race he has a physically stronger affinity for, his soul actually contains elements of all four supernatural races. He's shifter, vampire, sorcerer and fey, all rolled up in one powerful package. All of the quads are. Each of them took on a stronger aspect of one of the races, but they could switch if they knew how to tap into their abilities. The longer they continue to join in their quad bond, the murkier their race distinctions will become. Max's true mate could have been from any of the supe races, and it just so happens that it's you."

No! No! No! No! NO! After everything I'd been through. After accepting that he would never be mine ... to find out like this. It couldn't be true, right? There was no possible way.

He must have read the agony on my face. For the first time I was unable to stop my emotions from showing. Maximus always was my weakness.

"Yes, it's true. The true bond couldn't form between you before because he was not linked close enough to the other races within him. He hadn't joined to his brothers. And then the fake mate spell interfered. It would have faded eventually. That vampire is too strong. Luckily Cardia continued to be a good little soldier. She reinforced the bond. It was in her blood, and every time he fed from her, it secured their fake bond."

Cardia was an evil bitch. Couldn't be happier that she'd lost her head. Bet she'd never expected that one when she signed up for her fake mate role.

"It is a shame that she died," Kristoff said, showing not an ounce of sadness at all. "She delivered a lot of vital intel to me and Larkspur. He almost won because of her. Sometimes kids can come in very handy."

Was he still talking about Cardia now, or Giselda? The witch was still MIA, and according to Jessa she was as evil and crazy as her father.

The sorcerer stood but I barely even noticed. My body continued swaying, and despite the burning oil seeping into my body, I was shivering, parts of me freezing while other parts burned.

Kristoff wasn't done monologuing yet. Nope, seemed he still had more to rage about. "I had so many plans, and all of them thwarted by the power of those quads. It's not natural. They should not exist. So now we have moved on to the less satisfactory but necessary plans for revenge. I find great delight in knowing that I have the power to make them suffer. They took everything from me: my power, my position, my daughter. Maximus didn't save my child, and now he won't be able to save his own either."

My head lolled forward as he left the room. I knew I had to fight, but there was no way to stop the darkness from descending over me.

My last thought was of my daughter, and whether I could keep my promise to protect her.

A multitude of pain and fire slashed at me even as I drifted in a sea of unconsciousness. There was no true rest, but I managed to keep a section of my wolf energy wrapped around my womb, doing whatever I could to halt the spread of poisonous oil from continuing its insidious journey through my body.

Wetness splashed against me, rousing me to a semi-conscious state. "You need to wake. Your subconscious is hiding from him. Call for your damn mate or I will kill your child."

The sorcerer's voice was fuzzy and I barely recognized the words, but something resonated within me. I needed to call for Maximus.

I really didn't want to. I didn't want him anywhere near this crazy guy who'd been trying to take him down for months. But I had to think of our daughter, and the fact that Maximus would be expecting me to reach out to him. Maybe I could let him know it was a trap.

In my confused, probably dying state, I wasn't sure where to start. In the end I decided to just throw my spirit at the tenuous and emotional connection I'd always felt toward the vampire.

Maximus! I need help. Kristoff has us and he's poisoned me with something. Some sort of oil. I'm trying to protect her but I think I'm failing. He wants you to come. It's a trap. Please...

Whatever else I wanted to say was lost as a spasm of pain rocked through me and I screamed. My stomach started to heave and I couldn't stop the vomit from expelling everywhere. There was nothing much left in my gut and the bile burned the entire way up. The darkness was in my chest now, and as I continued heaving, the taint of evil pressed in on me.

"That's good," Kristoff said, pushing my hair back from my face. With a snarl I found the strength to rip my head back, out of his grip. "Keep calling for him. He'll come, and I'll be waiting."

I had no more strength, no more fight. Holding on to the last facets of who I was, I slumped and started praying to the gods, to the fey, even to Josephina, Jessa's dragon. She was pretty much a god. *Keep my baby safe.* Instinct was telling me that even if I died, she was developed enough now to live outside of the womb. Developed and strong enough. Someone had to save her for me, it was my most fervent desire.

Something cold and wet hit my face again, but I had no strength to open my eyes. I barely felt the pain of the chains cutting into me now. It felt as if the blood were sloshing sluggishly through my veins, thick, inky, and evil. A shout penetrated the muffled nature of my head. Kristoff again. Trying to get me to call for Maximus.

Too late, buddy. You didn't leave me with enough energy to do anything but sit here, fucker.

My mom hated that word, but I think in these circumstances she'd understand.

As my thoughts started to get weird and vapid, the wolf rose. She was often dormant within me, a byproduct of so many years caged. It had tamed a lot of the fire in her, and me also, but we were still wolf, and she did not want us to roll over and show our bellies.

Mate, she said.

If Kristoff's crazy ramblings were right, then I finally understood why she always said that.

Mate.

I coughed a few times, and my heart was doing this crazy slow beat. My wolf continued to batter me with growls and "I told you so's."

Yes, he's our mate. I'm sorry I always acted like you were wrong.

I sent reassurances to her and all I got in return was another growl. What did she want then? Why did she keep repeating "mate" to me in that way?

Icy cold water slapped me hard, and there was a burn in my arm I wanted desperately to rub at but couldn't. With a burst of heat, my mind came to life and my eyes flew open. I gasped, trying to fill my lungs with air. Everything was fuzzy in my vision, but there was no mistaking the sorcerer's evil, pointy, ugly-ass features.

"They're here," he said gleefully. "There's no point in this show though if you die before they get here. That will limit Maximus' suffering, and I can't have that. I've shot you up with a special blend of adrenalin. It will boost your shifter side and keep you alive just long enough."

Mate. My wolf sounded a bit smug now, which was really unbecoming of a majestic spirit such as hers.

I could feel Maximus. I'd always been hyper aware of him, something I tried not to think much on. Pretty much all made sense now.

This was the first time in hours I'd been able to properly focus, so I attempted to picture the massive vampire in my mind, aiming to touch the connection between us. *It's a trap.* My thoughts were desperate, but I was going to use whatever had been in that shot to reach him. *Kristoff plans to capture and torture you. Don't come alone.*

I repeated the warning over and over while my eyes remained locked on the insane sorcerer. He was standing just two feet away, staring at a spot over his shoulder, listening and waiting. I didn't know much about magic, but I had no doubt that he had this place rigged with all kinds of security and warning systems.

A coughing fit shuddered through me and I gagged a few times as my empty stomach protested. Even though I could hold my head up now, I wasn't doing great. *Hang on, baby girl.* I had to keep reassuring her. I was helpless to do anything else but shower her in love and warmth from my spirit. Thankfully my wolf was there also, adding her own magical spirit to the protection we were creating around her.

Kristoff still had not moved, continuing his statue impression.

I heard a series of crashes, and something fissured inside of my chest, like all the love and emotions I'd ever held toward a stubborn, giant, alpha vampire burst free from me in search of its mate. Damn you, emotions, you get back here.

I couldn't lose myself like that again. I wouldn't. Last time it had almost cost my sister her life, and I was not okay with that. I would not be my mother. I refused.

But still, there was no stopping the speeding of my heart and pulse. No stopping my head from turning toward where I could feel him coming from.

Despite my current state of dying and stuff, there was no way to deny that Maximus still had the tightest hold on me. And he was coming for me now, just like Jessa had promised. They never left a pack member behind.

How ironic to finally find the family I'd always craved, who accepted me unconditionally and fought for me, only to be moments away from death.

Screw you, fates … screw you.

CHAPTER ELEVEN

Maximus Compass

Rational thought had long since faded from my mind. Instinct was all I had.

"Are you ready, brother? You remember the plan, right?" Braxton was calmer now that he had Jessa back, but the beast still shone from his eyes.

He cared about Mischa. I was way past that. Caring was an insipid word compared to what I felt at this point.

As we stepped through the final magical portal, Braxton growled, his eyes flashing from yellow to blue. He was in protective mode: no one touched his pack and lived. Which was why he had incinerated all evidence of the supe smuggling operation before we left.

Jacob, Jessa, and Tyson then went back to Stratford to alert the council of what we'd found. The supes who'd been in the cages around us were escorted to the sanctuary, where they would be able to decide where to go next. Louis, Braxton, and I went after Mischa.

I was desperate to find Mischa, and desperate to kill the son of a bitch who took her. Louis had picked up a magical essence from the fey stones Kristoff used to purchase Mischa, which he had then used to amplify a connection he sensed between me and Mischa. His step through had led us to a land of cold, stark, desolate expanses of wilderness.

"Russia," Louis murmured as we moved freely. I did recognize some of the landscape now. We were in northern Russia, near the supernatural prison town of Kreatsky.

The wizard who'd run the smuggling ring had admitted that Kristoff was more than just a simple "buyer," he'd actually been instrumental in setting up the entire thing. He was the one who made deals with the demons. I tried not to think too hard on it, considering he had Mischa and I was already fearing for her safety.

Goddammit! I focused on putting one foot in front of the other and trying to mentally reach for Mischa. The connection was there, strangely tenuous but it was there. Weirdly enough, it almost felt like the more Cardia's bond faded from my body, the stronger the connection was between Mischa and me. And my baby. They weren't dead, I knew that much, but the flickering of the bond was causing me great concern. Mischa was hurt. The taste of dark magic and blood was strong across my senses. And since it wasn't coming from me, it was definitely from her.

"Hurry!" I bit out, increasing my pace and forcing the mage to step up. He was the one directing this search party, and I hated following when I wanted to charge ahead.

"Patience, vampire. There's dark magic washed all across this area. It is very hard to pinpoint the actual location when I am sifting through all the waste."

My answer was lost in the growls as I lunged for him. Braxton caught me before I managed to make contact. "We need him! You can't kill him yet."

Louis shook his head. We were sprinting across the tundra now, slipping on mud and ice. "No idea why I bother with you all. If it wasn't for my love of the Lebron girls, I'd have cast you all into the dead plains long ago."

I flipped him off before baring my fangs, a direct threat he would recognize. Most supes did their best to run and hide when vampires lost it like this, but Louis simply grinned as though I amused him.

My murderous thoughts were halted by another thrumming along the connection leading me to Mischa. It flared to life in an odd way, and I wondered what that meant, almost as if she'd been unconscious and was now awake. But bonds didn't work like that. Being unconscious was no barrier to them, so it had to be magic.

"I've got her," Louis said in a hurry. "She's projecting very strongly. I don't even need the bond between you two to follow the trail." He was staring at me now. "A bond which I'm finally starting to understand."

Great, because I didn't understand it at all. The only thing that made sense to me was the baby's essence connecting us, but somehow that just didn't feel right.

"You will explain all of this to me after we save her," I growled. There was no time to worry about it now, she was in trouble. We had to get to her before it was too late.

My boots smashed against the cracked ground. The land around us was barren, and not just because of the harsh winters here. Death lingered in the air and among the scrawny scattering of plant life, like something was leaching it of life.

None of us spoke, until Louis ground to a halt. "Where is she?" I said, my head swiveling as if I was missing something. There was still nothing here. For miles I saw nothing but plains of withered land.

"They are below us," he said, dropping to his knees. I felt the stirring of magic. I didn't have the same senses as the shifters. Their beasts were more innately connected to magic than vampires, but for one of my race I had always shown a strong affinity for the fey energy which was within all of us.

Louis' magic was so strong that even humans would feel the vibrations of energy he exuded. As he pressed his hands to the ground and magic started to sink into the earth beneath him, I took a step back as the dirt began to ripple and collapse. Of course my one step was pretty useless when most of the land around us plunged down, taking the three of us with it. I braced myself for the drop, not sure how far we would fall. It ended up being about twenty feet down. The light was dim down here, but not too dark for vampire senses. I saw the ground approaching, and landed lightly.

Braxton and Louis were right beside me. None of us had any trouble with the drop; it wasn't part of the security here. If Kristoff had been really trying to keep us out, the drop would have been miles down. Nope, this was just the first step to infiltrating his underground bunker, and now he definitely knew we were coming.

The connection in my chest intensified. It was almost as if I could hear her calling me with the faintest of whispers across my mind.

On my way, Misch. Hold on for me.

The area we were in now was a large cavern, filled with rock formations and scattered stalactites on the ceiling, stalagmites on the floor with flat tops. Water had dripped through these caves over the years, although it felt cold and dry.

"No wonder Kristoff was always in the pocket of the human leaders," Louis said. "This mine is filled with diamonds."

The single beam of light from the hole above, the one we'd just plunged down through, highlighted the gems scattered about. Everyone in Stratford was wealthy. We had plenty of mines of our own, and the trolls kept us well fitted with gold and gems, but this was so much more than that. This was enough to buy countries. No doubt Kristoff used it for many things.

Diamonds were also the key ingredient in lots of spells and curses. There was nothing more solid to use as a conduit.

Braxton was striding around, stepping into the shadows. His voice echoed back to us. "I always knew Kristoff was filled with secrets. His power is unstable."

"Which was why he tried to frame us and then get us killed. Power has sent him crazy," I said. "No doubt he was responsible for the supes we chased in the forest around Stratford. A distraction we were stupid enough to fall for. Then he could make sure there was a doorway there for the girls to stumble across. It called for them, and they answered."

Braxton strode back into sight. He nodded to the left. "There's a path over there. Goes for a long way. I couldn't see the end."

A path which had better lead us right to the sorcerer. "What's the plan? We know he's waiting for us. He has more than enough power to hide himself if he wanted to, so he wants us here."

Louis ran his eyes over me. "Do you still have the staff?"

I reached into my back pocket and pulled it free. The powerful relic was still masquerading as a small twig, a few inches long and scraggly like an offcut of a tree.

The sorcerer took a moment to stare between me and it. "It has connected with you. Maybe you will find it a symbiotic relationship, but if you notice at any point that it's starting to control you, you're going to have to let it go. Its power knows not good nor evil, it's all about the wielder, but it will try to influence you if you let it."

"You want me to use it here, take control of Kristoff? He surely will not expect us to have this staff."

Braxton clenched his fists. "There's no doubt this is a trap. He'll have a plan, and then a backup plan. Do not react without taking a second to think about it. Mischa's life is at stake."

"I know that!" I snapped, taking a step back, rubbing my hand across my face, trying to quell my fury. Shit. Damn. Fuck. Yes, I knew that I needed to be calm when we made it into his prison, but something about the thought of Mischa and our baby being here with a crazed male ... not knowing what he had been doing to her. My mind was partly gone already and I was going to be hard pressed to keep my cool at all.

"Don't let me do anything to get her hurt, man." I swallowed my pride and admitted what everyone here already knew: "I would never directly hurt her, you know that, but I won't be able to stop myself with Kristoff, and when magic is involved ... I can't stand the thought that she might get caught in the crossfire."

Who knows what magical backfire this bastard was planning.

Braxton dropped his hand on my shoulder, giving it a brief squeeze. "Mischa is part of our pack now. She's important to us all. Plus Jessa would kill me if anything happened to her sister. We won't let him win, he won't take her from us, and he *will* pay for what he's done. I can promise you this."

"I can also," Louis said, no inflection in his tone. "I've picked up his magical trail. Stay close."

Just like that we were moving again. I blanked out my mind, allowing it to settle into a mild hum of fury, the twig-size staff of Gradiella gripped in my right hand.

The scenery didn't change as we stepped silently with a brisk pace. Dull lighting, icy and untouched rocky cavern, visible tendrils of dark magic. I couldn't tell what these tendrils were doing, but no doubt they were part of a security system. Louis took care of them. He was in the lead, doing something with a wave of his hand to break the bonds.

"By breaking them, are you letting him know how close we are?" Braxton was half shifted, so his words were very low and rumbly. "I'm not sure shouting our presence so loudly is a good thing. A slight element of surprise could really help here."

Louis grinned; his teeth shone in the half-light. "For most sorcerers they'd have no choice but to break them. These securities are strong. I'm not breaking so much as pausing them temporarily. He would have to be paying very close attention to even notice. It's just like each of these magical pulses are skipping a beat or two before resuming."

Braxton and I exchanged a wry smile, definitely thinking the same thing. Thank God Louis had adopted Jessa. We needed his experience. Even though Tyson would rival him one day in power, he didn't today. We were too young. It was frustrating to realize there was nothing we could do to speed up the aging of our powers. Despite the current wicked levels of energy we wielded, for our full potential to be reached, only time would help.

The temperature did a rapid plummet then. The staff responded by heating and growing larger. "I think we're close to the spider's lair," I murmured.

All of us remained focused, our footsteps barely audible as we crossed the final part of the cavern. We found ourselves staring at a pair of large wood and iron doors, twenty feet tall, which seemed impossible considering how low the ceiling had been at times in here. But clearly Kristoff had found a way.

"This reminds me of the cave where Larkspur's doorway was," Braxton said as he reached out and brushed against the door. "There's silver, iron, and fey crystals embedded in this metal. It's going to be hard to break."

He grinned then, and bringing his hand back I noticed it was partially shifted into dragon claw. He swung and smashed into the lock as hard as he could. I expected a massive clank as he hit, but Louis' sent out a spell at the same time that deadened the noise – a spell which brushed past me with a real kick of power, adding strength to Braxton's dragon swing.

Whatever they did worked. The metal lock shattered and the doors swung silently open. Braxton and Louis took a second to observe the other side.

I was done with waiting. Staff in hand I strode through the opening. Louis was right on my heels, and as energy whooshed past me, I knew he was using his power to check for traps. Trusting my team, I continued to trek through what looked like a courtyard. Unlike the underground tunnels, this area felt almost like we were outdoors in the Middle-Ages. Cobbled ground, large fires burning in round concrete containers scattered around, even some animals roaming; chickens and ducks were scampering about. The illusion of sunlight and warmth was strong, but I saw through that. It was still rock above us. We were far beneath the Russian sky.

In the distance was a castle. Made of dark grey stone, the center structure was squat and square, with two towering round pillar-style wings on either side. Everything looked fortified, built to withstand a battle.

And a battle was what they were going to get. I strode closer, trying to discern a weakness or entry point. I needed to get in there. Mischa was inside.

Noticing something on one of the round towers, I forewent the main entrance and instead ducked along the left side and started to climb. The castle had clearly been built with the help of magic, but had a roughhewn design which gave me plenty of decent handholds. The window I was aiming for was about halfway up, a good fifty yards high.

I scaled the side in minutes and pulled myself to the edge of the huge arched opening. There was no glass or protective covering over it, which gave me easy access into the castle.

Diving inside, I was up and scanning around the tower room I'd landed in. Took no time to tell that this was an alcove connecting to a hall. I started along the landing, following the path which circled around to reach a twirling, stone staircase.

Relying heavily on the tugging connection to Mischa in my chest, I started to descend. With each step the pull was stronger, until everything inside of me wanted to run, to claim, to find what was mine and to protect her. I needed to protect her. It was ingrained into my very psyche.

Generally, I thought of myself as an easygoing sort of vampire. As attributes of my race went, mine were very mild. I could go a long time without blood and was less cold and clinical. Vampires were able to strongly compartmentalize their emotions, making them lethal killing machines. *Machine* was an apt way to describe them, actually, but I'd always been different. I felt strongly. I cared too much. I loved my pack with a ferocity that scared me at times, and I would die for them in a heartbeat. I'd always thought the love I'd had for them was the strongest emotion I could feel. Now I knew better. Now I knew what true, uncompromising, unconditional love was, my love for an unborn child, and in part for the woman who carried our baby.

The scent of my brother and Louis lingered behind me, but I ignored this to focus solely on what lay ahead. What did Kristoff need all this space for? How long had he even had this place? His history was shady. He was never one to let others know of his past, always afraid someone would discover a weakness there.

Giselda was no better. I didn't know her well. Beside tussles between her and Jessa, she'd never been on my radar. I heard the rumors though, and saw the way she was at Stratford gatherings. She was more often than not found on her back, her sexual appetites more reminiscent of vampires than magic users, but I had never felt any reason to go near her. Her blood never smelled right to me.

The further I descended, the darker it grew. There were no windows or openings, just solid stone twirling deeper into the earth. A faint tinge of copper was assailing my senses; blood had been shed recently. It was not that close, but I was particularly attuned to the scent. I hurried my steps as the tugging was practically yanking me down the narrow staircase.

Rounding a corner I was hit hard with a wall of magic, similar in design to Stratford's securities. It had Kristoff's magical essence all over it.

Louis pushed past me. None of us spoke. The tension was high as he ran both hands across the slightly shimmering barrier. I had to force myself not to move. My body was straining to fight, to charge, but I could not waste energy on fruitless endeavors. Thankfully I didn't have to. It took Louis about eighteen seconds, a few muttered spells, and one curse, but he eventually smashed through the barrier. The magic shattered, tinkling around us in shards.

"Should have upped his game," Louis murmured as we stepped forward. "He took my magical design for Stratford and simply tweaked it in a few places. Worst case of fan fiction I've ever seen."

I almost cracked a smile at that. Kristoff, who was many years older than Louis, would not be pleased to hear such a statement. Not only had Louis bested him in attaining sorcerer level, but had also been the youngest before Tyson to rule the magic-users' seat on the supernatural council. Now he'd reduced Kristoff to nothing more than a fanboy.

Fitting.

As we stepped across the barrier threshold, all three of us ground to a halt at the stink of death and dark magic. That faint blood I'd been scenting was strong now, overwhelming even, and there was another oily scent that I was having trouble placing.

"Lunarti oil," Louis growled, and took off. I was right behind him, Braxton at my side.

How the hell did Kristoff get Lunarti oil? It had been banned for at least a hundred years, ever since the last supernatural war. During the war it had been popular due to its ability to kill slowly, the ultimate weapon of slow-death torture. Supes would fill magical weapons with it and then shoot them out across the opposing side. One drop was enough to kill within a week.

It was expensive and extremely hard to brew. You needed to be a level five sorcerer, minimum, and you had to be demon-touched, fluent in dark arts. I had never known anyone to successfully brew it. The few who tried were either dead or in one of the prisons.

As we dashed rapidly along the lengthy hallway, I caught glimpses of a large circular room, dark stone covered with a few tattered tapestries. The blood and oil was so strong now, and my heart was pounding far too fast. I refused to think about what might have happened in this room, what I might find when I finally stepped out of the hallway. The tugging in my chest felt extremely physical now. I doubt I could have stopped running even if I wanted to.

As Mischa's scent wrapped around me, the roar building inside of me ripped free. Louis was at my side. He wore tense lines across his face, which was more than a little concerning. If he was worried...

A figure stepped into the open door, and the manic grin on his face did nothing to calm the fury within me. Louis stopped me a second before I was about to smash into him.

"No," he said. "He's demon-touched. Don't strike at him, you'll be fueling his power."

My chest was heaving as I stared down the slimy magic user. He had changed a lot since I'd seen him last. He was frail now, his body bent and withered. His skin was grey and haggard, and I was pretty sure more than a few teeth were missing. His dark hair that used to be wild and thick was now thin and matted. Barely a few strands covered his crown.

"The evil you house within is starting to reflect on the outside, wizard," I said, softly and without inflection. I would never let him see the pain and panic tearing at my insides. He wanted my suffering. It was what we were here for.

The manic grin disappeared and his face screwed up he blasted out at me with magic. "I'm a sorcerer!" he screamed.

I dived to the side, narrowly avoiding a blast of whatever darkness was spiraling from his fingertips. My grip remained strong on the staff. I knew very little about it. Would it work against a demon-touched? It wasn't supposed to be built on demon energy, but it had been housed in their realm for many millennia. Who knew where its loyalty lay now.

The moment Kristoff's darkness died away, I was back on my feet and charging. I couldn't directly attack him. To touch a demon-touched allowed them to siphon off some of your energy, allowed the demon to taste your soul, and then you would forever be on their radar. Demons were rare, mostly utilized by magic users who went completely dark. If they were strong enough, they controlled the demon. If they weren't, the demon controlled them. If the demon managed to free itself from the host, it would have a short time to find another, or cause mass destruction before it was drawn back to the land between.

Kristoff must have wanted his revenge badly, because he'd cursed his life irreparably by merging with the darkness. He was forever lost. No redemption.

Not that he'd be around long enough to worry about redemption.

He didn't move as I went directly for him, side-stepping at the last moment and swinging the staff in a wraparound movement. I urged it to expand to its full size again, needing the extra distance.

Heeding my call, it shot out to six feet in length. I jabbed it at Kristoff's shoulder, knowing I only needed to connect for a second to gain control – providing demon-touched were not immune to such magic.

Just as the staff was about to make contact, the sorcerer flashed away, disappearing and reappearing across the room.

"Well, that's a new trick," Louis said, his right brow lifted comically. "Demons are an underrated bunch. They've got a bad rep, you know, with all their evil murder and such. Such a shame no one ever talks about all that untapped potential."

Braxton snorted. "Yeah, if we make it out of here alive, we should definitely take a stand against demon discrimination."

Louis grinned and clapped his hands together, forming a wall of magic between us and Kristoff. The sorcerer's flash across the room to escape my staff had given us an opening. He was now trapped against the rounded wall.

Now that he had enough space, Braxton wasted no time. He stripped off his clothes and let the shifter magic burst from him. "Dragons are immune to demon taint," he said, before allowing the change to wash over him.

My eyes flicked across to Kristoff. He was slamming his body against Louis' wall, doing everything possible to break through. He started scratching away at it, looking like a manic rabid dog, foaming at the mouth and everything.

The sorcerer at my side grimaced. "He's damn strong. So much more than I've ever felt in his presence. This demon does not feel like one of the regular sorts. It's got an ancient energy that makes me uneasy."

"Ancient like from the original darkness?" I growled.

Louis tilted his head, his eyes dissecting the crazy male. "He wouldn't be so stupid. If that was the case he would have literally released the darkness, and once the darkness is out, it's not so easy to return it. Especially in a world filled with energy and light. Darkness craves the light. It will taint everything. It cannot be allowed to go free."

It was in that second Braxton let out a roar, his massive body crashing forward to stand right at the wall of magic, opposite Kristoff.

"We can't kill him," Louis stressed again. "The demon is bound to its summoner. Once that vessel is destroyed, nothing will bind it. Even though it will return to The Great Divide soon after, the damage it could do, even in a short time, would be devastating."

Well, that was damn unfair. I needed to kill Kristoff. It was on my bucket list.

A flicker of energy crossed my mind, and a murmur caught my attention.

My entire body lurched to the right.

Since stepping into the room, I'd been ignoring the Mischa bond inside of me, focusing on killing Kristoff first. But she was calling for me and there was no way for me to ignore her low plea.

"Max…"

The breathy whisper came again and everything that made me who I was crumbled inside. Where was she? Why couldn't I see her?

My chest was burning. I felt the very real tangibility of our bond now. It was a hot, tight spot which must have lived there for a long time, so long that I'd never even realized it wasn't really mine but something I held for Mischa. I let it fling free and the heat burst to life inside of me. It spread like dripping lava, burning through me, burning away everything I used to be and leaving something else behind.

I knew where to find her.

With Louis and Braxton keeping the demon-touched under control, I sprinted across the room to the far wall, a wall which looked like normal stone, but there was a doorway here somewhere.

I began to run my hands along it, feeling the slightest draft. With no patience to figure out how it worked, I took a few steps back and slammed my shoulder against it. It groaned and shifted minutely. Taking a few more steps back, I slammed my body into it again, this time shifting the wall an inch backwards. That was enough for me to wedge my hands into the small gap and force the space to widen.

On the other side I caught sight of a lever. I nudged it and jumped out of the way as the entire wall shifted to the side. Without pause I dashed down the stairs on the other side. When I was halfway down, I heard the cracking of Louis' spell shattering. Kristoff must have busted through.

Braxton roared, and as much as I wanted to go back and help my brother, I had to get to Mischa. She was hurt badly. I don't know how I knew it, but I did. The moment that heat in my chest had expanded, so had my connection to her. This was not just about our baby, this was something so much more. If I didn't know it was impossible, I'd be wondering if she was my true mate.

But it was impossible.

Even if my bond with Cardia was fake – and I'd reached the point now where I was really hoping it was – there was no changing the fact that Mischa and I were from different races. We couldn't be true mates. But we could choose to be bonded and hope neither of our true mates ever came along. I could think of worse things than having her in my life and my bed every night. Actually, if I was truly honest with myself, there was nothing I wanted more. I wanted Mischa in my life as my mate. I wanted everything about her. She was my choice.

The stairs were narrow and dark, preventing me from running down as fast as I could. The air was filled with blood, oil, and human waste. Every nerve in my body was shot. Knowing that she might have been touched with Lunarti oil was killing me.

The stairs rounded out and I stepped into the basement, which was set up as a prison. There was more than enough light for me to count twelve cells, six on either side.

"Mischa," I said loudly. "I'm here for you. Hold on for me."

I stepped down the middle path. The floor was stone, dirt and debris scattered across it.

"She's over here," a soft melodic voice said. I followed that voice, using vamp speed to get there in an instant. It could be a trap, but since the staff was a formidable weapon, and it was in my hand, I wasn't too worried.

The female who'd called out to me was pressed against her bars. She was thin to the point of wasting away, her long blond hair matted with blood and soot. She was tall, almost six foot, and swaying in her attempt to remain standing. Her very white-blond hair contrasted with her cocoa-colored skin – striking in every way, but they were not the beautiful features I was looking for.

"Mischa is here." She pointed to the cell next to her, and I growled at the sight of my wolf shifter sprawled across the ground. She was on her left side, arms wrapped protectively around her belly, and she was unconscious, her skin pale and waxy. The scent of death was hovering over her. *Fuck!* If not for the occasional shiver racking through her, I would have wondered if I was too late.

I dived forward and wrenched at the bars of her cage. There was a crack and the door dropped off with ease. These cages had not been built to withstand vampire strength.

The female's words shattered any calm I'd been hanging onto. "You have to save her. He used some kind of oil."

A bellowing roar shook me and I almost dropped to my knees as the agony of Mischa's pain slammed into my senses. Needing to touch her, I went to her side, and with as much care as I could manage, wrapped my arms around her and gently lifted. She whimpered weakly, which scared the hell out of me, but at least she was alive.

Blood coated her. Her skin was like ice, her pulse ragged and unsteady. I didn't need the stranger's words to know she was in grave danger. I could smell the Lunarti all over her, even in her blood. It had been burning through her for a while now, infiltrating deep.

Her heart started to stutter then, and with a growl I spun and ran for the door. She was fading, and I couldn't live in a world without her and our child.

Knowing I had to do something to stabilize her before we traveled, I paused at the base of the stairs and lifted my wrist to my mouth, scouring across it with my fangs. Vampire blood was strongly regenerative. It could help to heal minor wounds, and would maybe slow the deadly path of oil through her body. Lifting it to her lips, I let the red drip slowly into her puckered mouth. I had to open my wrist a few times, getting as much of the liquid life into her as I could. I didn't have time to examine her closely, but I could smell burned and seared flesh. The more of the healing blood she got, the better.

She moaned again, her lips closing around my wrist, and then the burning spot in my chest exploded. There were bursts of magic in the room, and I expected to see glittering lights drifting down around us. But there was nothing. This magic was internal.

Everything in my body tightened, and with no warning the bond in my chest snapped into place.

My legs weakened, dropping me to my knees. I managed to keep Mischa safely tucked to my chest, and as I held her close a furry beast loped across my mind. Mischa's wolf.

Sweet fey angels! It was the bond, a true mate bond. It had cemented between Mischa and me, and for the first time I could feel her in my soul, feel her beast and mine connecting. It was nothing like what had happened with Cardia. That bond had been a tingling in my blood, a sense of where Cardia was at times. With Mischa it was as if her soul and mine merged together and there was a small part of her residing inside of me.

And now, more than ever, I could tell how close she was to dying.

Not on my damned watch.

I was up and on my feet so fast the room spun. Footsteps clattered at the bottom of the stairs, and my head whipped around to pin the intruders with my gaze. *Thank fuck.* It was Braxton, back in human form.

"Kristoff escaped," he said. "When the wall shattered, my dragon went for him, and the demon must have realized he was in trouble and disappeared."

The sorcerer would be back. That much I knew for sure. He had not achieved his goals here today. He would come for these girls again. Braxton was looking at me strangely and I wondered if I looked different. Was the burst of emotion rushing through me already showing on the outside? Was the bond visible between us?

I was in panic mode, but there was something I had to tell my brother first. "There's another female here. She's in one of the cells; can you get her? I also dropped the staff back there somewhere." My voice was almost unrecognizable, low and thrumming with emotion. "I need to get Mischa to a healer. She's in a bad way. He used the oil on her."

Louis must have been close behind. He stepped into sight. "There are few healers in the world who know how to deal with the effects of Lunarti. The best I know is Chan. He's in Shanjoin, near the Chinese prison community. I'll open a step-through."

By the time Louis had the portal open, Braxton had the white-haired girl in his arms. She'd told him her name was Justice before passing out. Seemed she'd been doing everything in her power to remain conscious. To help Mischa. Or herself. Either way.

"The staff was gone," Braxton said, his brows raised, his eyes beaming yellow. "And the girl is human. Why the fuck would Kristoff be keeping a human locked down here? He's practically starved her to death."

Human. That was not what I'd expected. Granted I'd taken no time to try and figure out her race because I simply didn't care. Mischa was my focus.

Gathering her frail form closer to me, I reached out with my senses toward our baby. Fear like I'd never known clenched my chest. What if there was no life there? Generally, the weakest would be affected by the oil first.

When a strong thrumming heartbeat filled my mind, I coughed a few times to hold back my tears. Yep, I was about thirty seconds from breaking down and crying into Mischa's still form. I hadn't shed a single tear for Cardia. Not one. But it felt as if I had a million for Mischa and our child.

Please, don't let her die, I prayed as the step-through took us across the world again. I hoped Louis was right about this Chan, because if he wasn't he'd just signed Mischa's death warrant.

CHAPTER TWELVE

Mischa Lebron

My body was hovering on the thin edge between life and death. I could feel the cold tendrils of the next life tugging at me. But I would not give in. I needed to fight for my daughter because she was not free of my body yet. She needed to live.

I worked hard, holding on to all the anchors I had left in this world. The strongest was this stunning cord in my chest, white and shimmery, shot through with strands of silver and purple. The power in that cord held essence from all of the supernatural races. I sensed the wild shifter energy, the cold power of vamps, the earthy magic users, and the elemental ties of fey. It was everything, and it was keeping me bound to this plane.

Pain was my constant companion, and in some ways I clung to the agony. It was another thing connecting me to the body, which was already starting to feel like it didn't belong to me any longer. My wolf howled, wrapping her strength around us both. She was a fighter; she was helping me fight.

I continued calling to Maximus in my mind, through our bond. A few minutes ago something had happened. A warmth had washed through my tired and cold limbs and that had brought me closer to the land of the living. Closer to him. But then death had tried to steal me again.

It felt like years that I hovered with one foot in either veil, drifting in and out of the pain, not enough free thought to worry but enough to hold on to life. The darkness of the oil was seeping closer to the womb at my center, and it was this I fought to hold back. It would not touch my daughter.

A slicing pain cut through me then and I screamed out. Somehow there was still enough strength in my body to scream and thrash. Strong warmth wrapped around me, holding me close, caressing my skin.

Soft words were whispered but I could no longer hear or understand such things. There was nothing in my world but pain now. I couldn't even hold onto the last tendrils of protection around my child.

Then, as more murmurs surrounded me, some of the pain faded from my limbs. It was very minute, but even this tiny lessening of agony was enough for me to calm. I could feel the fire tingling its last spark of life before dying off completely. As the agony left I was able to sink into the darkness further.

Mischa. Don't leave me. My sister's voice was soft, barely registering in my mind, but my soul felt her. *You're safe. We'll keep you and your baby safe.* Her warm reassurances were enough for me to let go of my tenuous hold on my child. She spoke truth. I could sense that my daughter was safe now. The darkness would never touch her.

"Mischa!"

The sharp tone of whomever was using my name cut through the nice squishy place I was living in my head.

"I swear to God, Mischa Lebron, if you don't open those gorgeous green eyes I'm going to start cursing. I'll do it. I know how you feel about the f-bomb. I might even pull out the c-bomb."

Even in my semi-conscious state, I now knew exactly who was demanding me awake. No one loved to curse like my twin. I swallowed roughly, my mouth bone dry. "You wou— " My rasp was cut off as I started coughing. A smooth, cool object was placed at my lips and small dribbles of water soothed away some of the dryness.

"I've never heard you use the c-word," I finally said, opening my eyes to find my twin's worried face hovering over me. "I bet Lienda would kick your butt if you did."

Jessa scoffed. "I'd like to see her try, and I was talking about cockswabbler of course. What did you think I meant?"

Even though every muscle in my body, including my face, felt tired, I still managed a smile. Which disappeared with Jessa's next words. "Of course, the other c-word is quite appropriate for Kristoff."

At the mention of the sorcerer's name, memories crashed through me with the force of a freight train. My hands flew down to my stomach, which was covered with blankets. Despite the panic in my body, I was easily able to detect a strong and steady heartbeat within.

I still had to check. "What happened? Is she okay?"

Jessa's eyes dropped to where I was still clutching my stomach and pure joy lit up her face. She placed her hand on mine and our twin bond flared to life. That energy washed through me and into my daughter, who started to wiggle and kick.

"It's a girl? I'm going to be an aunt to a beautiful baby girl?" Jessa said, her voice thick with emotion. "When did you find out? Does Max know?"

At the mention of his name, everything inside of me stilled. I hadn't forgotten anything from my time in Kristoff's messed-up lair, including his little reveal that Maximus Compass might be my mate. My true mate. Was that why I could feel him so strongly in my chest? I would swear we already had a bond in place, it felt so real.

I had to tell someone. My eyes darted around the room, confirming we were alone, and I couldn't scent anyone close by. "Jess, I need to tell you something, but you can't freak out on me, okay?"

She regarded me for a moment before nodding. "Lay it on me."

Without wasting any time, I detailed everything that Kristoff said. About Cardia being his daughter and a fake mate. About the Compasses' mixed heritage and how they could tap into any of the four races that they were born from. Jessa's mouth was hanging open at this point, her hand wrapped tightly around my own.

She shook her head. "That explains a lot. Kristoff's plans were always about power, he wanted it no matter what. The dragon king thing was the perfect ship for him to board. Then when that plan failed and he lost his chance to rule with dragon dickhead, he went bonkers. Not to mention he's demon touched."

Huh. "What's demon touched? Tell me everything that happened? How did I get here?"

Here was a small, very white, very sterile looking room. Nothing in it but my bed, the chair Jessa sat in, and a single set of white shelves in the right corner. I would have guessed it was a hospital, except the bed I was in was large and comfy. Thick quality linen, not the usual hospital starchiness. Although, supe hospitals were probably much better fitted out than human ones.

Jessa sighed then, and a few tears sprinkled her eyes. "We almost lost you, Misch. You and our little girl. Kristoff used Lunarti oil on you. It's this horrible demon-brewed stuff which burns through your skin and pollutes your blood. It was almost through your whole system. We had to bring you to Shanjoin, in China, to Chan, this healer Louis knows. He's been healing you for almost a week."

"Holy. I've been out for a week? I don't … remember."

I ripped the covers off my body and examined my leg. There were red and purplish marks up and down my thigh, ugly and scarred. I ran a hand across them and could feel the tugging of the disfigured skin.

"When Max saw your leg he lost his mind," Jessa murmured. "Let's just say this is not the first room you were in."

"Where are the Compasses?" I asked, casual-like.

Jessa shifted on the chair, running a hand through her dark hair. It was a mess of tangles. "Max is asleep in the room next door. I made him get some rest a few hours ago. Had to pry him away though, and he's going to be pissed that you woke up when he wasn't here. He has not left your side for a week."

Jessa reached out and grabbed my hand. "He's going to want to tell you this, but the mate bond kicked in between you both. You're definitely his true mate. And we all owe you the hugest apology from how we treated you in the sanctuary."

My silly heart started fluttering then, the mate bond pressing in on me. I couldn't believe what she was saying, and yet I felt the truth of it in my heart. In my soul.

I needed to see him, needed him here holding my hand too.

Jessa's blue eyes were shrewdly watching me, probably waiting for me to fall apart or something, but after everything that had happened, almost losing my life and my daughter's, a true mate bond with Maximus was the least of my worries. It was kind of a gift.

"The rest of the boys are back in Stratford. Braxton took Justice to the sanctuary. She's going to stay there until we deal with Kristoff. He clearly wanted her for a reason."

I sat straighter, relief flooding through me. "Thank the gods. She was so kind to me, Jess. I promised I wouldn't leave her there, and then I passed out before I could tell anyone."

She shook her head at me. "Most supes would have died long before anyone arrived. You did good, sister. Very good."

I let my weary body drop back against the pillows. "Braxton must love being separated from you."

Her laughter was brief. "Yeah, he's not too happy about it, but he's dealing. The boys can't all leave for too long. Their power is needed to maintain the securities. It's okay if they arrange something first, but right now, especially with crazy-Kristoff, they're the only ones keeping America and Vanguard safe. They pop back and forth to check on you."

I remembered something then, and lifting my hands I was actually surprised that no cuffs bound my wrists. Jessa followed my gaze.

"Ah yes, another nasty little surprise from that cockswabbler. Those cuffs took Louis and Tyson about eight hours to get off you and Justice. We couldn't do anything until they were removed because your essence was tied to Kristoff and we were afraid he'd do something to hurt you worse."

"Has anyone figured out why he had Justice there? She's hu—"

I was cut off by a scraping at the door. We both turned to find a tiny man standing there. He was barely five feet tall, wearing a black and white, draping robe, with a cross design on one lapel. He was definitely Asian in descent, and had an older face, looking early sixties. I wondered briefly if he was human. If he was a supernatural, he was ancient.

"Nice to see you awake, my dear." His voice was low and soothing, strumming along the wind like chords on a harp. "I wasn't sure my skills would be enough this time, but I'm glad to see that your supernatural strength is kicking in for the final healing."

My eyes fell to the scars on my thigh, a reminder me of how close I'd come to losing my life. I might never have seen Jessa again. Held my daughter. Known for sure I was true mate to Maximus.

So many things to live for. It was overwhelming.

Chan crossed the room to stand on the opposite side of my bed, his eyes also landing on the burned skin. "I'm sorry I couldn't do more to heal the physical wound. The oil destroyed all the skin and tissue there. This was the best I could do with the time I had. Continued healing will improve how it looks."

With a shake of my head I lifted my eyes and let them rest on the kindly fellow. "Please, don't apologize. This scar is nothing. As long as my baby is safe, I wouldn't care if I wore these marks all over my body." I reached out and grasped his hand and it was warm and dry. "Thank you so much, from the bottom of my heart. Thank you for saving her."

He gave my palm a squeeze before releasing me. "You're welcome. You carry a very special child here. I was pleased that none of the oil touched her in any way. I don't know how this miracle happened, but it was a blessing for you both."

Whatever my wolf and I had done must have worked. We had stopped the oil from touching her. "What do you mean special child?" Most probably he meant the power of a Compass offspring, but the way he said it felt like something more.

Before he could answer there was another set of footsteps at the threshold to the white room. I felt the pull in my chest; warmth flooded my mind and body. I knew before I even looked up who it would be – Maximus Compass, in all of his beautiful glory.

I couldn't stop from locking onto his face. He returned the gesture, zeroing in on me, eyes as black as pitch with a slight shine to them, the sort of darkness which would reflect its surroundings.

He didn't say a word as he stalked across the room to my side, he was dressed casually, but somehow made jeans and a long-sleeved Henley look like a million bucks. By now Jessa and the healer had disappeared. They probably just left normally and I was too entranced by Maximus to notice, but it sort of felt like they'd evaporated into the air.

When the vampire was at my side, we continued to stare, the energy between us practically humming. I might have been new to the supernatural world but I had always known this was more than normal, more than a chemical attraction or infatuation on my part. This was fate. This was a soul connection. A week ago I'd have been determined to run from it, afraid I'd let this weakness cost my child, the same way Lienda's had. Now I wasn't so sure.

How could I ever deny him when everything in my body wanted him so badly? If it was only about me, I would not hesitate for a second to throw myself into everything he was. He was a male of worth. I knew that. Even if he'd made some really bad decisions. But I had to think about our daughter too. She deserved my full focus, especially while she was young.

I would bide my time and see how things eventuated, no rushing in.

All of my musings were cut off as Maximus sank to his knees at my side. He was so tall that even on his knees our heads were almost level with each other. "I died a thousand deaths in the past week.

Every scar on your body. Every second of pain you endured." His head dropped as something akin to shame and anguish crumbled his broad features. "I have failed you as a lover, as a friend, as a father to our child, and as a true mate. The bond kicked in when I saved you, when I used my blood to try and slow the Lunarti oil. A bond I should have always known was there, and which is my greatest joy to receive."

I swallowed roughly. Already he was testing my resolve. His perfect words. His true sorrow. I couldn't stop myself from reaching out and touching his temple. His eyes shot up to clash with mine. "It's a girl, Max. We're having a daughter."

He froze, and then a single tear escaped from the corner of his dark eyes. I watched it trail down his face and fought the urge to lean in and catch it on my tongue. My wolf wanted me to do that, but the human side in me didn't understand. Maximus reached out and laid a gentle hand on my stomach, which seemed to have doubled in size in the past week.

"You have blessed me beyond reckoning. We'll be a family, Mischa. I can't lose you again." He took a deep breath. "I know you need time to learn to trust in us again. The true mate bond is not fully in place. I can't hear your thoughts yet, and I believe it's because you're not quite ready for the connection. I can wait as long as you need. Just know that even before this bond snapped into place, I already knew I couldn't live without you. I had already chosen you."

He'd finally said the words I'd been waiting months to hear. He chose me. My greatest wish. He was right though, there was much we needed to overcome.

"Max..." I started slowly, carefully choosing my words. "This bond brings me great joy, but also fear. I lost myself once to you, and it hurt people I love. Now I have a daughter to worry about. I can't lose myself again. But it's impossible to deny this thing between us. Maybe we should just start with rebuilding our friendship."

Some of the brown was bleeding back into his dark eyes, and I was confused for a second as a grin swept across his features. "Mischa Lebron, you and I are going to be best friends. But we're also going to be true mates and lovers. You can run from this as long as you need. I understand why you don't trust in us yet, but you will. I promise you that in the not very distant future you will be mine in every way."

A snort escaped me. "Arrogant much?"

He cocked his head to the side. "I like to think of it as confidence and trust in our bond. And you don't have to worry about our daughter. Together we'll keep her safe. She'll know more love than is possible to handle. No one will lay a hand on you or Agnes again."

I fully lost it then. Laughter busted from me in a torrent of mirth and I had to hold my stomach for fear that I would go into labor. Eventually I caught my breath. "We're not calling our daughter Agnes," I told the twinkly-eyed vampire.

"What about Mavis? ... Cecile?" His cocky grin and dimples were on full display. "I've been looking into human names. They have some really fun ones."

I shook my head, and even though I knew it was a bad idea I couldn't stop myself from reaching out and wrapping my arms around his shoulders. "Thank you for saving us. I'm really looking forward to the best friend thing."

And I was. Maximus was my family, and this felt right.

I heard him clear his throat as he wrapped me tightly in his arms, and before I could protest he rose to his feet, pulling me from the bed and into his arms, holding me so gently, my feet dangling inches from the ground.

With his warmth and scent engulfing me, everything from the past week crashed in on me. My chest got tight and the lump in my throat was choking me as I fought to control my emotions. Squeezing my eyes as tightly as I could, I tried to stem the rising tide, but tears still slipped out and ran down my cheeks with reckless abandon. Sobs were rising with them. I tried to stop them, but the moment Maximus sensed my tears and started whispering soothing and beautiful words to me, I completely lost it.

For the first time in my life, when I fell apart someone was there to catch me. It was the most incredible feeling ever. I'd never had that, never had support. I was not alone.

Finally his words turned desperate. "Mischa. Misch ... please stop crying. I cannot stand to see you in so much pain. I *will* kill Kristoff when I find him. I'll make him suffer for every second of his time with you. He'll be praying for death before I'm finished with him."

Eventually my tears dried up, but I didn't let him go. I wanted a few more moments to enjoy the warmth of his huge frame as it wrapped around me.

In the human world I'd never felt particularly small or delicate, but male supes had a way of making you feel positively petite.

Maximus' chest shook a little then and I felt his laughter. "How're you doing with the 'just friends' thing? Because the line's getting a little blurry for me."

I could tell he was joking. Kind of.

Then, as he pulled back and lifted a hand to wipe away the last of the wetness on my cheeks, his smile fell. Something hot flickered across his face and flared to life in his eyes. I had a second to squeak before his lips crashed down onto mine, and then I was lost in the taste and scent of the vampire, lost in the male who should have been mine from the start but was cruelly stolen from me.

I'm not sure how long we kissed. It felt like weeks. Had to be at least a few hours, because by the time his soft lips released mine I was dizzy and breathless. My head spun, and I knew that my legs would not be capable of holding me up. Which I didn't have to worry about because he continued to hold me, with not even the slightest falter, despite the amount of time he'd been carrying my weight, baby belly squished between us.

I opened and closed my mouth as I tried to figure out what to say. I knew I should protest or something, but my brain was mush. I really just wanted to kiss him again.

Maximus dropped his forehead onto mine. "I'd say sorry, but I'm really not," he said, and as he leaned in closer I knew he was going to kiss me again. And I wanted him to. Badly. But this was not taking it slow. I was already losing myself, and that was not okay.

I pushed at his chest, and he released me, placing me back on the bed.

"Slow, remember? I've already let the weakness of this bond between us crush me. I need to know I'm strong enough to be mother and mate."

Something primal lit up in his gaze then. He liked me using the word mate. "I haven't quite figured out how we're true mates yet. Theories are being bandied about, but nothing concrete."

Right! I had information to share with him.

For the second time that day I explained everything Kristoff said to me. With each revelation Maximus' body and face hardened, he was soon very statue like. As I finished with details on his fake bond with Cardia, he let out an angry snarl and took off. He moved so fast I missed the first step and only caught the tail end. He was already out the door and all I could hear was the whoosh as he stormed away.

Jumping from the bed, I winced at some of the lingering pain in my body. Ignoring it, I waddle-ran as fast as I could, following him. The hallway outside of my room seemed to run the length of this building. There were a bunch of rooms off it, but I didn't bother with any of them. I would have heard Maximus open a door.

He'd gone straight ahead.

It took me no time to make it into a living area. The building was very much in the styling of upmarket warehouse – huge ceilings, all open concept, a couch in one corner and an enormous kitchen with island bench in the other. There was also outdoor-indoor dining, leading out onto a covered patio area.

It was night. I hadn't realized. There was no window in my room, no way to judge time. As I continued along, Jessa popped into view. She must have been in the kitchen. Big surprise.

"What's up?" she said, joining me. "Did you tell him about the true mate bond and Cardia?"

I nodded. "He deserved to know. It was his life as much as mine that got screwed with."

My sister took my hand as we continued hurrying out of the warehouse. I would have loved more time to observe the industrial space. Exposed beams. Rustic wall art. Huge fluffy rugs on cement floors. But all I could see was the huge shadow out on the manicured lawn.

"Give me a second with him," I said, hugging Jessa tightly.

She laid a kiss on my cheek. "You got it, sister! No one will ease his pain like you. Just go with your instincts. You have good ones."

I snorted. "Yeah, maybe. Hard to tell sometimes."

A gentle punch landed on my arm. "The sanctuary was not your fault. True mate bonds are serious stuff. They literally drive supes insane. Had we known there was a chance you were true mates, we would have expected you to act as you did. Even worse, actually. The fact that you managed to stay as strong as you did was pretty incredible. And then all the times after, the way you fought Larky ... I'm proud to call you twin. You have a quiet strength, but that doesn't make it any less valuable."

I don't know why her words resonated so strongly with me. I didn't need her approval; no one should crave the approval of others, but she was my twin and the strongest, most kick-butt female I knew. She was life goals. To have her call me strong, to not see me as weak, kind of made me reassess the negative way I'd always treated myself. Confidence crashed through me and for the first time I started to truly believe I might be a worthy mate for Maximus.

That I might be worthy of the miracle child within me.

Leaving Jessa with one last hug, I stepped out into the humid air. I'd never been to China and was unfamiliar with the thick smoggy scents assailing me. The heavy air had undertones of cherry and something sweet and floral.

The yard was quite large, long and thin, with lots of landscaped areas filled with small hedges and bushy plants. The moonlight washed across the grass and created the most beautiful of pictures. My hand actually twitched for a paintbrush. I wanted to capture the splash of light, the shadows of the world, the perfect alignment of different plant heights scattered about. My mind took a mental picture and I knew it was something I would preserve on canvas another time.

A small stream trickled through the yard. I followed the bubbling brook until I reached Maximus. He was standing beside a koi pond. I couldn't see any fish in it, but the darkness hid much from us. I was at his side, our arms grazing as we both stared down into the twinkly depths of the water.

The moment didn't feel uncomfortable or tense, and despite the fact he was clearly still fighting his vampire temper, I wasn't getting a heavy rage vibe from him.

When he finally turned to me his eyes and face were calm. "I've been saying this far too much to you, but I am so very sorry, Mischa. I don't deserve you."

In that moment I realized how much we'd both been beating ourselves up over something that was really outside of our control. It was time to stop. He was a supe who always looked out for others, the protector, so of course he would be hard on himself in this situation. And something told me I was the only one who could relieve him of his guilt.

"Max, we can't change the past. I wish we could, you have no idea how badly, but I'm ready to move forward. Together. You are no more to blame than me. Both of us have suffered, and I don't think either of us should give Kristoff or Cardia any more of our thoughts or emotions. We let them go now."

I sucked up my courage, and reaching out took his hand. In my life I'd rarely ever initiated physical contact with others; the fear of rejection was strong within me, but it was different with Maximus. It always had been. Which was partly why it had hurt so badly when he'd turned away from me at the sanctuary. The trust had been damaged between us, but maybe not as much as I initially thought.

We stood there hand in hand for many minutes, the moon reflecting off the pond, the stars twinkling above us. Maximus untangled our hands to reach around me and drag me into his side. "This feels right," he said. "Cardia and I ... we were never right. The magic was there. The connection was there, but the rest could not be produced. I never wanted to touch her. You ... I can't keep my hands off you."

"Kristoff did say the more you bonded with your brothers, the stronger your shifter side would become and the more our mate bond would kick in."

He chuckled. "Hope it doesn't get too strong too fast. I'm trying to figure out how to win you over with my romantic side." His eyes flashed black for a moment. "The vampire though, he wants me to throw you over my shoulder, hide you in a secluded location, and feast on every part of you."

I couldn't suppress the shudder which rocked from the tip of my head right down to my toes. And a few places in between. The newly-formed bond between us had our mutual attraction stronger than it had ever been. My body felt needy in ways I had never known before. Not even the first time with him.

"I've never been able to resist this pull between us," I admitted. "And it's so much ... stronger now."

Maximus threw back his head and laughed. "From the start I promised myself we'd be nothing more than friends. It was too complicated. There was too much to lose. And yet I couldn't stop myself. If it hadn't been for the treachery with Cardia, I'd have come back to you again."

In some ways it was nice to know that the hold he had over me, the emotion I'd deemed as a weakness, went both ways. Maybe together we could learn to find a balance.

My legs, especially the one with the burn, were starting to ache. Maximus noticed the way I was shifting from foot to foot. "Time to get you back into bed," he said, sweeping me up into his arms.

I opened my mouth to protest his carrying me again, but decided it wasn't worth wasting my breath. This was just the way with these males. It was how they cared for us.

As he strode back into the house I tilted my head up to see him. "So what's the plan now?" I'd been suppressing the last week, pushing it way down into the cave which held my darkest moments, focusing on the unbelievable fact that Maximus was my true mate.

But the memories were no longer staying suppressed. "We need to hunt Kristoff down before he hurts anyone else. Justice will never be safe either."

Darkness descended across Maximus' golden features. "*We* will not be doing anything. I'll be hunting that bastard down while you're safely behind Stratford's securities. The healer said the baby was close to being ready. The trauma almost set you off into early labor. You could still have her at any time."

With a sigh I acknowledged his concern. "Okay, I'll agree to that for now. Protecting her is our top priority. But Kristoff must suffer. He must die."

Maximus grinned at me, flashing the slightest hint of fang. "Oh, my sweet Mischa. Do not worry yourself. Pretty soon there'll be no world in which Kristoff will exist."

My wolf started to howl, and even baby girl kicked me. Looked like we were all in agreement. Kristoff was living on borrowed time.

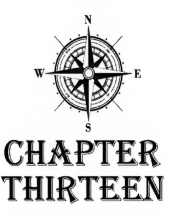

CHAPTER THIRTEEN

Maximus Compass

Our time was up in China. We needed to get back to Stratford. As peaceful as it was here, in the sanctuary of Chan, the ancient healer, I was feeling an urgency to get Mischa and Jessa protected behind the securities of our home town. I knew Kristoff would come for them again, not to mention my brothers were having trouble with the bear shifters.

Braxton had contacted me this morning. They'd had a bit of a tussle outside the town hall. The bears were demanding a representative on the council, despite the fact these leaderships were pre-ordained long before the actual supe took power.

At this stage, the next five leaders who'd step up after us had not been chosen, normal considering we were only in the first month of our twenty-five years, so there was plenty of time to figure out who'd step up next. The way the bears were acting, they were blowing any chance they had of one of their kind getting the role. Leaders were decided by the collective of all the supernatural elders, and this behavior would be taken into account.

Our leadership selection had been a little different. Normally they'd never allow any as young as us to have such power, but being quads, and having our unique bond, allowed us strengths others could never achieve. Still, the bears seemed to think we had cheated our way into our spot, that it was not deserved. But even if that were true, they should know better than to just demand a leadership position. It didn't work that way. Supernaturals could be liberal in a lot of ways, but we respected our leaders. Otherwise they would squash you and not look back. It was time for us to bring the heavy on the bears, time to put them in their place, before anyone got hurt in the midst of their rebellion.

I'd left Mischa a few hours ago to sleep. She was still exhausted, recovering. Scars written across her body and soul. The bond between us had settled in strong and unwavering, except for the small part which prevented us from seeing into each other's mind. Maybe I needed to figure out how to unlock the part of me which was shifter. Or maybe there were still tendrils of the fake mate spell in my soul.

As my thoughts turned to Cardia, flickers of the red vampire haze shrouded my vision. So much made sense now. The unease I'd felt around her. My lack of interest in our relationship, even in the bedroom. The way she'd not responded to the dragon king's call. So many lies. A complete world of lies. It had almost cost me Mischa. What if I hadn't come back to Stratford in time? What if Kristoff had gotten his hands on her and I never knew about my child? I would not make that mistake again. The pain of the bond with Cardia was almost gone now.

Whatever spell Kristoff used was wearing off. Her death had freed me.

As screwed up as it was, now every part of me was glad she was dead.

A familiar scent drifted toward me and I turned to find Jessa crossing out of her sister's room. She'd barely left her side while she recovered. Their twin connection was strong and fierce. When she reached me, she wrapped her arms around me in a hug. As I pulled her closer, I thought of all the times I'd wished she was my true mate. Now I couldn't be happier that she wasn't. I loved Jessa, she was my pack, my family, but Mischa held my heart.

Jessa pulled back a little, leaving one arm draped across me. "Braxton contacted me. He said we need to stop in at Sinchin prison before heading back to Stratford. Which will actually work out timing wise – Louis is off dealing with more of the supe smugglers, cracking a few skulls and shit, so he'll not be able to get us until tonight."

"What do we need from the prison?"

She shrugged. "No idea. Apparently he'll contact you soon, when he has more details."

Jessa bounced on the spot a little. "I really can't wait to see Sinchin. I've read the books and seen the pictures, but there's nothing like experiencing the ingenuity in person."

Her enthusiasm had me smiling, a real smile. That had been missing from my life for some time.

"It'll be good to meet the leaders there," I finally said, turning to stare out into the garden again. Chan had it set out in such a peaceful, *feng shui* design. It encouraged you to stand and stare at it. "We should have done a quick world tour when we were first initiated as council leaders, but everywhere was such a mess that it was postponed for a later date."

Wars don't end when the final battle is over. Rebuilding lives is sometimes harder than the fighting itself. And the supernatural prison world still needed some serious rebuilding.

"I can't quite believe you guys are leaders already. Feels like it got here so fast," Jessa said, her blue eyes huge as she shook her head.

I laughed. "How do you think we feel? I could have done without the few years skip ahead in time. Our community deserves great leaders, and so far we aren't there. We don't know enough, and despite our power we're lacking. We were barely schooled in leadership, management, or supe control. You know we prefer to use our fists to sort out drama, but now we have to be diplomatic and use our words."

Jessa laughed this time, her light chuckles floating into the morning air. "Brax is trying so hard to be diplomatic with the bears, when all he really wants to do is go dragon and rip their guts out."

"They need their guts ripped out," I growled. "Haven't we had enough trouble recently? Why step in now and demand a leadership spot? Why create discord in a community already trying to recover? That's not the sign of a leader."

Jessa nodded. "They're using the argument that you four are not trained, and that you've all been absent quite a lot in the short time you've been leaders. They say you're too young and not experienced enough."

It was always the same. Those who don't like the way things are done try and shout loud enough, hoping someone will hear them and respond. With any luck, it would all be blown over by the time we were back in Stratford.

Jessa had the same thought as she patted me on the arm. "It'll be fine, no one really wants to take you four on, and I know you'd never hand your power to someone else." With a wink she turned away. "I'll go and wake Mischa, tell her we're getting a once in a lifetime chance to see the famous Sinchin prison."

I was looking forward to it too. Sinchin had never lost a prisoner, never had a major incident, and maintained peace better than most around the world. Vanguard was in the top ten, but we could learn a lot here. I just needed to phone my brothers first and find out exactly what we were going there for. I didn't like surprises, not in this sort of instance. Forewarned was forearmed.

The twins were wide-eyed as we took the first steps into the prison community that bordered Shanjoin. It was a mountainous range, like many of our hidden prisons, isolated in the south of China, to the east of the Tibetan Plateau and heading toward the Sichuan Basin.

The locals were expecting us. Many had gathered around the small dome-style huts which comprised their buildings. This community looked quite primitive, no modern buildings or amenities, but magic was thick in the air, which was a pretty huge indication that they were concealing much here.

The air was thinner and I reminded myself to keep a close eye on the girls. With their pregnancies they would have to be careful of the elevation. The fact that supes adjusted to different climates easily was the only reason they were here today.

Hadie, a leader here, had met us at the front of the community. She was taking us to the Sinchin entrance, where we would be greeted by a council member, her vampire mate.

As we followed Hadie, I had to reach out and take Mischa's hand. There was far too little touching going on here. She flashed me a stunned expression before a true smile lit up her face.

"Are you okay?" I was staring but I didn't give a damn. It was the first time I'd seen her out of borrowed bedclothes in some time and she looked absolutely beautiful.

Her dark hair was clear off her face, braided in a single line to her shoulders, giving me an unobstructed view of her clear green eyes. At the moment they reminded me of the ocean on a bright, hot summer day. Her body was rounded with pregnancy, but that only made her appeal greater. That was my child she was carrying. My body virtually hummed with the need to get her naked and relearn every part of her. Our one time together was not even close to being enough. I needed days, months, years. I needed forever.

Her smile grew. "I'm great, thank you. This place is amazing, isn't it?"

She turned away as Jessa started gushing about Sinchin. Both girls were talking a million miles a minute, which gave me some extra time to continue my stalk stare.

The changes in Mischa fascinated me. The female we'd first met last year had been young, skittish, and lacking in confidence. Now she was all woman, exuding poise and security in who she was.

Larkspur's daughters would have a hard time taking advantage of this version of Mischa.

Hadie joined in with the girls' chatting, and also introduced many of the townfolk who'd come out to meet us. I was forced to remove my eyes from Mischa and focus on Hadie. She had a heavy Chinese accent, but she spoke carefully so we wouldn't miss a thing. Very courteous and polite, exactly as I expected.

Her soft voice traveled through the crowds: "They have all been waiting for you to arrive. We have heard many stories of the brave supes who destroyed the threat of Larkspur. You are ... somewhat of a celebrity."

We'd done no more than anyone else in our position. It had been our calling, our gift to counter a threat from long ago. Still, the crowds clearly didn't want to hear those truths as they pressed in closer to us. Gifts were presented, both girls receiving huge bundles of wild flowers which grew in the mountainous ranges, their colors ranging from the palest of pink to the most vivid of orange sunset, flowers which I was sure would be nowhere else in the world. I received a dagger from a tiny, wrinkled sorcerer. He must have been many hundreds of years old, the centuries imprinting fine and deep lines across his face.

The dagger was about fifteen inches in length and a few inches wide. It had been handcrafted from a single piece of steel and stone. The hilt was inlaid with diamonds and rubies. The double edges were visibly sharp, and something told me they were enchanted to never dull. This was a gift worth more than money. It was a treasure.

I bowed low and he returned the gesture. "Thank you, I am honored by your gift. I shall use it to govern my community."

His eyes flicked across to Mischa, who was waiting at my side, a genuine smile lighting up her face. He stared at her for a few moments longer than was polite, but there was nothing there to rouse the vampire. His actions were respectful. He spoke without turning away from her.

"Use to protect mate and child. Forged in heart of dragon mountain. Built with tears of fallen souls."

Then he wrenched his gaze from Mischa and turned away, hurrying off with far more agility than one would expect from such an ancient supe. I stared after him for many long minutes.

"Well, that was cryptic," Mischa said.

Cryptic was right, but the words weren't completely foreign to me. I caught Jessa's eye and the glint of recognition was there also. It was written in our early history that the birthplace of the dragon, a giant scaled serpent, was in the heart of a volcano. It was said that the center of this volcano mountain was unique. One side was molten lava and the other was a spring of the purest water. Along the center, the two merged and a crystal crust formed, which led supes to believe the water side was magical, tears of gods, souls of their fallen. The dragons were made of fire and gods.

Braxton liked to point that out regularly – literally born of the gods. Arrogant bastard.

Hadie handed me a scabbard and a thick, woven cream-colored cloth. "Take care with Sersie's weapons. They're known to be magical in nature and sharper than any blade forged. You'll want to wrap it up before placing it close to your body."

Trusting her, I followed those instructions, taking care not to scrape against the blade before I deposited the secured sheath in the large pocket on the side of my army-style pants.

"That's one beautiful knife," Jessa said. She sounded a bit put out. "Why do they always give them to the dudes? I want a knife from the heart of dragons' birthplace. I'm going to ask Josephina next time I see her."

Mischa and I exchanged a smile. That would be Jessa using her contacts to get a weapon better than everyone else's.

Mischa leaned in close and whispered to her sister: "Don't you think the fact that your mate is a dragon shifter, your best friend is a dragon queen, and your children are supposedly going to be the most powerful of all supes, that you kinda have the powerful weapon thing locked down."

Her voice was low in deference to the "secret of Jessa's twins." They were the first trueborn dragon shifters – not dragon mated supes – and their presence needed to stay as hidden as we could keep them. We didn't need a bigger target on our backs. Someone would surely have the genius idea to take them out now when they were vulnerable.

Jessa scoffed. "That's power of others. I like power for myself. I'm feeling decidedly less badass since gaining twenty pounds and losing my dragon. Now I'm almost as useless as a regular supe."

I had to chuckle then, and the dark glare she leveled on me did nothing to halt it, even though it was wise to be very careful of Jessa. She could kick ass with the best of them.

"You've lost nothing, Jessa babe. You're going to be mom to two powerful dragon twins. That honor would not have been bestowed on anyone unworthy."

She looked slightly less put out, but I could tell I hadn't really placated her. "She'll get better once she has the babies," Mischa murmured to me. "It's a big adjustment for most, and Jessa lost a lot."

So damn understanding. Always worrying about others. It was time someone started worrying about her. We were distracted then as more of the town pressed in to greet us. It took an hour or more to speak with them all and continue on to the prison.

"Thank you for that," Hadie said. "It means a lot to them that you took the time to stop. Most leaders don't. They simply breeze through, have their meeting, and leave."

"It was our pleasure," I said.

Hadie said no more but I sensed an approval in her gaze which had been missing earlier. Nice to see the diplomacy was strong with me today. I had no doubt the calm in my soul had everything to do with having Mischa at my side. She soothed my inner demon.

The entrance to Sinchin was dark and cool, a cave which led straight into the base of the mountain. It was against this mountain that the community of Shanjoin was built, and right at the top was the prison.

We had to pass through several layers of security. Magical essence tested us for deception, revealing our true selves – no magical disguise would work here. A scanner for weapons picked up my blade, but Hadie overrode that to allow me to keep it with me. It also picked up four knives and some throwing stars on Jessa. That was my girl.

The next few levels tested a variety of other magical things, and then finally we had to donate a drop of blood to cross the final threshold. Sinchin was a living entity, and once it had your essence it would always be able to find you. None of us were particularly happy with this part, but there would be no entry without it. This prison, of any around the world, was the most entrenched in magic. This was the reason there had never been an escape.

As soon as our blood sank into the stone at the end of the entrance tunnel, an elevator door appeared. Somehow, in the center of a mountain, there was a stainless steel box which was going to take us all the way up the middle of the prison.

My eyes flicked across to Jessa and I wasn't surprised to see a blade in her hand. Like most shifters, steel boxes made her uncomfortable. Mischa too, but they'd be okay for a few minutes. The view at the top would be worth it.

As we stepped inside, I drew each of them into my side and draped an arm across their shoulders. Hadie said nothing as the three of us remained locked tightly together during the ascent. My vampire almost purred at the contact of having my pack close. Should have guessed I was part shifter. I had so many of their instincts and pack-like tendencies. It all made sense now.

It took only a moment, despite the fact this mountain was practically miles in the air, to reach the top. With an almost silent whirr the doors slid across and the cool air washed in.

"Please give yourselves a few minutes to adjust to the altitude," Hadie said. "It can be a little disconcerting, especially when pregnant."

Jessa and Mischa both ignored her warning. Looking very much the twins they were, they marched out together, crossing over the large expanse of grassy hilltop to reach the closest edge. Both of them were wide-eyed and slack-jawed as they stared. I had to hold back my grin; at times there were worlds between their personalities – which was understandable, they had very different upbringings – and at other times they were so similar.

I understood why they didn't wait though, there was no way to stop yourself from crossing the huge space to stand on top of the world. The Sinchin prison was set atop one of the largest mountains in this region of China. On top here, it was about three miles total in diameter, shaped like an elongated egg. The views on all sides went on forever – mountains, greenery, urban landscape – even the sea could be seen at some points. It was almost as if this was the center of a million worlds and there was so much for the eye to see.

As I stepped to her side, Mischa turned sparkling green eyes on me. "This is so incredible. I can see everything."

She spoke quietly, almost reverently. Standing here was like standing amongst the gods. Very spiritual and mystical in nature.

As she turned to the view again, a sigh left her. "I wish I had my paints. I'm not sure I'll be able to truly capture this back home."

I straightened. "You paint?" There were so many things I didn't know about her.

Originally I hadn't wanted to know her too deeply. I'd felt as if the more pieces of herself she gave me, the more I'd want to keep them.

Everything was different now. Now I wanted every single part of her.

Jessa spoke up before Mischa could. "She's amazing, Max, you should see her paintings. She's taken over my room at Dad's and has turned it into an art studio. Misch definitely sucked up all the artistic talent in this twin genetics, that's for sure."

Mischa's cheeks pinked as she continued staring out into the vast space.

"I would very much like to see your paintings," I said.

I wanted this piece of the Mischa puzzle. I was adding it to my collection.

A throat cleared behind us and we turned as a unit to find Hadie with a tall, dark-skinned male at her side. He was not quite my height but had the bulk of someone used to combat. I took a step forward and we clasped hands in a brief shake.

"Thank you for visiting," he said, his voice low and naturally rumbly. "My name is Lock. I'm one of the leaders of this community, and the vampire leader on the Asian supe council."

Lock. The name was familiar to me. He had fought in the last supernatural war and had been singlehandedly responsible for taking down an entire pack of shifters.

"It's a pleasure to finally meet you," I said. "I'm Maximus Compass, and these are my pack mates, Jessa and Mischa Lebron."

He gave a brief nod to the girls before focusing on me again. "We're grateful that you've taken the time to stop by. I've been hoping to speak with you about a couple of prison exchanges. We have some local supes here, and you know we don't like to leave them in the country of their residence."

I nodded. Braxton had already filled me in on this part. "We have some space in Vanguard for transfers. I'm not sure there are any up on exchange right now, but I can double-check with our prison manager."

Hadie turned toward the girls then, starting a side conversation. "We do have some art supplies here that the prisoners use. Would you like to see if there is anything suitable?"

She'd heard our conversation.

Mischa's eyes widened and she turned to me. "Do we have time?"

Fuck. Joy lit up her features and it was like being punched in the gut. I couldn't stop myself from reaching for her and pressing my lips to hers. I needed to kiss that pretty little mouth.

She kissed me back without hesitation, and it was only the knowledge that others were watching that kept me from claiming her right then and there. There were only so many times you could tempt a mate bond before it forced you together. I needed to slow this down. She wasn't ready. Trust was not where it should be between us. I needed to prove my loyalty to her, my worth.

I pulled back, leaving her flushed and breathless. I wanted to see her looking like that many times.

"Go, we have plenty of time. Lock and I have leader shit to talk about anyway."

The vampire laughed then, his rumble turning into a boom of mirth. "Leader shit might be the most accurate description I've heard to date."

Mischa had her hand pressed to her lips, and seemed to want to say something, but then Hadie gestured for the girls to follow her. Jessa hooked her arm through her sister's, and soon they were stepping over to a large building close to the edge of the east side. I watched them until they were out of sight.

"Congratulations on your child. I had not heard there was more than one mated Compass, or more than one young due."

I turned back to Lock and gave him a nod of thanks. "Yes, Braxton and I will be blessed as fathers very soon."

"My daughter has just had a son with her mate," he said. "I thought I could not love any supe more than my child until my grandson arrived. He owns my heart."

I clasped him on the shoulder. "Congratulations to you and Hadie. That's truly wonderful news."

I couldn't wait to meet my daughter, to hold her close and promise her the world. The thought that Kristoff had nearly ended her life kept me from peaceful sleep, and had oceans of anger churning within me.

Chan was a healer without equal. He had worked miracles to keep them both alive. Although, at one point he'd suggested that Mischa might not make it, and that we should remove the child in order to give the baby a chance to survive. It had been a hard decision, but at the time my instinct said to keep them together, that mother and daughter were stronger that way. They had proved me right, fighting off the effects of the oil, pushing through the pain together. True warriors. My perfect girls.

"Let me show you through the prison," Lock said, distracting me from the dark memories filling my mind. I couldn't dwell on what I'd almost lost. For now I was grateful.

I followed the vamp in the opposite direction of where the girls went. Despite the roundish shape of this space, this was the largest of edges.

"Magic keeps the breezes up here to minimum. Otherwise we'd be buffeted," Lock said, giving me the tour. "We house five hundred supes here. The other prison, in North China, has about a thousand. We have quite limited space."

He led me right up to the edge and then whistled loudly. He repeated this action twice more. We both waited, silently staring out into the horizon. Standing this close to the edge felt as if I were standing on the clouds. A flapping could be heard now, distant at first but getting louder and louder, until two beasts flew into view – large eagles, but like no eagle a human would ever have seen.

"Beautiful, aren't they?"

"Yes," I said. "Where do they stay when you don't need them?"

Lock gave a waving hand signal to the birds and they swiftly landed behind us. They were massive, standing at least a foot taller than me, and twice as wide. The span of their wings was almost comparable to dragons, and the incredible power of their bodies was unmistakable.

"I don't know where they go, but they always come when called. They're the true guardians of this prison. They're tied to the mountain itself, and the prison makes sure they're protected and cared for."

This "living" prison, and the mythical guardian eagles which allowed supes to travel to the cages, was something no other community could boast. The origin story of Sinchin stated that these birds were a product of the prison's magic, that they will never die and cannot be manipulated by inmates.

Lock crossed to the closest eagle and reached out a hand. Large obsidian eyes followed his movements, and as he approached the bird lowered his head and allowed him to touch. Lock then stepped around to the side and pulled himself up onto its back, settling in close to the joints of the wing. I wondered why he didn't just slide right off the silky feathers, until I noticed a small harness-style leather strap crossed over the middle. Lock gripped it to anchor himself.

"Make sure you extend the first reach, but then let him come to you," he said, warning in his tone.

Copying his movements, keeping myself as calm as possible, I approached the other bird. There was maybe a moment longer hesitation from my beast, but he soon lowered his head and allowed me to mount. I settled myself onto his strong back, and surprisingly enough it was comfortable and easy to grip my legs.

"Prepare yourself, young vampire," Lock said with a grin. "This is not for the weak of disposition."

I returned his grin. "My disposition is as rock solid as Sinchin."

Not to mention I'd spent plenty of time on the back of my dragon brother. We'd made Braxton take us flying many times. That's what he got for being the lucky asshole with a dragon soul inside. Still, as the eagles spread their wings and ran for the side of the mountain, nothing quite prepared me for that initial drop off a mountain thousands of feet in the air.

It was freeing in a way that would be impossible to explain. It was something everyone needed to experience for themselves. I wished we lived closer so I could do it all the time. Mischa and Jessa had to give this a go, they couldn't leave until they had. With some strong thrusts and tilting of their bodies, the eagles circled around and started to cross to the prison.

As the cells came into sight I had to shake my head. Now that was what I called some truly secure prisoners.

CHAPTER FOURTEEN

Mischa Lebron

Jessa sat beside me while I painted. For once she was quiet and tranquil. Clearly something about this place gave her a sense of calm. Not sure what that said about my sister, considering this was a prison, housing a bunch of deadly criminals. Still, if I ever committed a crime, this was where I'd hope they would send me. The beauty would occupy me for many years. Of course, I was yet to see where the cells were, so maybe I'd change my mind about that. But for now it was perfect.

Most of my mind was occupied with building layers of images and then painting them into place. Still a part of me was stuck mentally repeating that kiss from Maximus. It had come from nowhere, in front of others, and he gave zero cares. He had kissed me like he couldn't stop himself, and my heart was still pounding.

He was disarming me, tearing down every wall I'd ever built to protect myself, walls I'd been building since I was old enough to feel the sharp sting of rejection, of hatred, of prejudice toward anyone different to the norm. The human world might have a lot of wonderful in it, but there was also a lot of hate. The supe world was segregated too, but not in the same way. Humans were the same species, the same blood and organs beneath their skin, and they still found ways to separate themselves out. The supe races were actually different species and still managed to live in communities together, to build a world which protected humans and other supernaturals. Yes, they had wars, but it just didn't seem as bad. Or maybe I'd not been here long enough to see it. Hopefully it was just not as bad.

"I'd hate you, except I think art is a useless skill. Now, knife throwing, that's a great skill," Jessa said, her head thrown back in the sunlight. There was no malice in her words, something else I appreciated about supes. If a human was jealous of my paintings, they'd have sneered and acted like art was the worst thing anyone could bother doing. Jessa did none of that, she just spoke truthfully. I had a skill she admired but didn't think was any use. So she wasn't jealous.

Still ... I had to chuckle at her.

"You're the queen of the backward compliment."

She shrugged. "What can I say, you have a true gift from the gods. I'd swear that's a photo sitting there, not a picture painted with tiny little brush strokes. But that isn't going to save your life if someone comes at you armed."

Truth. Still, my artistic abilities had saved me on more than one occasion. Not in the way Jessa was saying, but the ability I had to paint scenes in my mind allowed me to notice little details. Sometimes that saved me from being attacked, or let me know when someone was trying to trick me.

I should have known it with Larkspur's daughters, but grief and abandonment issues had completely wiped out my artistic side. I didn't paint for months, which was like the first time ever. I'd been a bit broken then. I wasn't sure all the cracks were filled yet, but things were getting better.

I was about halfway done with the painting when a whoosh noise drew my attention. We'd been in the building with Hadie when Maximus and Lock had gone to the prison. I still had no idea where the cells even were, and the last thing I expected to see was a pair of dragon-sized eagles fly over our heads. They went into a glide, landing in the center of the large oval space. Jessa was already on her feet, her body half crouched and blade in hand. She only relaxed when she noticed Maximus and Lock on their backs.

I was standing too. Somehow my wolf had taken control for a second and shot me to my feet. My back ached briefly as it adjusted to the weight on my front. Every day the width of my tummy doubled. Maybe I was carrying twins too. Or my girl was very cozy in her well-padded room.

Maximus' face was lit up as he gracefully launched himself from the huge bird. It was nice to see him with such a carefree expression, dimples flashing.

Damn dimples. Jessa was right. They were weapons.

He took his normal long strides, reaching us in seconds. "I hope neither of you are afraid of flying on the back of giant eagles, because you have to see this prison. It's ingenious."

Jessa scoffed. "I was a goddamned dragon. You can't have forgotten already. Old age is gonna do a real number on you, my friend."

He ruffled her hair before laying a kiss on her cheek. "I remember, babe. Don't worry, I know you're an expert flyer."

Ah, so the question had been for me, and I really had no idea.

"Guess we're about to find out," I said, standing taller. I was not missing out, even if there was a chance the flying motion would have me wanting to vomit over the edge.

Maximus reached out and took my hand, touching me on instinct. I was totally down with this instinct thing.

My eyes remained locked on the fascinating beasts as we walked closer. Jessa moved toward Lock. He reached down and hoisted her up with ease. Maximus led me to the other, and without any hesitation placed both hands on my waist and lifted me onto its back, right behind this little brown leather saddle.

"Normally you'd have to let the eagle come to you first, but he trusts me now, so as long as you're with me, we're fine," he said as he leapt up behind me, settling in close.

It was good to know the bird wasn't planning on attacking me anytime soon. Maximus wrapped his arms tightly around me then and all other thoughts disappeared. He ran a soft caress over my belly, before reaching forward and clenching a large hand into the loop of the saddle attachment.

"Hold on," he said softly. Then with a sharp whistle from Lock the eagle spread its wings. The sudden change in footing sent a lurching sensation through my stomach. The eagle was fast, trotting along on two legs until it reached the edge of the mountain, and without a moment's hesitation dropped right off the side.

I couldn't stop the shriek bursting from my mouth. My stomach roiled wildly for many seconds, before eventually the flight went from falling to gliding and I was able to swallow a few times and stop my breakfast from reappearing. Then the beauty of the world stilled everything inside of me. I forgot about the torture, about the last few months of fear and loneliness. I forgot about my stupid decisions, and my heartbreak at losing the only guy who'd ever held my interest for longer than a few minutes. In that moment I was no longer Mischa Lebron, damaged and broken. I was a creature of the sky and I was free.

I lifted my arms up and closed my eyes as the gliding sensation washed through my body and into my soul.

"You look like one of the gods," Maximus said, his voice low and strained. "The light is surrounding your face, and there's so much serenity shining from you."

He dropped his head then and buried it into the space between my shoulder and my neck. I could feel him inhaling deeply, as if breathing me in. There might have even been the scrape of fangs, but no bite. Which was sort of disappointing.

He lifted his face, lips brushing gently against my cheek. "You need to open your eyes now, gorgeous.

Sinchin cells are just around this curve of mountain."

I shifted slightly so I could see his depthless brown eyes shimmering back at me. His face was so close that it would take nothing for me to lean forward and press my lips to his. The cocky grin on his face said it all. He knew I wanted to kiss him.

Dammit, why were the Compasses so irresistible?

The eagle started flapping harder, increasing the bumpiness of the flight, which was enough distraction for me to look away and focus on the mountain. It was almost as breathtaking as the male behind me.

I loved seeing Sinchin from this angle. We had made it to the top through an elevator magically built into the center of it, but the actual mountain itself was hundreds of miles wide, and had large ruts and ground-out sections everywhere. There were huge cliffs of bare stone; others were overrun with grass and wildflowers, like the ones we'd received earlier from the people. Small animals were dotted around, mountain goats and other mammals feeding and climbing.

As the eagle crested around the side I realized this part of the mountain was almost a straight up and down wall. The rest was designed in the normal tapering pyramid shape, smaller at the top before gradually easing out to the largest section at the bottom. Not here though, this was completely vertical and smooth, no handholds or anything.

That's when I saw them, right near the top – scattered prison cells built into the rock face. They started right across the top, and moved along in rows. Hundreds of them.

Maximus started to explain it to me and Jessa, who was hovering close by with Lock. "There are five hundred cells, each occupied by a single prisoner. The magical barriers extend out about six feet in all directions from the edge of the rock. That way they can't touch the mountain itself to try and escape. They'd have to jump, which some prisoners have chosen to do, but apparently the mountain never lets them leave. If they jump, they disappear into the ground below and are never seen again. No one knows what happens to them."

So literally the prison cells were ten-by-ten square holes in the side of the mountain. There looked to be a pallet bed and small restroom facility in each. A shimmery, clear dome extended out from each of the holes, which was obviously that barrier Maximus was talking about, which meant the supe could walk right out and stand on ... nothing. I could see some of the prisoners sitting right on the edge of their clear barrier, staring out into the distance, legs dangling out into the abyss below.

There was a real mix of supe races. Some I couldn't tell from here, but others were clearly from the demi-fey contingent.

"How do they get food and supplies for activities?" Jessa asked.

Lock picked up the conversation now. "Mostly everything in this prison is controlled by the mountain itself. Whoever created the spell inside this giant rock was one powerful magic user, because over time it has become a sentient being. Once a day the rock wall at the back of each cell opens, allowing the prisoners to leave. On the other side is a large football-field-size space. The inmates have time to eat, use the gym, and work on creative products. We allow them to take paints to their rooms, because many of them find the view comforting in their time of incarceration."

"When new prisoners arrive, they go into the same lift we used," Maximus said. "But the prison takes them straight to their cell, no detours."

Lock nodded, his eyes drifting across the expanse of cells. "Yes, there's actually very little use for us here, except to make sure everything continues running smoothly. It's why I'm generally the only one around the prison. The other leaders don't bother themselves with it so much."

I had to shake my head – prison was a bleak life. Understandably. Some of the inmates deserved to be here, no doubt; others probably deserved worse, but it was still sad to see life wasted in such a way. I wished people could just enjoy their blessings and not seek to harm others. Maybe there would be a world one day where prisons were not the sole reason for our supernatural communities.

"We need to return to Stratford now," Maximus finally said. I noticed then that the sun had shifted quite dramatically in the sky. Time had flown by so quickly.

The eagles banked off; many of the prisoners' eyes followed us. Some even waved, like we were visitors who'd stopped by for tea. In no time the birds had deposited us back to the mountaintop, before taking off again.

"If the mountain provides everything for the prisoners, why do you need the birds?" I asked.

Lock watched them fly away before turning back to me. "The wall only opens once a day. Some of the prisoners have special needs and need supplies more regularly than that. The eagles are provided for this reason."

Fair enough. Hadie emerged from the building then. In her hands were our flowers and a rolled scroll. "I wasn't sure if you would have time to finish the painting," she said when she was closer. "So I had one of the mages magically seal and bind it for you. When you get home you can open it and the spell will dissipate. It will be as you left it."

I blinked back a few tears. "Thank you," I said, reaching out and taking the gifts from her. "You two are so very kind. We really appreciate you taking the time for us today."

Hadie and Lock smiled broadly, seeming very pleased. I was glad I got to meet them. Kind-heartedness was something I truly treasured.

"Yes, this has been a wonderful visit." Maximus stepped forward and shook both of their hands, before reaching out and relieving me of my *very* light items. "I'll return with my brothers at another date, but until then we'll be in touch about the prison transfer and the trade on commodities. I'm sure something can be worked out on both ends."

The leaders thanked us many times and then it was time to go. As we took the death box back down, Maximus told us that the mountain didn't allow any step-throughs inside or on top of it. We would have to call for Louis once we were clear of the prison. He would then take us straight back to Stratford, which was probably a good thing. I was tired again; the burn on my leg had been aching on and off for an hour or so. It was getting harder to ignore.

In the elevator, as Maximus closed his arms protectively around Jessa and me again, I found myself sinking into him. It was nice to have someone else support my heavy butt for a few minutes. His hand rubbed up and down my spine, which was both soothing and ... well, not so soothing. It was bringing my body to life, tingles, aching desire ... the usual. Even as the doors slid across and we exited, he didn't drop the arm around me. Jessa was freed from his embrace, but I remained at his side, being supported. How did he know? Somehow the guy could read my mind, even when the bond between us was not complete. True mates generally had a mental connection, but ours was not there yet.

My thoughts were shelved by the appearance of a certain violet-eyed sorcerer already waiting for us on the outsides of Shanjoin. All of us waved our farewells to the townsfolk and then followed Louis back to Stratford.

I was looking forward to a nice, uninterrupted sleep in my own bed. Tendrils of nightmares had woken me more than once the last few days. With healing sapping so much of my strength, the dreams hadn't been too severe, but something told me that once I was able to deal with the physical injuries a little better, the mental would come swinging at me with full force. Especially while Kristoff was still out there, breathing air better intended for others. He was my nightmares brought to life.

My parents hugged me for at least thirty minutes. Every time one of them pulled away, they'd get all teary-eyed and yank me back in again.

Jonathon was babbling, which was so unlike my stoic father: "The boys were keeping me updated. I was doing everything I could to figure out where Kristoff was, but Jessa assured me that if anyone could find you, it was Max."

I might not have known my father for most of my life, but he was everything I'd expect an alpha wolf shifter to be. Or werewolf – what I thought humans who shifted to wolves were before I came to Stratford. You know, when they were mythical creatures and not my life.

Jonathon definitely had that powerful, strong and deadly aura. When you screwed up he came down on you hard with the sort of authority that had my wolf whimpering in the corner. But when he loved you, he did it with every part of himself and made you feel truly treasured – the sort of relationship I'd always hoped to have with my father.

Lienda was sobbing against me. "When they told me you were taken by Kristoff, I didn't know what to do. Jonathon wouldn't let me come after you, so I spent my time praying to the gods and trying to stay busy. I rearranged upstairs."

She had her arms wrapped tightly around me. Despite her thin build, her strength was clear and admirable. It was taking some getting used to, this animated, caring version of my mom. I was used to the scared, mourning, full of rules and strict as all heck version. Have to say, it was a huge improvement. I think the overly strict thing she'd been pushing was her way of keeping me safe, but I could have used some love there as well. You know, for balance.

For the most part I had forgiven her, but there were still slivers of me working on forgetting the neglect from my childhood. Now, more than ever, I understood her actions – why she'd been torn to pieces for so long. Losing dad must have been like losing her soul. I'd only been away from Maximus for an hour and already I felt uneasy. There was an ache in my chest that refused to budge. It actually took some strength to not run out the front door and find him.

No! I am stronger than this.

"You have to see the room," Lienda said, pulling back and taking my hand. I realized she'd been talking the entire time and I'd missed it. Forcing myself to focus, I limped along after them. Jonathon gripped my other arm when we reached the stairs.

"We should get another healer to look at your injuries," he said, his defined eyebrows arching forward in concern. "Surely there's more they can do. You're still in a lot of pain."

He could sense that through the shifter bonds. He was the alpha of all wolf-shifters in Stratford. Not to mention it was probably written on my face. "I just need some rest. Chan did an amazing job. He saved my life and my daughter's."

Lienda gave an excited little squeak. "I can't believe I'm going to have two granddaughters! Such wonderful news. And both of our girls are true mates to Compasses. We're going to have powerful grandbabies, that's for sure."

My parents had been overjoyed to find out Maximus was my true mate. They'd apologized many times for their treatment of me in the sanctuary. I never realized this true mate thing was so insane. The moment everyone found out they just completely excused my actions with Larkspur's twins. I didn't really like that. I still thought it was no real excuse, and I would continue to remind myself that I needed to do and be better.

Lienda's eyes were locked on me as we walked. Her ocean-colored irises were quite green today. She wore her blond hair in a braid. Pulled back like that, with no makeup on, she looked about my age. She had always been beautiful, but now with the new warmth she was exuding, she was stunning. When we reached the second floor I was led along to what had previously been a spare room. It was the one between Jessa's and mine, the only bedroom without its own bathroom.

Two smiles beamed at me as Jonathon clicked down the handle and nudged the door open. They let me step through first, and I couldn't stop my gasp.

It was a nursery. A perfect little sanctuary for any child to grow up in. Everything was done in creams and pastel colors. Lienda had made sure it would suit a boy or girl. It was absolutely beautiful.

There were two cots and a single bassinet, all hand-carved masterpieces, painted white, with ivory-colored linen to complete the picture. Shelves lined one wall and already they were filled with cloth diaper and lots of baby ... stuff. I needed to figure out what all of it was soon. These supe pregnancies went by so fast. I'd expected to have a lot more time, but apparently *she* could arrive any day.

Lienda was waiting near the door, rubbing her hands together like she was nervous. "Do you like it?

We figured that even if you didn't end up living here when she was born – and knowing Max you won't – we still wanted a room here for yours and Jess's babies. To stay over. Their own space in the Lebron house. They're all Lebrons too."

It took me a few moments to compose myself before I could finally talk. I wrapped my arms tightly around my mom first, and then my dad. "It's perfect. Thank you so much. I couldn't have done this without your love and support."

There was more than one sob, and they weren't all from me. "We're so proud of you, honey," Lienda said, smoothing my hair back from my face. "I have a lot to make up for. Things were really hard for you when we were away from Stratford. Now that my mind is clear I really understand how hard, but I have always loved you more than anything in this world. You and your sister are my blessings, and I'm so proud of the adults you've become. Thank you for choosing us to be your parents."

Cue the waterworks.

Eventually I sorted myself out, dried my eyes, and the parentals left me alone in the nursery. Despite my bone aching exhaustion, I couldn't leave the room yet. I found myself in the corner on the padded glider chair, rocking gently, a soft green teddy clutched in one hand, the other holding a small book which had been on a nearby shelf. I started reading it out loud. The story was for very young babies, about a fox and a hen, and the friends we make in unexpected places. It was sweet, and I imagined my daughter would love this book when she was a little older.

Once I was done I moved on to the *Magical Faraway Tree*. This was an Enid Blyton classic that had been one of my favorites growing up. Lienda had read it to me when I begged her, which had been most nights. Huh, I'd actually forgotten that she did that. It was nice to remember that growing up with Lienda hadn't been all bad.

I read until my eyes were barely open and my voice hoarse. Eventually sleep won the battle and I must have drifted off in the surprisingly comfortable chair.

CHAPTER FIFTEEN

Maximus Compass

This meeting was taking forever. We'd been back from China for about three hours, and the entire time I'd been stuck in Vanguard with my brothers and a bunch of the elders, discussing everything that had happened with Kristoff and the bears' riot, and planning the town meeting which was to take place tomorrow morning. We'd called an emergency meeting to fill in the townspeople about what was happening.

Not that most of them were really in the dark. Especially about the bears. Those fuckers had been loud and clear when they started throwing supes around the town center this morning. A few of them were in the holding area of Vanguard right now. I planned on taking a little visit to question them as soon as I got out of here.

Byron, an ancient lion shifter who'd been council leader many decades ago, was on his feet, roaring in the typical manner of his breed. "He has to be brought to justice! Kristoff has stolen power, broken out prisoners, and taken the wolf alpha's daughter and tortured her."

Jonathon was in the room now; he had arrived late after tending to both his daughters. I knew my brothers had had a hell of a time dealing with him when they got back to Stratford with only Jessa, especially after explaining about the supe smugglers and Mischa being purchased by Kristoff. The only thing that had halted his wrath was Jessa. She'd told him that Braxton, Louis, and I were hot on her trail, and that he was better situated keeping Stratford protected in our absence.

Still, I got the feeling that when he had me alone the next time I was going to experience the brunt of the alpha's ire. For more reasons than one. It bothered me that I had not spoken with him since finding out about the baby; he'd surely known for much longer than me. He would have had plenty of time to stew over my abandonment of his daughter. Supes did not just leave their pregnant partner to deal with life, even if she had only been a random hookup. Which she never was. Not even for a moment.

I wondered what Jonathon thought about the fact that we were true mates.

I wanted to take back so much of the last four months. It was one giant screw-up after another. But there were no do-overs in our world. I just had to focus forward and be the mate she deserved.

I pushed down thoughts of Mischa, or at least attempted to. I wanted to go to her. Our bond was so new; it was chafing at me to get to my mate and keep her safe. Parts of me continued to worry that the reason our thoughts were still private was because of the spell from Kristoff, the one which had falsely tied me to Cardia. I needed to figure this out, speak with someone who might know. Louis said there was a lot going on inside of me; the quad nature of my soul was struggling with all the complex facets of our four-way tie to the races. He believed I needed to tap further into the shifter side. When I let go of my more vampiric ties, I'd be able to secure the last vestiges of my true mate bond.

He was guessing though, and it was scary to think Louis didn't have the answers. If he wasn't powerful or educated enough to know, then who would be? Braxton flashed yellowish eyes at me then, as if he sensed my thoughts, and I was reminded how ancient his kind were. Dragons. Maybe I needed to speak with Jessa and in turn Josephina. The golden dragon was the queen of all beasts, a godlike creature now. Maybe she would know something.

I sat a little straighter; that was definitely a path to follow. Here's hoping Jessa would be able to get word to her, and the dragon queen could make it here soon. I couldn't be taking off to Faerie with a child on the way. I'd be gone for weeks in Earth time, and I needed this dealt with before the baby arrived. And until then I had to focus on the task of rebuilding my relationship with Mischa. I needed to get her out of her parents' house and into mine. To keep her safe. To see her beautiful face each morning and fall asleep with her in my arms each night. It was not natural for us to be apart like this.

Braxton caught my attention: "So we are all agreed on this matter. We will form 24/7 patrols for the outer regions of Stratford. No one will go alone, and if anything suspicious is discovered we call for backup. The sorcerer was powerful on his own, but now that he's demon touched, there are very few who can stand against him."

Louis spoke from his place next to Jacob. He was with us at the head of the square table. "The magic users are working on some spells to hold the demon and return him to the land between the realms. Until we have these, Kristoff must remain alive. He's the anchor keeping an ancient and powerful demon from exploding into the Earth realm and wreaking destruction across the humans."

"How far away are these spells?" I asked him. I needed Kristoff to be dead. His continued presence was an insult to my mate.

Louis tilted his head in my direction. "I have to gather a few more ingredients and then they can be completed. A day or so."

I gave him a nod. Hopefully the simmering rage inside of me could hold out that long.

Jacob stopped tossing his fireball around and let out a loud exhalation. "So now that we have a path to follow on Kristoff, what're we going to do about the bear shifters? They've been a pain in the ass for years now, and I'm all for kicking their entire pack out of Stratford."

Braxton shook his head, but before he could answer others chimed in.

"Yes!"

"Get rid of them."

"Play by no one's rules – tried to attack the mate of our council leader..." The last one was from Jen, a vampire. She was referring to the incident when Jessa was inside of Vanguard. She'd been attacked by a bear shifter.

Braxton got to his feet and let out a bellowing, "Quiet!"

The wrath of the dragon was in his gaze and his energy filled the room like a swift wind. Silence descended in an instant, and I couldn't help the grin which crossed my face.

"The bear unrest started with Kristoff, and possibly Vlad inside of Vanguard," Braxton said to the room. "These two stirred trouble, promising the bears that when they got rid of us as potential council leaders, one of the bears could have the future shifter position."

Vlad the Impaler had been one of the oldest and more famous of the prisoners in Vanguard. During Jessa's stay in the prison, he'd tried to torture and kill her. Thankfully her dragon saved her in time, and Vlad had not been seen since.

"Do we have any idea where Vlad might be?" I asked, "There have been no sightings of him. He wasn't with Kristoff. Surely he would have popped up by now." We knew those two had been in cahoots together.

Louis cleared his throat and the room fell silent. He had that sort of effect on supes. "I have been thinking on this, and the scenario which makes the most sense is that Kristoff sacrificed him to summon the demon. It's not an easy task to break the barrier into the demon part of the land between, and bringing one forth with such ancient energy ... almost impossible. He would have needed very dark energy, magic and a sacrifice. And who better to sacrifice than a supe who has the blood of thousands on his hands?"

Shit. That made sense. On one hand at least we didn't have to worry about that crazy fucker again, but on the other, this made the demon so much more powerful.

Tyson's face held no emotion, but his eyes were shimmering with magic. The mage was pissed. "So you're telling me Kristoff tried to have us imprisoned and killed, and when that didn't work he jumped on team Larkspur? And then when the Larkspur thing failed, he decided to go the demon route. Is this all about making sure we can no longer rule the US council? Is it about punishing us?"

Braxton nodded. "Yes, as far as I can tell he has numerous plans in place, and power is always his goal. Power and revenge. His hatred for us has grown exponentially. He can't control it any longer, and it has resulted in him making a huge mistake. Multiple mistakes. He's been caught out now. No council around our world would take him on, no community would welcome him. He's being hunted as a criminal. We should be extremely cautious with him now. Desperation causes supes to act irrationally, and he's already on edge with the demon inside. Don't expect him to act as he would normally. There's barely any supe left in him."

Jerak, the troll who led the demi-fey, leaned forward in his chair. "Have we heard anything of Giselda? Does he have more children scattered around waiting to initiate a plan?" I'd barely had a moment with Jerak, having run out as soon as we received our leadership, but he seemed to be a solid leader. His people respected him, which was not an easy task with so many different demi-fey falling under the one leadership.

Tyson shook his head. "Nope, she's disappeared into the wind. Checked with their relatives in Italy. Never showed up."

Great, so that psycho witch was out there in the world, causing havoc.

"I'll add her to the watch list," I said. "Someone will pick her up eventually."

We had an international watch list of criminals, updated by the various prison guards and town leaders. Yellow-hued names meant they were wanted for questioning. Red names were far more serious cases. Red meant these supes were more than just suspects, they were known criminals and you needed to take care when approaching. Understandably, most of our kind didn't appreciate incarceration and fought when cornered.

Braxton clapped his hands. "We need to wrap this up now. All of us have to get back to our people and rally up some members to join the border patrol. We're going to need half a dozen or more from each of the races. Educate your people well and then send them across to George." He pointed to a sorcerer at the far end of the table. "He's working out the rotational schedule for everyone. In regards to the bears, they'll be given a strict warning tomorrow in the council meeting. The ones who are in the holding cell will remain there until we figure out this Kristoff thing. He does not need any allies roaming around."

Jerak stood then and gave us all a brief nod. "I'll send across a selection of demi-fey to assist in this matter. I know we keep ourselves slightly separate from the problems of the other races, but Kristoff is a blight on the world. You have our support to destroy him."

All of us returned his nod; he turned and strode from the room, an ogre and pixie trailing after him. Chatter filled the space as everyone got their shit together and started to leave. These supes were all leaders in Stratford. Each of them would go back to their race members and find those who wanted to volunteer their services. I had no doubt they'd have more than enough volunteers. Supes were brave by nature, and on instinct would abhor the demon-touched sorcerer who had chosen this path.

Soon it was just Louis and my brothers left in the room.

"I'm going to find these last ingredients," Louis said, shoving back his hair. "My gut is telling me that it's going to take something extra strong to take this particular demon down. I want to have six backup plans in place."

I nodded. "Keep us updated. Hopefully it'll remain quiet here until you return."

He left then, striding out of the prison and taking the entrance to the land above. He would open his step-through up there.

Despite the fact that I needed to see Mischa, I forced myself to remain in Vanguard. "I think we need to speak with the bears," I said. "Find out how far this extends and how hard we're going to have to come down on their pack."

My brothers nodded, each of them joining me as we left the meeting room and crossed into the outer zone of the prison. We wore magical marks across our chests now, almost like a brand or tattoo, which allowed us free access to every area of Stratford and

Vanguard. The magic in the mark circumvented all securities and allowed us to touch and manipulate the energy running within the prison. As we walked, the four of us talked more about what Mischa had told me, how our souls touched all four races, and how we should be able to tap into each one.

Jacob looked thoughtful, his green eyes staring off into nothing. "That's why I don't fully fit with my fey brethren. I don't have all of their traits, and for the most part am grateful for that."

I nodded. "Mischa's my true mate, and this could mean yours could be from any of the four races."

Tyson gave a low whistle. "Still can't believe she's your true mate. I feel like absolute shit for the hell I gave her when she acted so weird in the Sanctuary. In hindsight, her actions were far above what I'd have expected from a true mate who had to watch her guy all bedded up with a nasty little vampiress." Another punch to my gut. "Not to mention that she was pregnant. And new to our world. She must have been in so much pain."

Tyson should have just stabbed me in the chest. Would have been less painful than his words. My chest was clenched so tight it took me more than a few moments to be able to breathe freely again.

"You speak only truth," I said to him. "This is a shame I'll carry for a long time. Even before the fake-mate spell from Kristoff, I was pulling away from her. Don't get me wrong, I always felt a draw to her, but a brief relationship wasn't worth causing possible unrest in our pack, especially since Mischa didn't know our ways. She wouldn't have understood. She was already attached and she was Jess's sister ... I couldn't see how it could work."

A hand landed on my shoulder; dark blue eyes shot into me. "You have to stop blaming yourself, just do better by her now. Shit was outside of our control. There was no way for you to know that she would be your true mate."

Braxton was right, but that didn't change my pain. Speaking of...

"I'm going to ask Jess if she can get in touch with Josephina," I said to the dragon shifter. "I still feel tendrils of that fake-mate spell and I want to know how to purge it completely. Mischa and I have the physical connection, but our mental bond has not clicked in yet, and I'm worried it's partly to do with Cardia. The dragon queen knows much. Maybe she can help us understand."

"Good plan. I know she's been dying to see her dragon again. It's been too long," he said.

Our conversation ended as we'd reached the holding cells. A few guards were scattered around; they gave us nods but didn't approach. We were the ultimate authority here, which is why it had been so easy for Kristoff to manipulate all of these supes when he was in charge. No one would have ever questioned him, and he'd done everything in his power to keep this prison hidden from us. That way we'd never see the shit he was pulling.

The holding cages were outside of the main prison, in the same row as the offices for the wardens and such. There were four bear shifters being held there at the moment, each in their own cage. I recognized all of them by sight. Stratford was not a huge city, and for the most part didn't have members join or leave regularly.

The bears were all big bastards, as was standard, but I was bigger than all but one – Donnie, the alpha of the Tressa pack. He was also the uncle of Melly, the douchebag male who had it out bad for Jessa. She wanted to be the one to take Melly down ever since he'd punched her while her back was turned. Jessa definitely liked to fight her own battles, but I knew Braxton was dying to rip that particular bear limb from limb. He was working on his patience too.

I focused on the alpha douche. Near seven feet high, he had the general hairy ruffled look one would expect from a bear who'd been hibernating for six-months. His beard was almost to mid-chest, and the dark coarse hairs went everywhere as he started roaring at us. I strode right up to his cage, and before he could say anything more, reached through the bars, clutched his shirt in my fist, and yanked him forward, slamming his head into the bars.

His roars choked off as I repeated the action twice more. Damn, that was satisfying. I'd had pent up rage and fear living inside of me for too long. It was nice to let the vampire free and enjoy some good old fashioned bear bashing.

"Shut the fuck up," I growled, noticing the daze leave his eyes and his mouth open again. "If I hear one more goddamn noise from you, none of you will make it to trial. I'll see to it personally."

He spluttered, but something in my gaze must have clued him in on how serious I was, because he knocked my hand away and took a few rapid steps back.

"You can't do that," the one to his left whined. "You're council leaders. Bound by rules."

Tyson snorted then. "We have lots of friends. None of them are council leaders. Most of them don't like rules. Won't be a problem."

Jacob started flicking his fire around again. That was usually the prequel to him using his flames to keep a supe extra toasty warm.

The general power we exuded was working its magic now. All four bears looked like they were about to piss themselves in fear, and that was exactly where I wanted them. No one talked louder than those trying to outrun our wrath.

Jacob took the first line of questioning, his fireball casting shadows across his refined features. "Why are you trying to push your people onto a council seat? You know it doesn't work that way, so what's your endgame?"

No one spoke for a moment and the ball of heat grew larger, encompassing both of the fey's hands. That seemed to be enough to kick one of them into gear.

"Kristoff teamed up with—"

"Shut up," Donnie roared at him. "Do not speak one more goddamn word. We have pandered to these weaker races for too long. Now it's our time." He turned to us again. "You'll get nothing from us. We know Kristoff's plan will come to fruition and our rewards will be great. My father, and then myself, should have been the council leaders. This has been a long time coming."

I could tell by his set features that he would not break. Not easily anyway. But he had let quite a bit of information slip in that last little spiel. This was why there was so much animosity between Melly and Jessa. Her father had been council leader in place of his uncle, and there would have been much hatred in him about that. He influenced his entire pack, gave them grounds to fight against the traditions, gave them the heart to rebel.

We were going to end that now.

"You'll face trial in a week. Think during this time what you hope to achieve with this rebellion," Tyson warned them. "You're dividing our community, and for what? Even if you managed to usurp us as leaders, they'd never follow you. You lost all their respect when you spat in the face of our traditions. In the face of the previous council, and all the elders. The Book of Guidance will never accept you. Not to mention you're now allied with a demon-touched sorcerer who's wanted in multiple countries for crimes against supes."

With the truth of those words ringing through the cells, each of the bears paled. We turned and walked away. There was scuffling behind, and no doubt one of the bears wanted to talk, but for now they heeded their alpha's command.

It took us no time to leave the underground and stride through the forests that were our home. The weather was still cool, but I could sense the turn of nature in this wilderness, the new buds of flowers just waiting for enough heat to burst into life, the first flickers of foliage pushing through the black of winter-dead trees. Spring in Stratford was the best time of year, the birth of life, the time of rejuvenation. This spring I would have a child born to this world. I still couldn't really believe it.

"I'm going to find Mischa," I said to my brothers when we were close to home. "I have some convincing and begging to do. I don't want her at

Jonathon's any longer. She needs to be here with us, in the safety of our pack."

They all nodded, and I felt through our bond that each of them loved Mischa too. That she was accepted and trusted as a precious member of the pack. Braxton halted me, his hand on my arm, his eyes staring off into the distance. I recognized the mind-speak thing. Jessa was in his head.

"Mischa is inside with Jess," he said, turning back to face me. "They've been preparing dinner for us."

The four of us kind of froze, the same wide-eyed expression across our faces. Jessa wasn't exactly the domestic kind of female, she was more into eating food and kicking ass when she felt like it.

"Is this some kind of weird pregnancy thing?" Jacob was pretty much whispering, his eyes darting left and right like we were about to be attacked. "I feel like we should be on guard. Something is off here."

I sent my consciousness along the bond toward Mischa, but other than feeling that she was happy and not in any pain, I couldn't sense any more. She'd never shown me any signs of being someone who loved to cook, but then again, I'd worked really hard to not pay attention to her after our night together. I never even knew she painted, and that was clearly something she not only loved to do but was damn good at. I was going to find out everything about the enigma which was my human-raised, wolf-shifting mate. Everything.

Tyson was wringing his hands together. "We can do this, guys. We've weathered Jessa's crap before. Whatever she is about to throw at us ... we can handle it." He was all jittery; his reassurance meant nothing in the face of his nerves.

Braxton was practically pissing himself with laughter now. "I've seen you face down ancient ravenous beasts with more calm than you're currently displaying. I'll handle Jess." He was all confident as he strolled up to the front door.

I shook my head. "Poor, dumb bastard."

Tyson snorted. "And that's the last we ever saw of him."

Braxton flipped us off. He took a deep breath and pushed the door open. Not one to let my brother take the lead, I strode quickly to his side, Tyson and Jacob right behind us. The house was quiet; even with complete focus I could hear nothing. There weren't even any heartbeats or breathing noises. "Are you sure they're here?" I murmured. "Can't hear signs of life..."

We were creeping down the hallway, all of us on high alert. "She's definitely here," Braxton said, his voice deep and low. "I can feel the bond, even if she has me blocked out of her thoughts."

Well, great. Not only was Jessa up to one of her schemes, but she now had an accomplice to help out. Mischa. Two gorgeous brunettes with too many brains and plenty of payback to dish out. Not a great combo.

Actually, I was really looking forward to ... whatever was going to happen. I loved to see glimpses of the fire which burned deep inside of Mischa. I had no problem handling the heat.

The hallway had never seemed so long, but eventually we stepped one by one into the large circular living area. Jacob murmured something and fire shot from his hands to land in the huge hearth. Flames and warmth burst from the fireplace, filling the room with flickering shadows and light. Just as I was about to step across and hit the light switch, shadows moved and all four of us fell into fighting stance.

It was an ambush.

My fangs descended and I was about to charge when the room lit up. The brightness was blinding for a split second, and then the shouts started:

"Surprise!"

"Happy birthday!"

"Three cheers for our new council leaders."

It took me a minute to get myself under control again and tuck my overly starving and angry vampire back inside where he would wait for the next moment to rip supes to pieces. The room was filled with at least fifty of our friends and family. Our parents were across at a long table loaded down with food, talking with Jonathon and Lienda. Nash was stuffing his face full of chocolate. Our adopted brother was keeping Jo and Jack on their toes, but I knew they wouldn't have it any other way. Mom had only ever been able to conceive us; she'd have probably had twenty kids if she could have.

Mischa and Jessa were standing front and center, both of them radiant. The pregnancy glow was no myth.

Braxton moved quickly. He had his mate up in his arms in seconds. Jessa's laughter carried across the house and I could hear her clearly.

"Of course you four idiots would think this was an attack. First instinct is always violence."

Tyson and Jacob were at their side, already waiting for their turn to hug her. "You've never thrown us a ... a surprise party. I mean, what the hell is it even supposed to mean?"

Jessa tilted her head to the side, her eyes resting on her twin. "Mischa said it's something humans do a lot of. They surprise those they love with parties like these to celebrate their birthdays. We thought it was a great opportunity to celebrate all the good things."

I was moving then, unable to stop myself from crossing to Mischa. She remained frozen in place, no doubt my determined gaze making her nervous. And yet she didn't look nervous. Her cheeks were flushed, pretty and pink. She wore a deep purple dress which brought out the highlights in her blue-black hair. The outfit draped nicely over her rounded belly, and it was hard to believe she was almost ready to give birth. She was still so tiny.

My plan, as I crossed to her, was to simply wrap my arms around her and hug her close, show her how much I appreciated her beautiful, giving nature. She always wanted to make others happy. This surprise party was something special she'd done for me and my brothers, and I would never forget that.

Yep, my plan was just a hug. But the second I scooped her up and pulled her tightly into me, the hunger inside me roared to life. There was no stopping my lips from slamming against hers. I wasn't sure what reaction to expect, but she didn't resist me at all. She wrapped her arms around my back and opened herself completely to me. As she returned my fire with equal amounts of her own, it just about dropped me to my knees. The room faded away and there was nothing in my world except Mischa. Her weight was barely noticeable. I could have held her like this for days, kissed her for hours, but I knew she was probably growing uncomfortable with such a long, public display.

Humans weren't as blasé about this sort of thing. Supes wouldn't even look twice at a kiss like ours. I fought for the strength to pull my lips from hers, when all I really wanted to do was carry her to my room, strip her bare, and bury myself inside of her. The thought of her naked beneath me ... it was enough to destroy the small amount of self-control I'd been working on. Shit. I could do this for Mischa. When I finally managed to pull back, she protested with these cute little growly wolf noises and snuggled herself closer again.

Joy so pure it was actually painful exploded within me.

I felt her choose.

Choose me.

Choose us.

She did not pull away; she did not care about those who stared. This was Mischa loving me and I didn't deserve it, but I was going to take it and hoard it like the greedy asshole I was.

She was mine now, and I would never let her go again.

CHAPTER SIXTEEN

Mischa Lebron

That kiss. It was like ... holy sweet gods above. I had been kissed before – twice by classmates, human males, who immediately ignored me afterwards and pretended it never happened – and there had been one other time, a guy who didn't understand the meaning of the word no – he'd eventually understood my fist in his throat, but that was another story...

The majority of kisses in my life had been from this vampire. The moment his lips touched mine it was like losing my mind completely and not even caring. I never wanted to separate from him. Didn't care that dozens of eyes were locked on us right now. I needed him.

My mom was a damn hero. Now I really understood how much she had sacrificed to keep me and Jessa safe. It might have been cruel for me in some ways, lonely, but because of her I was alive to have this moment. To have Maximus. She had left part of her heart and soul behind to do that for me.

I owed her a huge hug, and possibly an apology when I was done kissing my mate.

"You drive me insane." His voice was low, raspy against my ear. My entire body went on high alert – hello, pregnancy hormones, time to meet the wolf whisperer. I was on fire, and he had barely even touched me yet. I had not forgotten one second of our night together. I remembered what he could do, and something told me that the next time we were together it would be even better. No alcohol, no worrying about Jessa and Braxton, just the pure attraction and emotion between us.

Was the belly going to be a problem? The thought struck me suddenly, and then it was all I could think about. I was far too inexperienced for this. I needed to speak with my sister. If anyone knew how to have awesome sex with a pregnant belly, it was going to be her. As far as I knew, she and Braxton were very much experts.

Maximus kept his arms tightly wrapped around me as he gently lowered me to the ground. The laughter and conversation around us burst back into my consciousness and I realized no one was paying attention to us, everyone was chatting and eating and enjoying themselves. I could stand here for a few more minutes staring into his eyes like a lovesick idiot. I had known for a long time that I loved Maximus Compass. Even during the months of denying our relationship and wanting to hate him for all the pain he'd caused me, I'd loved him.

The moment to say it wasn't now, so I said the next best thing.

"I know we're a day early, but happy birthday. Sorry about the no presents. There just wasn't any time to get you a gift." I'd panicked when Jessa had arrived in the nursery earlier, startling me awake with talk of what to get the boys for their birthday. Both of us realized there was no time to organize anything with the Guilds, so I'd suggested the surprise party. It had come together pretty quickly after that.

Maximus buried both of his hands in the hair at the nape of my neck, brushing his thumb across the bare skin below. "You've already given me far more than I deserve or can repay. But since I am selfish when it comes to you, I do want one more thing..."

My breath stuttered a little as I sucked in deeply. I don't think I breathed or blinked in the few seconds it took him to speak again.

"Stay here with me. Live in the pack house with Jessa and the boys. You're our family, you're my mate, and we all want you here with us."

Do not cry. I was ordering my tear ducts to obey me this one time, but I was pretty sure I was going to lose it anyway. I loved their house. From the first moment I'd walked into it to meet my sister I'd wanted to stay. I never thought this warm pack home would be for me. All of the love and joy and hope ... that was never for me.

The intensity of his gaze didn't waver. It was as if I was the only person in the whole world. As if he cared for no one else but me. It was a powerful feeling, one which had the words: "Yes, I would love to live here," blurting from my mouth before I could stop them.

Still, once it was out it felt right. A smile ripped across his face as he wrapped those long arms around me again and spun me around. The rotation was enough for my stomach to lurch in an uncomfortable manner, but I didn't care.

"We'll grab your stuff tomorrow. You can just sleep in one of my shirts tonight. Or nothing." He winked.

Gosh, golly, gee. Looked like Jessa was right about me needing some new curses.

All I could think about was being naked. With him. Shit. I wasn't going to look like I did the last time. My hand dropped onto the rounded belly and almost instantly knew it didn't matter. Our daughter was the reason for my new figure and I'd never be ashamed of her. And if I knew Maximus at all, which I liked to think I did, he wouldn't care one bit.

"We should just kick everyone out," I half murmured to myself, but he heard. A wicked smirk lifted his lips, and I couldn't help but reach out and lace my fingers through his. He tempted me in the worst kind of way.

"So, something tells me we are about to lose a second daughter to the Compass household."

I spun around to find my parents, arm in arm, smiling at us both. Maximus loped his left arm around me, pulling us closer together, before reaching out to Jonathon with his right hand. My father responded immediately and they did some sort of handshake thing. Not like humans did; theirs involved grasping forearms and some other stuff.

"I'm sorry I haven't been there for Mischa over the past few months," Maximus said, his tone serious. "But I plan to rectify that by protecting her and our daughter with my all. We're a family. A pack. Mischa is my true mate and I offer my soul to hers."

Okay, swollen heart, please don't burst in my chest from an overload of emotions. To hide the fact my love for him was leaking everywhere, I forced a lighter tone, teasing him with, "What about what I want?"

His eyes seemed extra bright as they ran across me. "I'm going to make you so happy you're never going to want to go anywhere."

He. Was. Destroying. Me.

And I was okay with that.

Lienda stepped forward and I could see so much joy and happiness on her face. Reaching out for me, I moved into her arms and she held me tightly. I'd had more hugs from her today than in a long time. "I'm so sorry, Mom," I whispered. "Sorry for not trying harder to understand your sacrifice, for not thanking you enough."

Her arms shook and she pulled back to see me better. "It was no sacrifice. You're my child. It's my job to protect you above all others. I did the best I could at the time, but I should have tried harder. I know you'll be stronger for your daughter. I know you'll shower her in so much love she'll never hurt as you did."

Maximus' hand landed on my lower back, offering his support. "Our daughter will grow up in Stratford with her cousins and family. She's going to be a little hellion, and I for one can't wait to see that."

Lienda and Maximus locked eyes for a brief moment and something passed between them. An understanding maybe … or at least acceptance. She was handing her child across to be loved and cherished by another, and he was promising her that he would do right by me. I never thought I'd see the day where anyone cared enough to fight for me, for my happiness. Looks like I was wrong. My cup was running over. It was too much.

A sharp twang across my stomach took me by surprise. I clutched at the side where it was most painful, and waited a few seconds for it to fade away. I'd been getting little cramps and aches like this for the past few hours. When I thought back, they might have even started in Sinchin prison, but that one was the worst so far. I had to breathe through it for a second or two.

Three sets of eyes were watching me closely now, and when the discomfort eased I offered a reassuring smile. "Just pregnancy pains, nothing to worry about."

Maximus gathered me back into his arms, his hands running gently across my lower back. "Don't be brave about this. If you think the baby is coming, let me know so I can get the healer. Shifters don't tend to have many problems, but it has been known to happen." He growled a little. "I wish Louis wasn't out of town. It would be much better if he was here. His healing is of the highest caliber."

I patted his chest, sending warmth and reassurance his way. "It's going to be okay, women have been doing this for many thousands of years. She'll come when she's ready, and no amount of worry beforehand will make it any easier or less painful for me when it happens."

He gave a groan, dropping his head back to stare into the ceiling. "Seriously, I think the stress of seeing you in pain might actually break me." Lowering his gaze, he brushed my cheek with his thumb. "I hate the thought of you hurting, even if the reward is a beautiful little girl."

Before I could reassure him, he swept me away and deposited me onto the couch. He murmured something about me being off my feet and that he was going to grab me some food. Bloody thoughtful vampire. I owed the fates a nice gift basket. They had been extra kind to me this time around.

Jessa crashed down on my right side, Tyson dropped on to my left.

"Looks like you and Max sorted your differences out," the wizard said. "'Bout freakin' time. I was two days from kicking his ass for you."

I chuckled, before giving him a one armed hug. "Thank you for looking out for me. Have you heard from Grace?"

His features locked down, and with a shake of his head he gave me a faint smile. "Nope, no word at all."

I knew that his heart ached for the healer witch to return. The way he spoke of her, it reminded me of the intensity of my first feelings for Maximus. I was extremely curious about the possibility of a true bond between them. I hoped she'd return soon so he could find out.

Tyson was distracted by someone on his other side, which left me facing a smug looking Jessa. We remained in a stare-off locked-eye position for some time, and I couldn't halt the rush of love I felt for her. She was my twin, the other half to my soul, the one who fulfilled me in a way that no other could.

"I really missed you growing up," I choked out.

She froze, her normally expressive features stilling into something unreadable. Then she threw herself at me, and as my arms wrapped tightly across her back, and she pulled me closer, everything felt right in the world.

"I missed you too," she whispered hoarsely, before pulling back so that we could see each other. "Even when my world was complete, when I had my pack, there was always something there, something in my soul screaming out for another. You're my soul-sister, and I don't want us to be apart again. When Kristoff took you from the land between … there are no words for that, Mischa. I'm not used to feeling so helpless, and the devastation … I wouldn't survive if I lost you now. Please don't ever make me live without you again."

Tears sprinkled her blue eyes, which had my own filling also. I rubbed away the wetness before it could trail down my cheeks. "We need to make a pact that no one ever separates us again. There is no force strong enough in any of the realms."

She nodded her head. "Agreed!"

We settled back together, our shoulders pressing close, each soaking up the twin bond. It was strongly flickering between us, and even though the mind barriers were in place to keep our thoughts private, when we touched like this, some of the thoughts still snuck through.

Jessa was so happy. With Braxton and her babies and me back in her life, everything was perfect for her right now. Through all her joy, though, were these small tendrils of fear, about Kristoff and the bears, that someone or something was going to come along soon and sweep this all out from under her.

"I won't let them," I growled out, my voice all fierce and stuff. Damn, my wolf was so stunning when she chose to burst free and assert herself. "I've never had this before, and I'll fight to keep it, Jess. I'll fight to keep all of you!"

A warm hand took mine and I realized Tyson had been listening to our conversation. "*You* don't have to fight them, Misch. We'll fight them together. All of us."

"Yes." Another low voice was nearby, Jacob, the fey's perfect golden features highlighted by the flickering fire. "Together, always. Pack."

My throat was so tight I could barely breathe. This was more than my poor little human-raised heart could handle, but screw it, I was taking this pack. I was keeping them. I wasn't sure I could even live without them in my life now.

The party was in full swing around us. Supes were starting to get loud with what I suspected was some faerie wine help. The four of us remained in a cocoon of pack bonding. I could see Maximus and Braxton making their way toward us, both with plates piled high with food. The boys had been waylaid many times by their friends and alliances. The Compasses were feared in this community but they were also pretty well-liked, which spoke of their strength and compassion. For ones so young, they handled the burden well. Much better than I could have hoped to.

When they made it back to us, a smile curved across Jessa's face, and I loved the way Braxton zeroed right in on it, as if there was no more perfect sight than her smile. Damn, those two had an epic sort of love, one that you'd read about in books, one day, when someone bothered to write about it.

I realized Jessa had started bouncing in her seat, and at first I assumed the smile and bouncing was about the food, but then she said: "I think Mischa needs some pack bonding time tonight."

What was she talking about? I knew immediately I was the only one in the dark. The quads exchanged a look, one which was hard for me to decipher, but there was no confusion there. Before I could start demanding answers, Tyson jumped up and reached out a hand to me. He hauled me up gently, and far more quickly than I could have done on my own.

"Come on," Jacob said, taking my other hand. Between the pair I was led toward the stairs. I glanced back at Maximus, confused about what was happening here.

I won't lie. My mind sort of went straight to the gutter, and then enjoyed playing there for more than a few minutes. But eventually I realized that I wanted no other than Maximus, even though I loved his brothers very much.

Jessa must have picked up some of my thoughts. She let out a chuckle before nudging me. "Sorry, girl. Unfortunately the boys don't roll that way."

Braxton growled before shaking his head. He knew Jessa had eyes for no one but him, and I felt the same way about Maximus. I sent a pouring of love toward the vampire along our bond. He might not hear my thoughts but he could feel my warmth. A surging burn of emotion returned to me, and the fire in his gaze had me stumbling.

Lucky I had two gorgeous dudes on either side of me to keep me standing. My curiosity turned toward where this pack party was heading. When we reached the second floor I was amazed at the size of this level. It was huge: fifteen foot ceilings, giant log beams, and round spaces which spanned out and led to half a dozen huge timber doors.

We walked together all the way to the very end. No one seemed concerned to be leaving their own party, and I figured supes didn't go crazy about things like that. No one was watching or judging, they were just having a good time.

Tyson placed his free hand on the door and I felt some sort of electrical current run along our joined palms. "We don't let any but pack in here," he said. I started trying to lean around him to see inside. What were they hiding in here? Torture chamber? Secret sex den? Candy store?

Damn, please let it be a candy store.

It was dark inside. Tyson released me to cross the room and open the curtains along the far wall. Behind them was a window that spanned the entire wall, like floor to ceiling, and it looked out into the forest. Actually, this side of the house was practically in the forest, so staring out that window was like sitting amongst the trees. The night sky was sparkling above, so many twinkling stars.

As I pulled my eyes from the view, I finally noticed the bed. *Oh my.* A rush of heat flushed out my cheeks, but I seriously didn't even care. The bed was massive, like the size of three king sized beds all pushed together, and twice as long.

Jessa rushed to me and wrapped her arms around my shoulders. "This is where we sleep when we pack bond. This is what strengthens our love and ties. This is where we cry and heal and support one another."

I was blinking, unable to take my eyes off the lush mountain of blankets and pillows. Suddenly I felt exhausted. I wanted nothing more than to crawl in the middle there, burrow myself beneath the warmth, and stare out into the forest. Without warning, supes around me started to undress. Not all the way, but shoes and jackets were being thrown to the side. I was guessing there was other furniture in this room, things I hadn't noticed and didn't care about right now. Right now was all about this moment with my pack.

Maximus stood close to my back. I could feel him removing his jacket and boots. I only had on a dress and tights, so it was simple enough to drop off my sweater and kick free the black, shiny flats. Jessa and I then crawled across into the center. The mattress was like a cloud of orgasm. I sank into it and never wanted to come out. The four large shadows of the Compass quads followed us across. There was a ton of space on either side, but as Maximus settled in beside me, Braxton on Jessa's other side, I knew that the boys would stay close to us. This was a bed built for a pack to grow, for children and other partners to come into it. It was a family puppy-pile, and my wolf was so freaking happy she was purring.

I could sense Jacob and Tyson on either end. All of us had our heads tilted back to see the stars above. Jessa and I were on our sides, facing each other, a comfortable way for us to sleep with our baby bellies. I couldn't wait to sleep on my stomach again. I missed it so much.

Jessa reached out and grasped my hands, and Maximus settled in close enough that I could feel his warmth and smell the citrus, metallic and forest scents he always carried with him, wild and untamed but so comforting.

I tried so hard to stay awake, to cherish this moment with my family. Something I had never anticipated I'd get. But then Jacob started to sing. There was no resisting his voice. It was soaring and beautiful and had bumps rising across my skin. Fey had a special affinity for music, and the absolute emotion in Jacob's voice literally took my breath away. As the song continued in a soft melody, my eyelids started forcing themselves closed. Arms wrapped around me and soft kisses pressed against my neck, just near the base of my right ear.

"Sleep, Mischa. We'll keep you safe." Maximus' reassurance was the last thing I heard before darkness crashed into my mind, and I was out.

I woke a few times through the night. Nightmares of Kristoff's torture, the effects of the Lunarti oil, and almost losing my daughter, hurtled into my dreams, snatching the peaceful slumber from me. But every time there were soft hands and warm hugs to bring me back, to remind me that I had escaped. I had survived. Kristoff did not best me, and I would not let his cruel actions continue to haunt me so strongly.

Despite the fact I wanted to be close to Maximus at all times, I liked that the quads switched positions around us to allow maximum bonding time for all. Even the possessive nature of Maximus and Braxton wasn't bothered by this, which showed the true trust in this pack.

It was near dawn when I felt Braxton and Jessa leave the room. The dragon shifter lifted his sleeping mate into his arms and strode out the door. I was still half asleep when Maximus scooped me up, and that's when I realized we were walking too, out of the pack room and into another one of the doors on this level.

Awareness returned as I realized I was in his room. Something panged in my heart as I wondered if this was the space he'd shared with Cardia. He must have noticed the look on my face. His somber expression was enough for me to pull myself together and school my thoughts.

"This is not the room I shared with her," he said, caressing the side of my face. "I switched rooms right after the battle. I didn't want the dark memories to taint my world any longer. There has never and will never be any other in this room or my life. It's all you, Mischa Lebron."

He set me on my feet, closing the door we'd just come through. My heart was lighter as I took a few steps into the suite. There was a roaring fireplace near a small sitting area. In the other corner was a huge king-sized bed, decked out with a dark, timber base and ornately carved headboard. I could see a sparkling bathroom through an open door to our left, and there, in an alcove near the far corner, was a beautifully-crafted cradle, dresser, and change table.

I stepped closer to the baby stuff, my eyes growing warm and damp by the pure perfection of it all. Like the furniture at my parents' place, everything here was hand carved and painted in shades of white and cream. Dashes of lilac brightened up the area: a lilac duvet in the cradle, and lilac stuffed wolf sitting on the dresser. There were also splashes of green. I turned wide eyes on Maximus. When had he had time to do this?

He answered my unspoken question: "My brothers helped set this up while you were recovering in China. After we've dealt with Kristoff, we're going to work out a proper space for her," he said, his eyes locked on me. "But this will do for now. She'll be close to us, and that sits right with me."

My mate was one very thoughtful vampire. Desire and love was bursting from me, and I really couldn't halt my legs as I scrambled toward him. He caught me with ease, his lips crashing into mine as passion burst to life between us.

"Thank you," I murmured between kisses. "Thank you for everything. For her. For us."

Maximus' eyes went black then, and my stomach did flip-flops. He moved in an instant, lifting me up and striding toward the bed. When we reached the thick mattress he laid me on my side and spread out next to me. His mouth was on mine, and I lost myself in the hot, hot kisses he was dishing out.

There was no way to stop, my body was on fire. I needed him to touch me, every part of me.

"Tell me if you want to wait until after she's born," he said, running his hand across the bump. "Not sure I can stop, but I'll try for you."

I wiggled closer, my hormones screaming inside. "If you stop, I'll probably combust, and that can't be good for anybody."

He grinned, all shiny teeth and wicked dimples. Without any hesitation, he devoured me with a thoroughness that I remembered quite well. He had been like that last time, so attentive, so consumed by our lovemaking, as if he saw no one but me, as if he had never seen anyone but me. The first time we came together I'd been confused by that intensity. Now I understood. It was our bond.

Somehow my clothes disappeared, and so did his. His hands were large enough to thoroughly caress my body as he ran them down me. Everywhere he touched burned, until my skin was on fire, my lower body moving uncontrollably.

"Max, please. I need you to ... holy ... need."

Nothing made sense, but he understood, and the caresses soon turned much more specific. His tongue followed the path of his hands, and under his expert movements the pleasure inside of me skyrocketed and I exploded into a million pieces. It took me a long time to pull my shattered core back together. That had been so much more than last time. The surge of emotion and love in our bond was working strongly, adding an intensity and strength to the attraction between us.

I wanted to touch him, my hands reaching out to caress the velvety hardness of him. He groaned against me before stilling my hand. "I have no control when it comes to you, and right now I need to be inside you."

He turned me on my side, spooning his large body behind me. His hand came over the front to lift my leg. I felt his hardness against my core.

I had forgotten to ask Jessa about pregnant sex, but it didn't seem like Maximus needed any instruction. Lifting my leg slightly higher, he moved and in one smooth thrust slid inside of me. My moan was loud, that first sensation of fullness enough to have me already on the path to a second orgasm. Maximus was a huge guy, and the first time I'd worried that it was going to be impossible to fit all of him inside without permanent damage. Now I knew the only permanent damage was my addiction to him. Something I could live with.

Using his strength to hold me up, he continued to move slowly against me, sliding all the way in before pulling out just as far, each movement exquisite torture. I hooked my leg around him to give more access, which freed up his hand. He touched the center of my body and stroked the sensitive nub there in time to the thrusts of his body.

Holy shit. Hell. Fuck. It was time to pull out the curses. Gosh-golly-gee was not going to cut it here.

"Max," I cried out, the sensations so strong.

"Stay with me, Misch," he said, gutturally. "I've got you, baby. Come for me."

In that second I splintered apart, and the million pieces from before was nothing compared to the surging pleasure spiraling through every facet of my being. Maximus followed close after, his voice low and urgent as he thrust a few more times before groaning out my name.

It took a long time for my pulse to slow and my breathing to regain control. Maximus didn't withdraw from me and I loved the sensation of such closeness with him. Eventually we had to clean up. I found myself standing in a huge shower stall, multiple jets pulsing at me and Maximus worshipping my body like he'd never seen a woman before. Which, based on his skills, was far from the truth. His fangs were showing, and I tilted my head back for him, but he shook his head.

"Not while you're pregnant, Misch. You need to be at full strength. Very soon though I will taste you

..." his mouth was moving again, and I lost all coherent thought.

Eventually he wrapped his arms around me and we sank to the floor. He cradled me between his legs and we let the water beat down on us. I was trembling, but there was no fear or worry in my mind. I wiggled myself around a little so I could see his face, the water dripping from his long black lashes, the dirty blond of his hair darkening to a deep, rich umber. In that moment there was nothing between us, no secrets, lies, or hurt. We were just two supes, bonded for life and totally wrapped up in each other.

"I love you, Mischa."

He said it so strongly, nothing but surety in his words. Which made those perfect words seem so much more. His hands reached up and cradled my face and I let some of the tears leak out, knowing they were well hidden in the water streaming down my face.

"Even the strongest of mate spells could not come close to mimicking this bond between us," he continued. "You're everything to me and I love you so damn much."

My lips crashed into his, and I was crying even harder. "I love you too. So damn much."

Whatever barriers had been between us crashed and burned in that moment, and then I could feel him. In my mind. In my soul. The same way that Jessa and I were connected, that bond just settled into place.

Baby?

I laughed out loud, before pressing my head down to rest against his hard chest.

Our love broke the barriers.

He wrapped me up and peppered kisses across my cheeks and down to my lips. *Your love set me free.*

His love had set me free too, free from loneliness and pain. Free from a life half-lived.

CHAPTER SEVENTEEN

Maximus Compass

I awoke moments before the alarms started blaring across Stratford. There had been a breach. I could feel it in my connection to the town's securities. My eyes dropped down to the mess of dark hair beneath my hands. I'd had Mischa so tightly wrapped around me when we went to sleep that her hair was tangled around my arm.

Last night had been ... everything. The bond between us was complete, and she loved me. I was one lucky son of a bitch, that was for sure. The fact that she could forgive and trust me with her body and her soul, well, I would never take that for granted.

Of course, now it seemed that some asshole was going to rain on the parade, and I didn't need two guesses which asshole it was. Time to kill me a sorcerer.

Mischa started to stir as I unraveled our bodies and reluctantly pulled myself from the bed. By the time I'd checked the messages on my cell, she was sitting up.

"What's going on?"

"Perimeter breach. The scouts are on it, but they don't know for sure yet what's set off the alarms."

Tyson was out on the patrol line at the moment; he'd sent me a brief text with what they knew. Which was basically nothing.

Striding into my small walk-in-closet, I dressed quickly and grabbed my usual weapons. As I was leaving a glint of jewel and blade caught my eye and I realized it was the gift from the ancient Chinese supe. Instinct told me to grab it, so I strapped the sheath to my calf.

Returning to Mischa, I climbed onto the bed and crawled to her side, cupping her face, my fingers threading through the silky strands of her hair. Dragging myself out of bed was probably the hardest thing I'd ever done, I needed one last taste before leaving.

Her lips met mine and I was lost for a time. But I could only ignore the blaring of the sirens for so long, I needed to get out there and protect my pack and town.

"Stay here with Jess. She's downstairs. We'll secure the perimeter and then come back and find you."

I reluctantly pulled away from her; she followed me off the side of the bed. I handed her one of my shirts, which she threw on over her nakedness. "I really don't like the thought of you going out there without me," she said, her features drawn. "But I'm pretty useless at the best of times, let alone preggo."

I leaned down and kissed her one last time.

"Jess said I can borrow some of her clothes," she said when we parted. "So I'll get dressed and wait for you. Call me if you need anything. Keep me updated."

A satisfied grin spread across my face. She was protecting me, her wolf all bristly and fierce. Nothing warmed my heart more than that.

"I'll keep you updated, gorgeous."

With one last look, she turned and strode from the room, assumedly making her way upstairs to Braxton and Jessa's lair. I was relieved that the final piece of our bond was in place, now I could keep an eye on her while out on patrol. The pure rightness of our connection highlighted how screwed up my bond with Cardia had been.

I was definitely killing a sorcerer tonight.

Braxton was waiting for me on the front porch. Jacob and Tyson were already at the border. "Have you heard anything more?" he said.

I shook my head. "Nope, just that there was a breach of the force field on the west end. The patrolling group is checking it out."

Braxton's jacket scraped as he whirled his arms around. "I don't have a good feeling about this. I can sense demon energy."

My senses were on high alert too, and as we crossed through the town center I could see we weren't the only ones. The townsfolk were out en masse, some of them shifted into their animals, others calling spells and elements to their hands, the demi-fey using their strongest of magic to ready against the threat.

"Councilmen."

"Leaders."

Braxton and I received greetings and acknowledgements from most who crossed our path. I noticed Jonathon striding across to join us. "Girls okay?" he asked.

We both nodded. "Safe at home for the time being," I said to him. Couldn't trust either of them to stay put for long, but right now their protective instincts were working in our favor. They wouldn't risk the young.

My phone buzzed loudly. I quickly whipped it out and checked the message.

Incoming large group. Demon energy riding them.

I held Tyson's message up for the other men to see and we took off at a run. Others of the community must have received similar texts from friends or family. They soon joined us.

Braxton started barking orders: "Remember, do not engage the demon touched. Louis left spells with his people, so our role is to round all demon-touched into a group. Then the magic users will immobilize them and send their souls back."

No one questioned the dragon shifter.

"The only exception to this rule is Kristoff," he added as we approached our men on the border. "His demon is like no other. Only Louis has the power to banish it. Leave him to Louis."

Our group was about thirty strong, and there were another twenty or so already spread across the line. This was very reminiscent of the scene with Larkspur not that long ago. The only difference ... our enemies were already inside with us.

The Tressa bear pack was charging through the forest, coming in at the opposite angle of the force field. I expected they were going to try to take out the patrolling supes and then interrupt the protections around Stratford to let that asshole sorcerer in. Their pack numbered in the forties, and judging by the dark energy they exuded, at least a third of them were demon-touched.

I picked up my pace, full-on vamp-sprinting to reach the patrol group. Tyson and Jacob were front and center. Elements whipped around the fey, his face dark and pissed off.

Braxton was close behind me, and when he reached our side the quad bond kicked into place. It was easy now, instinct. All of us absorbed some of the others' power and our bodies changed to reflect this. Braxton shifted into his fusion mode, half man, half beast. If he fully shifted into dragon, the bond was harder to maintain, so he'd save that for the serious stuff.

"Is the fusion version immune to the demon?" I asked him, as we fell into formation on the front line.

He shook his head. "No idea. Hopefully I won't have to find out."

Supernaturals didn't use guns much. The manmade metals did not react well to our energy, and more often than not would backfire on the user. Instead we preferred swords, knives, and anything else sharp and pointy.

With that in mind, I pulled free the long blade which I often carried in a scabbard down my spine. This was my favorite weapon; we'd been through a lot together. Bushidō was her name. She was a katana blade I'd received from a Japanese-born sorcerer many years ago. He was my father's oldest friend, and he had gifted each of us with a specially designed blade. Master Koto had since passed on to the next life, which meant we were the last to hold one of his highly prized blades. So far it had never let me down.

A sorcerer started shouting from where he stood beside Tyson. "Those who are shifted into bear form are not demon touched. We'll focus on the ones still in humanoid skin. Keep the others off us."

The Tressa pack was almost on us. Most of them were in bear form. "The demons will be trying to open portals for more of their kind," Braxton said, his voice growly and at a level of bass no human vocal cord could reach. "Kristoff's demon has spread his seed in the bears and they are looking for more fertile ground."

We had to end this now. There was a delicate balance between the demon lands and the other realms. The more demons here, the larger the opening between the worlds. We could be overrun with demons in a matter of months if we didn't shut this down now.

I'm going to block you out now, Misch. Gonna kill me some bears. Be back soon.

Her laughter filled my mind. *We do need a nice rug for the floor. Stay safe. Call me if you need help.*

I sent her warmth and love before shutting down our bond. Despite her blasé demeanor, she really didn't need to see this battle. The bears were so close now, but I had enough time to turn to our people and say: "The Tressa pack is outlawed from Stratford. They're to be considered dangerous criminals. We aim to incarcerate them in Vanguard. If they resist, you know what to do."

With a roar I dashed to engage the bears, aiming for the ones who were shifted into seven-plus-foot thousand-pounds of furry beast. Bushidō cut through them with ease, severing heads and limbs in seconds. They had size on their side, but I was vampire, and our speed was second to none.

A gargoyle on my right cried out as a huge bear tore his stone arm off and catapulted it into the forest behind us. I snarled, and in a millisecond had sheathed my blade again, and with a crouching leap landed on the back of the massive shifter. My reflexes were almost doubled in speed while I was joined in the quad bond. My hands wrapped around the thick neck. The bear swiped across my arm, opening it to the bone, but that wasn't enough to stop me. I twisted and wrenched and tore its head completely free from its body.

The gargoyle inclined his head briefly in thanks, before turning back to jump into the fray. Losing an arm wasn't going to hold him back.

With a grimace I quickly tore some strips off the bottom of my shirt and used them to bind the freely bleeding wound in my arm. I'd heal fast, but the wound was deep and needed a little help.

The battle still raged around me. There were many bears littering the ground, but also some of our people. My brothers were fine. Braxton was battling two bears at once, almost lazily batting them away as they came at him.

"Stop playing with your food," I said with a laugh as I dashed past him. He flipped me off, and then in a double move even I was impressed by, stepped to the right and ripped both limbs from one bear and then used the claws from one of those limbs to sever the other's throat. Then he tore out their hearts. You know, just in case they weren't dead enough the first time.

He joined me then as we made our way across to the magic users. "Did someone send Louis a text or smoke signal or something?" I asked Tyson when we reached his side.

The wizard was right in the center, his energy joining with the others. They were holding the dozen or so demon touched for now, but none were banished yet. I wasn't sure they had the power, which meant we really needed Louis. I didn't know where the sorcerer had gone, and whether any modern technology worked there. But hopefully one of these magic users did.

Tyson nodded, his golden features pale. "Yes, he's on the way. He doesn't know if he got enough stuff for Kristoff though. Gonna have to wing it. These demon bastards are strong. I had no idea how damn strong."

From the corner of my eye I noticed a couple of bears break away from the fighting group and turn toward the magic users. I nudged Braxton and he roared. With a crouching leap, the dragon-man jumped clear over the sorcerers closest to us. Friggin' showoff. Not one to be outdone, I followed suit, amazed that I cleared the supes by a good few feet.

Bushidō was already out of her sheath and in my hand. I wasn't screwing around anymore. This shit had to end now. The bears had pushed too far. They were exiled from Stratford and would never hold a seat on the council if I had anything to do with it. A slight weakness was starting to filter through my limbs, and I knew it was from Tyson. He was throwing everything he had into the spell to hold the demon touched. Here's hoping it was enough.

"Melly!" Braxton roared. The huge bear he was engaged with was none other than the dishonorable cowardly puncher.

I shook my head, focusing on the other one. Melly should start praying that Braxton was in a generous mood, and decided to finish him quickly. The sun was rising across the horizon, low light filtering through to where all the fighting was taking place. Blood and bodies littered the ground for a good hundred feet around, and it did not make me happy to see so many of my people needlessly cut down in their prime. The bears had let their own need for power, and the bitterness of a lost leadership, cloud their judgment, and now their pack was going to be wiped from the world.

It was frustrating, and it pissed me off, but there were no second chances with a thing like this. It was either Vanguard for life or death. Associating with demons was an automatic life sentence.

Silver glinted in the sunlight as my blade sliced across the bear's meaty shoulder. This one was female. She roared, standing taller and swiping down on me with both paws. Her claws could easily eviscerate a supe if they connected. I darted to the side and slid across the bloody ground before coming up behind the shifter. She was slow to spin around; I had already cut along two major arteries in her body. She swiped at me again, jerky this time, and with a shake of her huge head, her legs collapsed beneath her and she hit the ground. Hard enough to rock it a little.

A glance to my left told me that Braxton had wasted no time on Melly. The bear was in about eight pieces, scattered around him. My brother was standing there, fury radiating off him, and I knew he was pretty close to losing his shit.

Brax, I called through our bond, trying to bring him back to me. *You got him, brother. Jess is gonna kick your ass for not letting her have that kill.*

The mention of his mate brought a flicker of life in his eyes. "Yeah, she's already pissed at me. But at least she's safe, staying put."

I had been blocking Mischa out as much as possible, mainly because the moment I felt her soft energy caressing mine I wanted to run to her. I couldn't do that. My people needed me here, and she was safe in our house.

Still. *You okay, gorgeous?*

A slightly irritated tone was in her reply. *I'm fine. I know you said you were going to shut the bond down, but I'd still like some updates. Ass.*

I chuckled, out loud. Her fire … I was starting to crave it.

Sorry. As you can see, pretty much chaos. I let the images filter through my mind, and despite her upbringing she did not flinch at the carnage.

Stay safe, Max. And come back soon. Jess is about five minutes from escaping. It's taking all of my distracting skills to keep her here.

I'll bet. Love you, baby.

I love you too.

Those soft words were enough to send sparks of warmth through me.

The demon touched were pretty much the last of the bears left, a dozen male and female supes, standing motionless. Although, I could see that some of them were starting to move, very slowly. The magic users were losing them.

A step-through opened then in the space just beyond the forest, behind the demon bears. Only one person had the power and ability to open directly into Stratford without worry for the securities. Louis was back. The sorcerer strode free; he was decked out in a long black cloak and snow-covered boots. Clearly those ingredients he'd been collecting were in the arctic.

His face was scary as he walked without pause toward the immobilized group of bears. The magic users holding them were definitely starting to struggle, and the relief on their faces spoke volumes. Louis had the strap of a satchel bag strung across his shoulder, the pouch flapping against his legs. He reached into the bag and withdrew a large jar of something.

When he was about a yard from the demon touched, he smashed the jar on the ground and thrust both of his hands skyward.

"Cresta demonica turnitalia reform."

His words ignited a fire in the very space he'd smashed the spell. The flames were tinged with a green-yellow hue, and they were suddenly eight feet high. The magic users who'd been holding the demons started to chant the same words as Louis. *Cresta demonica turnitalia reform.* Over and over. Each time the flames grew higher, spreading in a circle around the bears.

Louis clasped his raised hands together, and the smacking of palms was much louder than I'd expected.

His next words were echoing and heavy with power. "You have broken the cardinal law of supernatural peace time. You have invoked powers beyond your ken and now you must pay the price. The demons will not stop coming now that they have a portal to this world. The only way to close it down is to send you back as tribute. You, bear shifters of the Tressa clan, are sentenced to an eternity in the demon realm. You'll know suffering unlike any other. You'll wish for death. You'll never return to our plane. May the gods take mercy on your souls."

Misty wisps of energy burst from Louis. The fire roared a hundred feet into the air, completely engulfing the dozen shifters on all sides.

The roar of the flame was almost deafening. The magic users continued chanting the spell; the area was thick with magic and energy. The power from Louis waned then, and the flames began to flicker and die off. By the time the yellow and green plume was gone, there was nothing left in the middle except a black ring on the ground.

Louis spoke with urgency, striding forward to his people. "We need to sanctify and seal this space. There's a weakness here now to the demon world, and that cannot be left untouched."

The magic users scattered, most of them looking like two steps from death, but that didn't stop them jumping when Louis ordered it.

He crossed to us. "They're going to gather the ingredients we need. This should be all over soon."

Jacob and Tyson were by my side now. Braxton too. The four of us exchanged an uneasy stare.

"It's not really over, though," said Tyson. "Kristoff is still out there, probably creating more demon touched. What the hell was the point of this?" He sounded a little breathless, and I was glad that he'd been joined with us during the fight. Our strength as a unit of four had helped tremendously.

"Those demons were all upper level," Louis said. "Not as strong as Kristoff's, but I would say they were in his army of souls. I had to use most of the spell and energy I had to return them. That's why you all had so much trouble holding them." His flat eyes met Tyson's. "If you hadn't been here, and been able to tap into the quad bond, they would have overrun you. It was a good plan. I've never seen so many upper level demons on this plane."

A sense of unease was stealing along my spine. "So where is Kristoff then? Why wasn't he here adding his energy to the collective. With his demon they'd have succeeded. I mean, he couldn't have thought the bear clan stood a chance against us, so what was the point?"

For probably the first time in my life I saw Louis look uneasy. "I don't like it either. It was almost as if this entire thing was a distraction. But to what end?"

My own unease intensified, and with a start I reached through my bond to check on Mischa.

Misch. Everything okay?

My words shattered at the end of the connection, unable to reach her. I should have realized earlier, when the weakness first started invading my body, that it wasn't just about Tyson, it was also about Mischa. She was being blocked from me by a thick darkness.

I jerked my head to find Braxton. He stood with his eyes closed, small growls rocking from him.

"Jessa?"

He shook his head.

"Me either." I was growling too.

The vampire inside of me roared to life. I was already moving before another word was spoken. Looked like Kristoff had been using the bears as a distraction to get to the girls.

This time I knew he'd stop at nothing until they were dead. He hated us and wanted our suffering more than anything else, and targeting our mates was the worst punishment he could inflict on us.

We had to stop him before it was too late.

CHAPTER EIGHTEEN

Mischa Lebron

I was starting to agree with Jessa, being left behind while others went off to the battlefield really sucked the big one. Especially when it was our pack and they were facing an unknown enemy.

I'd just finished checking in on Maximus, and he was doing okay. Said the battle was wrapping up, but still there was some uneasiness in my body. I was sprawled back on the couch, television on, some movie playing in the background. Jessa was pacing the floor in front of me.

"You getting anything from Braxton?" I asked her. Maximus had me locked out again, although thankfully I could tell he was okay – a few bumps and scratches but nothing life threatening.

"He just killed Melly and now they're dealing with the demon-touched." She growled a little as she paced, one hand pressed against her belly, the other waving in the air. "That slimy asshole was supposed to be mine to torture, but no, Braxton had to go all dragon on him and rip his body into a dozen pieces."

The mental images of that set off a faint churning in my stomach. The damn thing had been upset since I woke. "He loves you, Jess. That's his way of showing you."

She snorted. "Reminds me of this cat which somehow stowed away and got in through the securities here. It used to leave dead birds on my doorstep. Presents for me. At times it feels a little like Braxton learned about love from that cat."

I burst into laughter at the thought of Braxton in dragon form leaving dead supes on her doorstep. Jessa must have picked up on the image too, and she lost it with me, both of us clutching our stomachs and hoping not to go into early labor. "Don't give him any ideas," she finally gasped through her laughter. "He would love to round up everyone who's ever hurt me and make them suffer. The man in him cannot stand my pain, and the dragon wants to inflict similar back.

It was really sweet, in a sociopathic kinda way. Truth be told, I felt that way about Maximus now. I wanted to kill Kristoff and Cardia – if she'd still been alive – for the parts they played in causing him pain.

Jessa froze in her pacing, and a beat later I felt a fissure go across the house. Our eyes locked, both of us still and patient, waiting to see what this change was from. Something powerful was close to us, and I knew by instinct it wasn't the boys.

I reached for Maximus, hoping he would tell me what was coming, but the bond between us was gone. Or not exactly gone, but completely muted so I could barely feel him.

"Jess, what could mute a true mate bond?"

Her blue eyes were wide and glassy. "Nothing that I know of. But I can't feel Braxton, so again, it seems as if the school texts need to be rewritten."

I swallowed hard, trying to calm the fear brewing in my chest. "Could a high level demon do it?"

I could feel him coming now, that same dark, oily energy from when he had held me captive. Kristoff had somehow figured out where we were. He was going to attack while our pack was busy with the bears.

I was on my feet with Jessa, both of us moving toward the stairs. "We need weapons," she said. "Follow me."

I expected her to rush up the stairs, but instead she veered off and led me to a small door on the side of the staircase. At first it seemed like nothing more than a simple wooden door carved into the wall, but when Jessa pulled it open, inside was a damn weapon factory.

We both ducked our heads and squeezed in together. The space was about six feet by six; weapons lined each wall. I'd been doing some training lately with a long blade, and that was what I grabbed. Jessa went for about eight different things, including throwing knives and a crossbow.

"So Kristoff is coming, right?" she asked as we stepped back into the main room.

I nodded. "Yep, definitely his oily stench."

Jessa didn't even flinch. Her face set into hard lines and she was all warrior.

"We can't let him touch us or the demon will have a portal to our soul – you'll always have to be careful of one of them trying to take you over. We're mated to Compasses, we should be safe. They're powerful enough to resist the demon ... but better for us to be safe than sorry."

I nodded, the tightness in my chest increasing. "I just wish our babies weren't so vulnerable right now," I whispered. "Even though they're safely inside, it's easy to hurt them and us because we can't fight properly."

Jessa's eyes crinkled as her face crumpled. "We have to keep them safe, Misch. I can't live in a world without my kids. It's just not an option."

It really wasn't. We had to protect them.

A groan near the living room of the house had us both on high alert. "Why aren't we running?" I whispered as Jessa crouched lower and started creeping from the room.

She glanced back for a beat. "He has the house locked down, energy coating the outside. It's what's blocking our mate bonds. We wouldn't be able to break through it without hurting ourselves considerably."

Of course. I should have expected that. He wanted us trapped like rats in a maze. Jessa was clearly not one to hide and wait for the enemy to find her, and I was down with that. The sorcerer had almost killed my daughter. He was top of my shit list.

Both of us silently stepped forward. My wolf was rising in my body, adding her senses to my own. I could scent the darkness of the devil in our pack house, and I wanted him out before he could taint everything.

Another twinge rocked across my stomach then, and I silently sent a request for her to please wait another few days before coming into the world.

Right now I had no time for labor. Jessa and I halted on the edge of the front hallway. Kristoff was just standing in the living room, looking calm and crazy as heck.

"Hello there."

Anger caressed me as I stared him down. There was nothing left in his eyes now, just a reflective darkness which was all demon.

"My name is Davind," the demon wearing Kristoff's skin said, bowing slightly to us. "I'm a king of my kind, and my demon-kin need freedom. Our world is a desolate and dead land. Earth seems to be the perfect plane to exist in."

Right, so Kristoff was no more. Davind had complete control.

Jessa straightened. "What do you want with us then? Shouldn't you be off bringing demons to Earth."

He turned those dead eyes on her and a grin lifted his cheeks. "If only it was as easy as that, but I see luck had doubly rewarded me this day. I was here for the powerful child within this one." He pointed at me. "But now I see that what I really should have been chasing was the two you carry ... dragon born."

Holy shit. Jessa's wolf burst to life in her eyes, and ferocious growls echoed across the room. "You'll never touch them," she snarled.

He still hadn't moved. His total calm was unnerving. "Unfortunately I need the power in their souls. I can use the two females to open a permanent portal between our worlds, and I think I'll keep the boy. He'll be mine to control. I'll never need fear another demon-kin or supe again."

The two females ... he was talking about our daughters, about harming their precious, tiny bodies and using their souls to power a portal. Jessa and I reacted in the same instance. She had the crossbow up and firing, while I flung my blade at him. With my wolf's help, it landed right on target.

Except this demon could disappear. In a blink he was in a new spot across the room. Jessa must have anticipated this because she had already started firing again, and two of her arrows hit their target, burying deep in his chest. Of course, that didn't seem to bother the demon.

He muttered something, and an echoing noise rocked through the room, and with a blast of something like a soundwave, Jessa and I were thrown back a few yards. As the energy crashed through us, I shrieked and clutched at my stomach. Next to me Jessa did the same.

"What's happening!" I screamed as sharp pains stabbed into me, tightening everything inside of my entire abdomen and lower back. Jessa started huffing at my side. "I would guess that this is labor."

WHAT. THE. FUCK?

Okay, no one had told me labor was going to feel like someone was peeling my insides out with a blunt knife. It was brutal in a way I had not expected. What had the demon done to us?

I crouched forward, trying to ease the ache. After about eight seconds – or eighty, it was hard to tell – the pain eased off and we both were able to breathe deeply.

Kristoff-demon still had not moved, except to yank out the arrows. "I've used a spell to induce labor. These children are no use to me while still inside of you. I would suggest you make yourselves comfortable somewhere. They'll be here momentarily."

Why was he still talking? Why wasn't he dead already? I could feel the pain starting to barrel through me again; there was no way to stay upright. I fell to my hands and knees, rocking back and forth to try and ease the agony.

Could this spell hurt our kids? Was this forced and violent labor going to crush them before they even arrived? Surely if he needed them alive for the start of his ritual, he would make sure nothing hurt them until then.

Jessa was at my side and I could see that she was struggling as much as me. I reached across and grasped her hand. We clung together through the next wave of contractions, before our bodies slumped forward. I sensed the oily presence closing in.

A stack of towels was thrown at our feet.

"I despise the disgusting reproductive and birth model of supernaturals. I'm going to prepare the spell, you two will birth the sacrifices. Everyone does their jobs, then you'll die without torture ... as a thank you."

What a polite little cockswabbler he was.

He strode away then, crossing to the fireplace in the center of the room. He started throwing things at it and muttering words. My focus on him disappeared as another contraction started. They were close together now, like thirty seconds apart, and I could feel my body starting to change, expanding and contracting with a speed that felt far too fast.

Jessa and I both pushed ourselves back to rest against cushions from the couch which were scattered across the floor. She handed me a couple of towels and I used them to pad the space under my butt and legs. We had to make sure our babies were delivered safely, and pray that we could stop the demon from touching them.

"I still can't reach Braxton," Jessa said, her face ashen, sweat beading across her forehead. "But they have to know something is up. They'll be here soon."

I let out a strangled scream as another contraction started, the worst one so far.

There was a strong heaviness down low now, and I fought the urge to push. It wasn't time, she couldn't come into the world yet. This crazy sorcerer would steal her, would hurt her. I could never let that happen.

With our hands locked, my sister and I started to breathe through the pain. I was learning to accept it more, and my body stopped fighting the strange sensations. We were settling into the natural rhythms of childbirth. As I'd told Maximus earlier, this was something women had been doing for thousands of years.

"I love you, Mischa!" Jessa said as her head fell back. "I'm glad you're here with me."

Her voice sounded weak; she looked wrecked already. Her babies weren't as far along as mine, and she had two, which meant this was far worse for her. I'd been close to labor, so the spell didn't have to push much. Jessa had been a long way from it.

"I got you, Jess," I said, gripping her hand tighter. She was half passed out, which I didn't like. Knowing I needed to aid her, I managed to place one of the towels across her lap and helped her wriggle free from her pants and underwear, before placing another clean towel beneath her.

"Okay, I'm totally not a doctor," I said. "But, girl, you most definitely have a baby coming."

I tried to joke to halt my worry. Jessa was bleeding quite heavily and I wasn't sure if that was normal or not.

She at least managed to flip me off before another contraction smashed into her and she let out a yelp. I couldn't do much more to help her because I was currently in the same position. This time I couldn't stop my body from pushing down with the next contraction.

My entire lower half was on fire. It felt as if I was being split in two, my bones moving and shifting to accommodate the child trying to exit my womb. I managed to kick off my pants and lay them across me. There weren't enough towels for my modesty. I needed the one I had beneath me so that my daughter would land somewhere softer than the floor.

Crazy demon dude was still busy tending his hell fire. At least that meant he wasn't standing right over us preparing to snatch my child the moment she entered the world. Which was strangely reassuring. I felt I could deal with anything as long as he didn't touch her.

A lot of wetness was coating my legs now and I was praying it wasn't blood. Because it felt as if I'd dumped half my fluids out. The contractions weren't really stopping now; my daughter was coming for real.

"I wish Max was here," I choked out.

Jessa nodded, coughing a few times as she tried to breathe through her pain. A wind blew up then, inside of the house, whipping around and whistling through the hallway. I thought it was the portal, but then Kristoff-demon whipped around and fell into a defensive pose.

Blackness descended as I screamed again and the need to push came over me.

Waves of power swept in with those winds, and a rush of relief hit me. I recognized that power.

"Mischa!" Maximus' roar was the best thing I'd ever heard in my life, but I also feared for him. This demon would let no one stand in his way, and I wasn't sure the boys could fight him. He was a king of their kind. Extremely strong.

I wanted to call out a warning to them, but every ounce of my energy was occupied with having a baby.

The boys filed into the room, and with a blast of energy Kristoff shot some sort of spell at them while at the same time trying to lunge for me and Jessa. Thank the gods that stupid ass hadn't wanted to see the mess of childbirth. That gave the boys enough time to reach us before he did.

Louis moved to the center and shot some return bolts of energy, deflecting Davind's spell. Even in my half-conscious state I noticed how drawn and worn out the powerful sorcerer looked, nothing like his usual unruffled state.

He was our best bet for this demon, but it looked as if another spell would do him in. With Tyson by his side, the pair managed to keep Davind from crossing the room to us, trapping him behind a barrier. It was at this point Braxton, Maximus, and Jacob raced to us.

The vampire skidded down beside me and tried to gather me closer. I screamed and pushed him away, the pains in my stomach intense. The movement sent it roiling, and I had to turn my head so I could vomit everywhere.

"What did he do?" Maximus' black eyes cut into me and there was true fear there. His hands were gentle on me, but he didn't try to shift me again.

I wiped at my mouth and cried softly, managing to string a ragged sentence together: "He wants the babies – sent out a spell to send us into labor. The demon has completely taken over Kristoff. He said the power of our young was enough to open a portal from his realm to this one. He's going to kill them."

My body locked down again; the pain was ripping me in two. My eyes met Maximus'. "It's time. She's coming."

He leaned down and kissed my cheek. As he pulled back I saw his fear strongly for a second, before he masked it behind a wall of calm. "Okay, baby, you can do this. You've done amazing so far." He cupped his hands for a moment and Jacob filled it with fresh water. Some of it trickled into my parched mouth before I had to get back to pushing.

"How's ... Jess?" I huffed out.

Maximus turned his head for a second. "She's doing okay. Braxton's with her and their little girl is almost born."

Shit. This was so bad. They needed medical help. We needed a hospital. Jessa and I had talked about supes having babies before, and she said generally they were birthed in your own home with the help of a healer. But I wasn't sure what happened with premature little ones.

"You need to push for me, Misch. I can see her head. Just a couple of big pushes."

I sucked in deeper, drawing on a strength I didn't even know I had. Gritting my teeth and bearing down as hard as I could, I felt the movement of my daughter through the canal, and I continued pushing right up until there was a final burning pain and then the pressure disappeared.

Blackness descended across my vision for a moment and I realized I hadn't breathed for a long time. As I sucked in deeply I heard a beautiful sound, the twin cries of babies being brought into the world. Seemed as if Jessa and I had birthed our girls at the exact same time, and they both sounded strong and healthy.

With that thought, fear ripped through me so strong it almost crushed my chest. My daughter was here. She was crying, and alive, and perfect. We couldn't let the demon near her.

Maximus' face appeared above mine wearing an expression I'd never seen before, complete and total awe.

"Misch, you did so well, sweetheart." He started kissing me and running a hand over my face. A wrapped bundle was placed into my arms, and then with one last kiss on my lips he pulled away. "I need to help Braxton. Jessa is struggling with her second little one. He's breech and we have to try and turn him. The healer is on the way. Hopefully they'll make it in time."

Fear for my sister and her son was strong. I waved him off, my other hand clutching my daughter closer. I took a moment to stare at the amazing miracle in my arms. I examined her beautiful face, perfect olive skin, her mess of black hair, her curls, and her huge blue eyes blinking at me as she tried to take in the new world around her. She was so perfect. The most perfect thing I could ever have imagined. At that moment I knew a love like no other, a love that could never be replicated. The love of a mother and her child was the first completely unselfish emotion I'd ever had. A love so strong and pure it was almost crushing in its intensity.

I reached across and gripped my sister's shoulder, giving her my strength, whatever I could spare. I sent it through our bond.

"You got this, Jess."

Jacob was sitting close by, a small bundle cradled in his arms. He was holding her daughter. He started to sing the low haunting melody he always sang to Jessa. It was their song, and it was a birth song for the fey. He was helping her welcome the little boy into the world. Braxton was crouched down in front of her, his hands trying to ease the baby around. Footsteps sounded and a male magic user dashed into the room.

"Out of the way!" He was abrupt, and despite being quite diminutive for a supe, didn't seem to fear Braxton at all as he pushed him to the side.

The dragon growled but didn't retaliate. The healer began to mutter something, Jacob's song still ringing out. Relief crossed Jessa's face then and I figured he'd helped with her pain. "I'm going to turn him now," he said. "Your children were not quite ready to be born. We must hurry, he's distressed."

Jessa started outright sobbing, her face crumpling. Braxton had his arms wrapped around her, and I thought a tear or two might have been sprinkling his dark blue eyes. I could tell he felt helpless, and that was not something the dragon handled very well. He wanted to fix this, but there was no easy fix.

A shout sounded from across the room. Kristoff had advanced and was in some sort of magical showdown with Louis. The two of them exchanged fiery spells while Tyson hurriedly mixed something into a few glass jars.

Maximus was close to me again, one hand tangled in my hair, the other resting on our daughter, who had fallen asleep on my chest. "I need to help him, he's losing." Maximus said, his voice low.

"Yes, do whatever you can. We can't let the demon near our girl."

Maximus kissed me fiercely, his expression both soft and scary as hell. Then he was gone across the room to take on the demon. I tried to lift myself up a little; some of the numb pain in my lower half had eased and I was starting to get feeling back in my body, but it was still hard to maneuver with the bundle on my chest. She had her mouth open now, pretty little rosebud lips moving as she suckled for milk.

My eyes switched between her and Maximus in a constant rotation. He was helping Tyson, the two of them standing close together, each holding a jar.

"Throw it now," Louis shouted. "He's breaking free. The demon's too strong."

Tyson and Maximus both threw in unison, and the three of them started chanting, odd words I'd never heard before but which rang with power.

Cresta demonica turnitalia reform.

A huge fire blew up then. It was odd, definitely magical in nature. It surrounded the demon-touched sorcerer and he took an involuntary step back.

"Not strong enough," Kristoff scoffed. "You needed at least three more spells."

The boys ignored him, chanting louder, magical weight behind each word. The fire started really blowing up, but it didn't seem to get any closer to the sorcerer. He laughed, stepping into the flames.

"Which one of you wants to die first? Your souls will bring forth a huge army, and then with the children's souls, I'll permanently open the doorway."

Maximus' entire face locked down into predator mode. His vampire was in control, but before he could react, Louis stopped him with a hand on his chest. He threw it off, but paused long enough to hear the next words.

"I don't have the magical power left," Louis said. "There's only one other chance to end this. It's not an option I wanted to take. It's far too dangerous, but I'll not let him touch the young, I promise you."

Maximus was silent and still, before finally nodding. Braxton shifted then. He hadn't moved from Jessa's side at all, but the boys must have called for him. Jacob crossed to me and placed Jessa's daughter down in my free arm. She looked a lot like my little one, only her hair was a shock of very white blond.

"Louis needs our energy, we'll be right back," Jacob whispered to me and Jessa. My twin was all ashen features and ragged breathing. Sweat beaded across her face, and her knuckles were white where she was gripping the pillow beside her.

"Help them," she murmured. "Don't worry about us, we're okay."

The healer was still performing magic over her. So we weren't alone, and it would be far worse if Kristoff got free. Jacob and Braxton joined their brothers and energy filled the room as their quad bond kicked in. I was distracted for a moment as the babies on my chest starting to fuss. They wiggled and cried, then two tiny hands found each other, reaching out and linking together. The sight had tears pouring silently down my cheeks, and I tilted my head to the side and met my twin's gaze. "They already know each other," I said, my voice breaking.

She nodded. "Yes, and their brother, the protector, is on his way."

Louis gave a shout, and my eyes opened wide trying to understand what he was doing. He was dashing across the room to directly engage the sorcerer. What? ... we weren't supposed to touch him. And Louis was so powerful that if his soul ended up demon touched, we were all screwed.

CHAPTER NINETEEN

Maximus Compass

I never knew a heart could be so full, and clench so tightly at the same time. When Mischa pushed one last time and my daughter slid into my hands, everything in my world changed. Everything. My daughter was this tiny little supe, and she was the most important thing in this life. Her and her beautiful, strong mother.

Now it was time to make sure they both remained safe. Tyson had explained through our bond that the only chance we had now was to shoot Louis with as much of our energy as we could, then he would take the demon into his soul and expel it back to the underworld. It was a very risky maneuver, which is why he'd never considered it as an option before, but it was the only chance we had. We just had to hope he was strong enough to do it, especially with his energy so drained. If the demon was stronger, we'd all be dead.

When I'd pulled free the blade, the one gifted to me in China, Louis had pretty much snatched it from me, saying it was the perfect channel for his power.

I didn't question him. I would give anything to keep my pack safe.

The sorcerer took off then. Tyson and I continued to shoot our energy into him. Braxton was right on Louis' heels; his role was important too. Kristoff crouched down, preparing himself for a fight. The pair of them clashed, sparks flew around the room, and energy ricocheted outwards.

Louis slammed a hand down on Kristoff's chest and shouted. "Now, Braxton!"

The shifter turned his hand into a dragon claw, and with ease struck out and severed Kristoff's head. The dark spirit of the demon gushed from the severed neck, but before it could dissipate out into the world, Louis lifted my blade and thrust it into the dead sorcerer's chest. He then closed his eyes and called for the demon-kin, taking control of the specter.

Louis was the strongest of sorcerers; this had to work. Braxton backed himself across the room toward us, and then as a group we surrounded the twins, who were still laid out on the ground. Jessa was about to birth her second child, and Mischa had the two little girls on her chest.

All of us kept our guard up, eyes locked on the mage. The battle he was fighting was internal, and there was no doubt it was a tough one. He shifted around to face us and the purple of his eyes was streaked with black.

"He's so strong," he muttered, sinking to his knees. "This is going to hurt."

Dropping my blade, his hands landed on the floor. He remained on all fours for a long time, then the darkness started seeping out of his mouth.

Flames burst to life beneath him and slowly the darkness faded, agonizingly slow, taking forever before finally Louis collapsed.

His body went still, no movement at all. "No!" Jessa screamed. "Louis!"

Tyson was up and across the room in a second. He reached out and felt the sorcerer's neck. We all waited breathlessly.

"The demon's gone and Louis is still alive," he finally called out. "His energy has been severely drained though. He needs to be placed into a healing sleep."

The medical mage lifted his head from Jessa. "I'll be done in moments, then I can help."

He wasn't kidding either. With one last guttural cry, Jessa pushed her son out into the world, and Braxton was right there to cradle the little one. The medic cut the cord and wrapped him up.

Before he could leave, I pointed him toward Mischa so he could do the same for her. I'd left the cord intact, not wanting to hurt her or our daughter.

I watched closely, but the male healer did not waste any time. He was quick and professional, checking all three children before dashing across the room, his hands already held out toward the sorcerer still unconscious on the floor.

I gently lifted the little white-haired girl off Mischa and handed her across to Jessa, who had both arms out. She wanted her babies. Braxton crowded closer to his mate and children, surrounding them with a ferocity to be expected from a dragon.

I gathered Mischa and our daughter closer to me. "I love you," I said, my voice desperate. I had come so close to losing both of them again. So goddamn close. The demon had planned to kill her, to kill my perfect, black-haired, blue-eyed daughter. It made me want to destroy him again and again. Hopefully both the demon and Kristoff found a lifetime of torture waiting for them in the dead lands.

Tears sprinkled Mischa's long lashes. She hadn't taken her eyes off our child for many minutes. "Have you ever seen anything so perfect?" she asked me. "We made something so pure and perfect."

I laughed and pressed my lips to the smooth skin of my baby's cheek. Someone had rubbed the gunk off her face, and I was surprised to see she wasn't all wrinkled and newborn looking.

"Do you know what you want to call her?" I asked, my hand gently rubbing across her soft black curls. I couldn't stop myself from touching the precious child.

"Did you have any thoughts? My mind is all frazzled right now. I can't think around the mass of love filling me."

I hadn't really had a chance to think about her name yet. I'd expected something to feel right when she was born. Staring down at her cream and peach features, my heart so full, my soul peaceful for the first time in a long time, I knew what I wanted to call her. "Lily."

Mischa's eyes widened, and she blinked a few times slowly before a smile spread across her face. "I love it. What made you choose that?"

Jacob answered from over my shoulder: "Lily means "chosen of my heart" in the ancient language. The stories say that the lily was a flower crafted by the fey gods for the one who held their soul. It's a sacred name. It's a strong name." His hand wrapped around my shoulder. "Good choice, brother."

Braxton and Jessa were still murmuring between themselves, before finally separating out. "We have named our two Jackson and Evie. Named in honor of our beloved family members."

Jackson had been the grandfather we were closest to growing up. He lived in Ireland now and was very reclusive, but he was one of our favorite supes ever. Our father Jack was named for him too. Evie was from the twins' maternal grandmother. Evelyn was a powerhouse shifter; she ran a pack in the New York area. Mischa didn't know her yet, but one day we would go there and introduce our Lily to her.

The healer had placed Louis on our couch and was working over him still, Tyson assisting where he could.

"Louis' vitals are strong," he said, from across the room, "but the healer isn't liking the lack of brain activity. For now he'll keep him in the healing sleep. Whatever energy he lost should be replaced soon enough."

We nodded, all of us taking a second to acknowledge the depth of gratitude we owed the sorcerer. The healer briefly checked out the girls and babies one last time. Jessa and Mischa just needed rest, time for the natural healing of their bodies to kick in. He spent extra time on Jackson and Evie, checking that their early forced entry into the world had done them no harm. Eventually, the babies all got a clean bill of health.

The healer left then. Tyson followed behind, carrying the sorcerer. Louis would remain under constant watch and have additional healing through the day. By this time Mischa was able to stand, with some help from me, Lily still gently clutched to her chest, sleeping, content. Jacob remained behind to help Braxton while I assisted Mischa up the stairs. It was slow going at first, but then her body started to move more freely.

"I'm probably trailing blood all over the place," she murmured.

"Don't worry about it, Tyson can easily clean it once he gets back."

Her bleeding had stopped and her body was healing. Which was a huge relief. Thank the gods that shifters bounced back fast from childbirth.

When we reached our bedroom, Mischa entered the bathroom. "I'd like to clean up," she said. "But I don't want her out of my sight. Do you mind?"

I turned the shower on for her, letting it warm thoroughly before gently bringing Lily into my arms and pressing her tiny body to my chest. She shifted, grumbling a little at the disturbance of leaving her momma's warm embrace. Mischa wasted no time stripping off her ruined clothing and stepping into the stream of water. It ran red for a few minutes before the blood was washed away.

She was cleaned up and drying off in record time, her face pale, exhaustion riding across her entire body.

"Do you want something to sleep in?" I asked her.

"Just some clean underwear bottoms," she said. "Lily will feed, and I'd like some skin to skin time with her."

Whether it was the mention of food, or just the sound of her mother's voice too far away, a small wail sounded from my little girl. Her face was suddenly red and scrunched as if everything in life was horrible.

Mischa's smile was so huge it lit up her entire face. Despite the fatigue, she looked happy, at peace. She crossed to the large bed and held out her hands for Lily. The little one went right to her and straight to her breast. The sight of Mischa feeding our child stirred something primal within me. My mate and child. Perfect.

"I'll go and check on Brax and Jess, and grab you some clothes," I said to her. It was a struggle to tear myself from the room. Moving with vampire speed, I was back within moments.

Mischa had her eyes closed, her head tilted back. One hand was gently stroking Lily's curls, the other wrapped around her tiny body. She must have sensed me; our bond was functioning again, and I could feel the strong emotions within her.

"Everything okay with the others?" she asked, her voice dreamy. I nodded, handing her a pile of clean clothes. She put them to the side to put on later. I quickly shucked off my own clothes, and in only boxer briefs crawled across the bed to settle in beside her. I wrapped my arm around her back and drew her closer into me. We lay like that for a long time, bonding together as a family.

"Tell me about you, Maximus Compass," Mischa said, turning her blazing green eyes on me. "Who are you? I want to know everything."

I stroked her arm and settled further into the pillow. We were true mates; she could see into my mind, and there was endless oceans of love between us. But in so many ways we were strangers. Unlike

Jessa and Braxton, we hadn't spent most of our years together.

"My name is Maximus Compass," I said with a grin, ridiculously happy to be cradling my family in my arms. "Six and half feet of vampire supernatural … well, sort of. I'm also partly shifter, magic user, and fey. I like weapons, especially blades, muscle cars – although a decent four-wheel drive can be fun. I like my music really fast, with a strong beat. I'm the protector, I chase down the criminals and keep my family and town safe. I love a black-haired wolf shifter and tiny little angel more than anything else in this world. I'll now be protector for them first. They're my life."

Mischa let out a breathy sigh, snuggling further into me. Lily switched sides and started happily feeding again.

"Mischa Lebron," she said softly. "Five and half feet of shifter, who for most of her life thought of herself as human. I love art, and nature, and hiking. I used to go out by myself for hours and explore whatever natural stuff was in the area around us. We moved so much when I was growing up that I never formed any strong relationships, except with the trees, and the sky. They were constant, they never left me. I've made a lot of mistakes, but for some reason the fates decided I deserved a second chance at happiness. Now my life is complete." She tilted her head back and I softly kissed her cheeks, and nose, and lips. "Thank you for giving me all of this, Max."

I had to kiss her again. Probably wouldn't ever stop, which was exactly how it should be. My love for her would only grow stronger with time. Our bond would strengthen. Mischa never had to worry about losing me, I was always going to fight for her, for us, because she was worth fighting for.

CHAPTER TWENTY

Mischa Lebron

One month later.

Lily gurgled as she wiggled on her spot on the floor. During the past four weeks our pack house had exploded into something resembling a baby factory. At the moment all four quads were down on their hands and knees crouched around three little supe young, trying to get them to smile.

Jessa and I stood back, just staring at the beautiful sight. The babies already had the boys wrapped tightly around their tiny fingers.

"Jackson woke up eight times last night," Jessa said around a huge yawn. "I swear he already has his father's appetite for boobs."

I snorted, shaking my head. "Dude, I did not need that mental image." I was lucky, Lily was such a content child. She slept in five to six hour increments, and then when she woke for her feed I'd bring her into bed with Maximus and me, and we'd spend the next hour bonding together.

My happiness was almost sickening. I never even knew that this level of happy existed outside of movies and books.

"You're such a strong boy," Tyson was cooing at Jackson. "Already protecting your sisters."

Jessa and I rolled our eyes at each other. It was one of those mimic twin things, and we did it a lot nowadays. But for real, these quads were crazy in love with the babies.

The front door slammed then, drawing all of our attentions. Jonathon and Lienda hurried into the room, followed closely by Jack and Jo and Nash. The grandparents were almost as bad as the quads, each of them demanding their daily hugs and kisses from the babies. One thing our kids didn't lack was love. It was bursting from everyone who stepped near them. So far Jessa's two hadn't shown any crazy abilities, but we were all waiting to see what the dragon born were going to pull out of their tiny onesies. Both of them had a swath of white-blond hair, which was odd considering their parents' hair was as black as night. Maybe a throwback to one of the grandparents. They all claimed it anyway. Lily's hair was still a mess of dark curls, and getting long already, brushing over her forehead.

Maximus left the grandparents to their kisses, his arms automatically wrapping around me. "We should sneak off," he murmured.

I laughed, elbowing him. "You need to be patient, Lily will go down for her nap soon." And despite the fact I missed my daughter when she napped, I did enjoy the bonding time with her daddy. Maximus and I were still newly mated and the urges were strong. Part of me still couldn't believe he was in my life like this.

Tyson shifted off the floor to allow Jack and Nash to take his place. The Compasses' younger brother was obsessed with the babies. So loving and kind.

"How's Louis?" Jessa asked Tyson when he reached us.

He shook his head. "No change. The medics are baffled. His energy has returned, and there are no visible injuries, and yet he doesn't wake. They're guessing it's something to do with the injury to his soul. It's still healing."

Jessa crossed her arms tightly over her chest. "I'm worried about him. Josephina said she'd look into it, but I haven't heard anything since."

Jessa's dragon had visited last week, bestowing blessings on the three little ones. She said they were strong of soul and energy, that they would make formidable supernaturals one day.

Now at least, with Kristoff and the bears out of the way, it looked like life would be a lot calmer in Stratford. I for one couldn't wait. I wanted lazy days with my pack, long nights of shared company, and my child growing up with more love than she knew what to do with.

I especially wanted a lifetime with a stubborn, gorgeous, dirty-blond vampire at my side. My mate and love.

I had a life so much better than I ever imagined. It was mine. I was blessed.

Something while you wait ;)

Thanks for checking out my story! Stay tuned for more Supernatural Prison stories. Including Tyson, Jacob and Louis. While you're very patiently waiting (lol), please check out one of my favourite authors and series. The Wilds, by Donna Augustine.

Chapter One

Have you ever wanted to be someone else so desperately that you wished for it with everything you had? Closed your eyes at night and prayed you would wake up as someone else? Would sacrifice anything to just not be you for another day? That's how I used to feel when I first came here, fourteen years ago a screaming child of four, crying as my parents walked out of this place without me.

I stayed like that for a long time, too, a black hole of emotion. I'd destroy any light that came too close. I cursed the world and everyone that dwelled upon it.

It was six years ago that I was lying in my private cell in The Holy Sanctuary for the Criminally Insane—or the Cement Giant as me and the other inmates called it—and had one of those moments, the kind where I could see beyond the confines I'd erected in my mind. The bars that had kept my mind in this dark place, as surely as the cement walls kept my body, weakened and rusted away.

I don't know why it happened. Maybe it was simply age or maturity, but the anger that had been pouring out of me like a spigot on full blast started to slow. I realized that this was it, the only life I was going to get. I could either let myself rot here in misery or I could find a way out. I'd already gotten one second chance. I'd survived when so many others hadn't. Was I really going to waste it here?

See the thing is, I'm a Plaguer, one who's had the Bloody Death and lived. That's not something many can say. When the Bloody Death hit the world a hundred and fifty years ago, it had a zero percent rate of survival. From what I've heard and read, one day no one had ever heard of the Bloody Death, and the next it ripped through the human population like a forest fire after a six-month drought. And just like a fire, it killed fast and painfully. People would be up walking around fine, only to fall bleeding on the street one moment, and gripped in agony and dead the next.

From the records left behind of that time, ninety-five percent of the population contracted the Bloody Death and all of them died during the initial outbreak. Not to mention that it didn't spring up and then disappear. No, it's been coming back every ten or twenty years. You don't have to be a math genius to know those odds suck. I guess it's a good thing there were so many humans to start with or we might have gone the way of the dinosaurs.

Everyone is fearful of when the next wave might hit. Maybe that outbreak will be the one to end us all. It's not like anyone knew where the Bloody Death came from, or why it still mysteriously showed back up from time to time, which added to the fear. The unknown and all that? Some people have a real hang-up about not knowing things. I don't understand that fear, but maybe it was because as a Plaguer, I've always known more than I wanted.

When rumors started creeping up about how a teeny tiny percent of the population, something like less than .001%, was surviving, most people thought it was a lie. Plaguers are so rare you can go your whole life never meeting one, but I'm living proof they exist.

The first couple of days after I'd survived the Bloody Death, I'd thought I was the luckiest girl to walk the Earth. I was young when it happened, only four and so full of childish delusions. Children can be like that before life teaches them better.

I still regard myself as lucky, but now I know survival comes at a cost. The Bloody Death changes you, makes you see things. They say these things aren't true, but I know better. They say all Plaguers are psychotic, contaminated and ruined, need to be locked away to protect society from the evil they spew about monsters.

I say they're blind. But maybe willfully so. I know what the Plaguers before me have said. I've seen the things they've seen. There's a reason no one wanted to believe them. I understand why they hide us in places like this.

The people here, they tell me that this is the only safe place for me. That I would be killed if I'd been born somewhere else, like the Wilds, which encompasses the vast majority of what used to be the United States now except for the small slivers pieced out to form the few smaller countries that exist.

I'd prefer to take my chances. I didn't survive the Bloody Death to only go on and live as if I were truly dead. If I was meant to be alive, I didn't want to walk this Earth—I wanted to truly live it, dance and revel in everything it had to offer, feel every sensation and emotion open to the human psyche. I would. Even if it took me until I was a hundred and I only had one single day of freedom, I would not die here; I would die living.

The door to my cell opened and startled me. It wasn't time for the daily release yet. I looked up from my bed, already dressed for the day in the simple white dresses we were given, to the guard.

"You're getting a visitor."

I let out a sigh. It was going to be one of those days.

About the Author

Jaymin Eve is the USA Today bestselling author of Young Adult and New Adult romance novels (both urban fantasy and contemporary). She has a passion for reading, writing and arithmetic ... okay maybe not the last one but definitely the first two. She loves surrounding herself with the best things in life: her two girls, a good book, and chocolate.

She'd love to hear from you, so find her at
Facebook:
http://www.facebook.com/pages/Jaymin-Eve
Twitter: @JayminEve1
Mailing List: http://eepurl.com/bQw8Kf
Webpage: www.jaymineve.com
Email jaymineve@gmail.com

CPSIA information can be obtained
at www.ICGtesting.com
Printed in the USA
LVOW12s1828310117
522741LV00004B/786/P